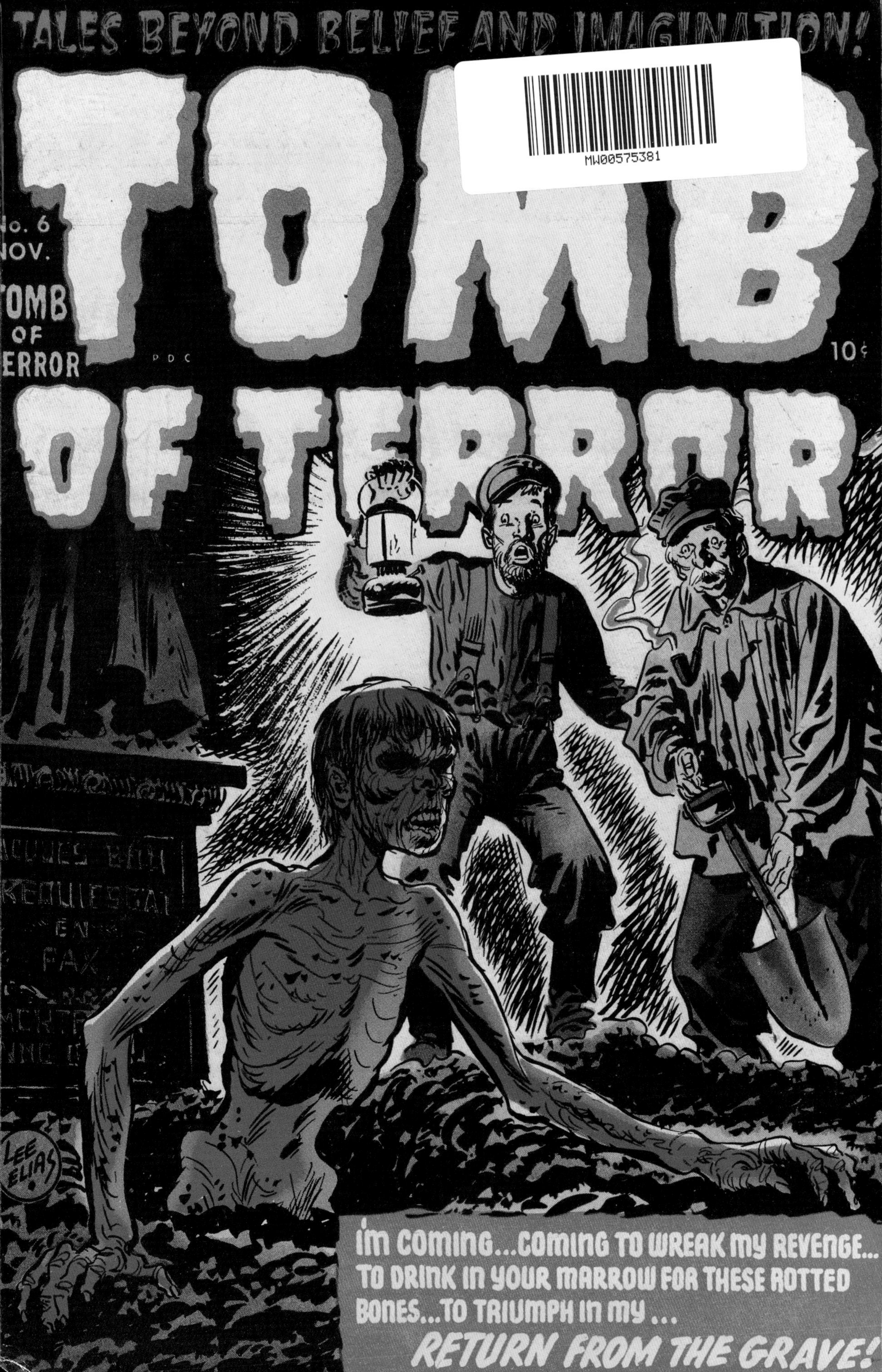
TALES BEYOND BELIEF AND IMAGINATION!
TOMB OF TERROR
No. 6
NOV.
TOMB OF TERROR
PDC
10¢
LEE ELIAS
I'M COMING...COMING TO WREAK MY REVENGE... TO DRINK IN YOUR MARROW FOR THESE ROTTED BONES...TO TRIUMPH IN MY ...
RETURN FROM THE GRAVE!

Terror, terror everywhere! The world whirls through a pool of panic . . . strange figures of other worlds parade in ghastly processions! All is a bedlam in the TOMB OF TERROR!

This is the storehouse of the unknown . . . this is the vault of the forbidden . . . this is the crypt of the loathesome . . . this is the TOMB OF TERROR!

Enter the eerie chamber . . . set foot on the horrible path . . . follow the slimy walls that go deep, ever deeper, into the inner depths of evil!

See all the ghastly creatures that mushroom forth in the TOMB OF TERROR!

Read the amazing story behind the most fantastic problem of the future! The science-fiction-horror saga that is another TOMB OF TERROR first! Read the incredible story of THE SURVIVORS!

Visit the most horrible inferno ever visioned! See a Hades on earth in the VOLCANO OF DOOM!

Torn from the pages of your daily newspaper . . . straight from the occult terror that is Tibet . . . told by the scientist who lived it! This is the story behind the headline—FOUND: THE LAIR OF THE SNOW MONSTER!

And the frantic account of a man possessed with all the evil spawned by Satan! A man who dared to cheat the stars! Read the suspenseful RETURN FROM THE GRAVE!

See the scenes of all scenes now in the . . .

TOMB OF TERROR!

FATE IS AN ENIGMA! AND IF NO MAN CAN FORETELL WHAT FATE HAS IN STORE FOR HIM HOW CAN HE BE EXPECTED TO KNOW WHAT AWAITS HIS VERY CIVILIZATION ITSELF!

THE SURVIVORS!

MIDNIGHT IN A LAND OF RUIN AND HORROR-- AND SUDDENLY THE THROBBING DRUMS HERALD THE ARRIVAL OF THE DEAD, WHOSE RAVAGED FACES AND FESTERING BODIES BEAR THE MARK OF THE . . .

VOLCANO DOOM!

"I SHALL BE BACK!" THE GREAT LEONARDO SAID, AND HIS ASSISTANT, ROBERTO, SMILED WITH HIDDEN CONTEMPT! BUT REVENGE IS STRONG EVEN IN DEATH--AND THE BEYOND CANNOT DENY A--

RETURN FROM THE GRAVE!

ROBERTO! I AM COMING FOR YOU! ONLY **YOU**, ROBERTO--YOU BELONG WITH ME IN THE NICE SMOULDERING EARTH! **ROBERTO! ROBERTO!**

YAAHH! HEAVEN HELP US!

OUT OF THE FROZEN LAND THAT IS TIBET CAME A TERRIBLE MONSTER THAT PREYED ON HUMAN FLESH--THAT MADE NEWSPAPER HEADLINES SCREAM...

The Morning Chronicle

FOUND: THE LAIR OF THE SNOW MONSTER!!!

TOMB OF TERROR, NOVEMBER, 1952, Vol. 1, No. 6, is published monthly by HARVEY PUBLICATIONS, INC., at 420 DeSoto Avenue, St. Louis 7, Mo. Editorial, Advertising and Executive offices, 1860 Broadway, New York 23, N. Y. President Alfred Harvey; Vice-President and Editor, Leon Harvey; Vice-President and Business Manager Robert B. Harvey. Entered as second-class matter at the Post Office at St. Louis, Mo., under the Act of March 3, 1879. Single copies, 10c. Subscription rates, 10 issues for $1.00 in the U. S. and possessions, elsewhere $1.50. All names in this periodical are entirely fictitious and no indentification with actual persons is intended. Contents copyrighted, 1952, by Harvey Features Syndicate, New York City. Printed in the U. S. A.

Do You Want a

SUCCESS-WINNING VOICE?

Give the Feuchtinger Voice-Method a chance to help you develop more

POWER VIGOR CHARACTER

IN YOUR VOICE

Add *controlled* strength to your voice and people will listen when you talk. A stronger voice may make you more interesting, more persuasive, more poised. What you say will have more importance, when your voice is full-toned, because people generally respect a BIG voice.

I can strengthen your voice—build it up to be one of your most valuable assets. Get the ring of confidence in your voice and it will help you get ahead in business, increase your income, develop leadership.

—Eugene Feuchtinger

Thousands are held back by a negative voice—

AND DON'T KNOW IT!

Your popularity and recognition depends, frequently, on your voice and the impression it makes. Don't be handicapped by just an ordinary common weak voice. You'll improve your personality by replacing "thinness" in your voice with new desirable strength. And, of course, I don't have to mention the direct dollars-and-cents cash value of a more positive voice for salesmen, executives, preachers, announcers, union leaders, politicians.

AMAZING DETAILS—Just fill in coupon and rush it back to me today

You'll find this training enjoyable as well as valuable—as have more than 150,000 other ambitious students during the past 51 years. Helps both your speaking and your singing. Self-training lessons, mostly silent. You get your results in the privacy of your own room. No music required. Everything is handled confidentially and all mail is sent in plain wrapper. *Take this first step* toward your personal self-advancement now, it's free . . . send for my fascinating illustrated booklet "How to Strengthen Your Voice to be More Successful." Simply fill in and mail this coupon today, (Cannot be sent unless you state your age.)

PREFECT VOICE INSTITUTE, Studio L-131
210 South Clinton St. Chicago 6, Ill.

FREE "Successful Voice" BOOK! MAIL THIS COUPON TODAY

PREFECT VOICE INSTITUTE
Studio L-131, 210 South Clinton St.
Chicago 6, Ill.

Please send me—free and without obligation—your inspiring and helpful illustrated booklet "How to Strengthen Your Voice to be More Successful," by Eugene Feuchtinger. Mail in plain wrapper. No salesman will call.

NAME____________________________

ADDRESS_________________________

CITY__________________STATE________

My age is:__________

FATE IS AN ENIGMA! AND IF NO MAN CAN FORETELL WHAT FATE HAS IN STORE FOR HIM HOW CAN HE BE EXPECTED TO KNOW WHAT AWAITS HIS VERY CIVILIZATION ITSELF!

THE SURVIVORS!

IN A SCORCHED DESOLATION, A NUMBER OF WEIRD, OMINOUS-LOOKING CREATURES ROAM ABOUT FREELY!
GRRRPH...!

...UNTIL THEY STUMBLE UPON A STRANGE STEEL DOOR IN A PREVIOUSLY UNEXPLORED CAVE!
GRRRPH!
CLANK!
BANG

THE STEEL DOOR IS NO MATCH FOR THE MONSTER'S GREAT STRENGTH! AND AFTER SMASHING IT DOWN, THEY ENTER INTO A STRANGE CUBICLE...
GRRRPH!

THE CREATURES REGARD THEIR DISCOVERY WITH QUIET CURIOSITY BUT THE AIR ADMITTED THROUGH THE NOW OPEN DOOR REVIVES THE HUMANS!
I... WHAAAA! MONSTERS!
WHERE ARE WE! AIIIEEK! THEY'RE HORRIBLE!

GRAB YOUR GUNS, EVERYBODY! THEY'LL RIP US TO SHREDS!
IT'S THEM OR US!
GRRRPH!

PANIC STRICKEN AT THE SIGHT OF THE GROTESQUE CREATURES, THE HUMANS REACH FOR THEIR WEAPONS! BUT THE MONSTERS, EQUALLY FRIGHTENED, INSTINCTIVE-LY RETALIATE!
AIIIEEE!
GRRRRPH!
RAT-TAT-TAT!

AIIEE! AGGGRRRAA!
GRRRPH!

WE'RE BEATING THEM BACK! KEEP SHOOTING!
GRRRPH!
AGGGRRAAA!
RAT-TAT
TAT!

THE MONSTERS TAKE A GREAT TOLL OF HUMAN LIFE BUT ARE FINALLY DRIVEN OFF!
THAT WAS GHASTLY, CARL! THE 20TH CENTURY WAS NEVER LIKE THIS! WHEN WE VOLUNTEERED TO BE SEALED IN THE TIME CAPSULE, I NEVER DREAMED WE'D COME OUT TO A RECEPTION LIKE THIS!
IT'S HORRIBLE... JUST HORRIBLE!

TO THINK THAT THIS AREA WAS ONCE NEW YORK! WHAT HAS THE WORLD COME TO!
WE'LL NEVER KNOW UNTIL WE GO ABOVE AND EXPLORE, PROFESSOR!

BUT THE MONSTERS...!
WE HAVE TO RISK IT, JAN!

THESE MONSTERS MUST BE THE SURVIVORS OF CIVILIZATION AS WE KNEW IT! A CATAS-TROPHE MUST HAVE TAKEN PLACE!
RIGHT, PROFESSOR. REMEMBER, NO VIOLENCE UNLESS WE'RE ATTACKED!

THERE THEY ARE! WE'LL TRY TO COMMUNICATE WITH THEM!
WITH THEIR STRENGTH, IF THEY PROVE FRIENDLY THEY MAY BE USEFUL!

THE CREATURES DO PROVE PEACEFUL AND THE SCIENTISTS ARE SUCCESSFUL IN ENLISTING THEIR AID IN DIGGING OUT THE BUNKER!
THEY WORK LIKE BULLDOZERS, PROFESSOR! THE BUNKER WILL BE CLEAR IN NO TIME!
THEN TO OUR EXPERI-MENTS TO FIND OUT WHAT MADE THESE CREATURES WHAT THEY ARE!
GRRRPH!

ALTHOUGH FORMIDABLE IN APPEARANCE THE STRANGE CREATURES WERE QUICK TO CO-OPERATE!
DO YOU REALLY THINK THESE INJECTIONS WILL RETURN HIS HUMAN CHARACTERISTICS?
WE'VE BEEN INJECTING THIS SERUM ALL WEEK, CARL! WE SHOULD GET SOME IMPROVEMENT SOON!

LOOK, CARL! ITS FEATURES!
YES! THE SERUM IS WORKING!
WAIT---! QUIET!

GRRRPH!...I... WHERE...GRRRPH! ...WHERE AM...I... GRRRPH...
HE SPOKE! MARVELOUS!
WE'RE SUCCEEDING! SPLENDID!

THAT NIGHT...
WE'RE MAKING PROGRESS, CARL! WE'LL CONTINUE THE EXPERIMENTS TOMORROW! IF WE'RE LUCKY WE MAY BE ABLE TO TURN ALL OF THESE MONSTERS BACK TO THE HUMANS THEY PROBABLY ONCE WERE!

BUT THE NEXT DAY...
THE MONSTER, PROFESSOR! MISSING!
ESCAPED! THIS IS HORRIBLE! WE'VE GOT TO FIND HIM!

LIKE MEN POSSESSED, CARL AND THE PROFESSOR HUNT FEVERISHLY...
COME, CARL! IF HE GETS BACK TO THE OTHER MONSTERS---! ALERT OUR CREW!
RIGHT! WITH HIM TO LEAD THEM NOW IT MIGHT BE THE END FOR US!
4

AND THE PROFESSOR'S GRIM PREDICTION MATERIALIZES INTO STARK, LURID REALITY!
THEY'RE COMING FOR US! AND HE'S LEADING THEM!
LET'S RUN, CARL!
TOO LATE FOR THAT! IT'S A FIGHT TO THE FINISH NOW!

AIIIEEE!
GRRRPH!
AGGRRAAA!
RAT TAT TAT

ONE LESS, ANYWAY!
AGGKRRAAA...!
RAT-TAT-TAT

AIIIEEEE!
GRRRRPH!

AGGGRRA... NO USE... CARL...
AIIIIIEEEK!
GRRRRPH!

CARL! HELP! AIIIEEE... NO... AGGGRRAA!

THE SUPERHUMAN STRENGTH OF THE GHASTLY CREATURES IS TOO MUCH FOR THE OUT-NUMBERED HUMANS AND THE ONLY SURVIVOR OF THE SAVAGE MASSACRE IS CARL!
DEAD! ALL OF THEM! AND I'LL BE NEXT UNLESS I GET BACK TO THE TIME-CAPSULE!
GRRRPH!

THEY'VE SEEN ME! I'VE GOT TO MAKE IT!

GRRRPH!
...NOT... FAR...NOW...!

SLAM!
MADE IT! THEY'LL NEVER GET ME IN HERE! I'LL SEAL MYSELF IN THE CAPSULE AGAIN!

BUT AS THE LONE REMAINING HUMAN SEALS THE TIME-CAPSULE, HE TURNS IN HORROR TO SEE THAT HE IS NOT ALONE!
GRRRPH! I...GRRRPH!
I...WHAAA! THE MONSTER WE EXPERIMENTED ON!

DIE, MONSTER, DIE!
GRRRRPH! AGGGRRRAAA!
RAT TAT TAT
6

GRRRPH!
HE'S DYING! I... WHAAAAA!

AIIIIEEE! THE PROFESSOR'S SERUM... HYPODERMIC NEEDLE!

CARL'S BODY IS PIERCED BY THE INJECTION NEEDLE CONTAINING THE PROFESSOR'S STRANGE SERUM! AND A HIDEOUS TRANSFORMATION BEGINS!
I....CAN'T GET UP... I...AIIIEEE...I'M CHANGING!

I...CAN'T...GRRRPH!... I GRRRPH!... DYING....

....GRRRRPH!! AGGGRRRRAAA...!

GRRRPH....!!
THE LAST HUMAN IS HORRIBLY DESTROYED BY ONE OF HIS OWN INVENTIONS...AND THE EARTH IS ONCE AGAIN INHABITED SOLELY BY MONSTERS!
The End.

"I SHALL BE BACK!" THE GREAT LEONARDO SAID, AND HIS ASSISTANT, ROBERTO, SMILED WITH HIDDEN CONTEMPT! BUT REVENGE IS STRONG EVEN IN DEATH--AND THE BEYOND CANNOT DENY A--

RETURN FROM THE GRAVE!

ROBERTO! I AM COMING FOR YOU! ONLY **YOU,** ROBERTO--YOU BELONG WITH ME IN THE NICE SMOULDERING EARTH! ***ROBERTO! ROBERTO!***

YAAHH! *HEAVEN HELP US!*

THE GREAT LEONARDO ALWAYS KEPT HIS ENGROSSED AUDIENCE IN RAPTUROUS CONTENTMENT AS HE SHOWED ONE BRILLIANT TRICK AFTER ANOTHER--
--AND NOW THIS WHITE PAPER SHALL TURN INTO A DOVE! SO!
OHH!
AH!

BRAVO! MORE! MORE! YOU ARE MAGNIFICENT! WONDERFUL!
THANK YOU! THANK YOU! FROM THE BOTTOM OF MY HEART!
CLAP
CLAP

OUTSIDE--IN THE WINGS WAS ROBERTO, HIS SERVANT-- MORE HIS SLAVE! HE HAD WATCHED HIS MASTER FOR YEARS AND YEARS--AND HE HATED HIM WITH AN INTENSITY THAT NO WORDS COULD DESCRIBE!
THERE BUT FOR THE GRACE OF FATE, WALK I! IT IS NOT RIGHT FOR ONE MAN TO HAVE ALL THE CREDIT WHEN OTHERS HAVE SACRIFICED THEIR LIVES TO HELP HIM!

AH-- IT WAS A GOOD NIGHT THIS TIME! OAF! DO YOU HAVE MY ROBE?
RIGHT HERE, MASTER!

OH, MY DARLING, I'M SO PROUD OF YOU! YOU WERE GREAT TONIGHT!
THANK YOU, LILA DEAR! SOON YOU SHALL GO ON THE STAGE WITH ME AS MY WIFE! THEN WE SHALL BOTH ACCEPT THE ACCLAIM OF OUR AUDIENCE!

I DON'T LIKE TO BE GAPED AT, DOG! WHY'RE YOU STANDING HERE IDLE? GO, AND ATTEND TO MY WARDROBE AT ONCE!
OWWW! YES--YES, MASTER! AT ONCE!

I SHALL HAVE MY DAY YET! I AM TIRED OF HIS INSULTS! HIS BLOWS! HIS INSUFFERABLE EGO! I DO EVERYTHING FOR HIM, BUT HE ONLY LAUGHS

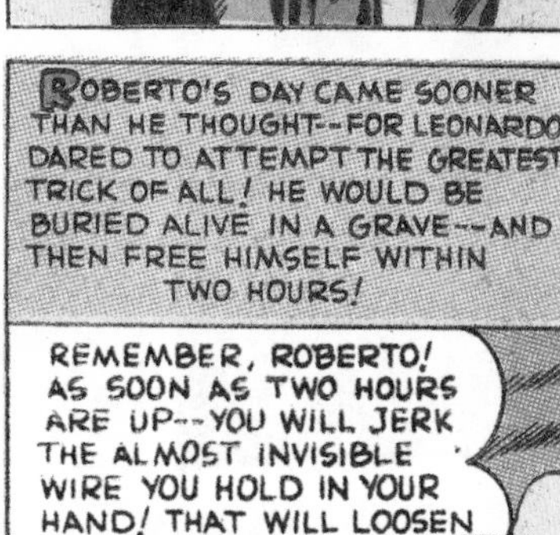
ROBERTO'S DAY CAME SOONER THAN HE THOUGHT--FOR LEONARDO DARED TO ATTEMPT THE GREATEST TRICK OF ALL! HE WOULD BE BURIED ALIVE IN A GRAVE--AND THEN FREE HIMSELF WITHIN TWO HOURS!
REMEMBER, ROBERTO! AS SOON AS TWO HOURS ARE UP--YOU WILL JERK THE ALMOST INVISIBLE WIRE YOU HOLD IN YOUR HAND! THAT WILL LOOSEN THE LOCK ON THIS COFFIN!
BUT, OF COURSE, MASTER!

2

I DIDN'T LIKE THE WAY ROBERTO LOOKED AT ME! I SHALL HAVE TO GET RID OF HIM VERY SOON!

HE SUSPECTS ME SOMEHOW-- **LET HIM!** IT WILL BE HIS LAST SUSPICION! HE IS DEAD FOREVER--**AS OF THIS MOMENT!!**

TWO HOURS CAME AND WENT AND NOW LEONARDO WAITED PATIENTLY FOR THE LOCK TO TURN IN HIS COFFIN--BUT IT NEVER DID!

WHY DOESN'T THAT FOOL HURRY! I'LL **SUFFOCATE** VERY SOON!

CAN'T BREATHE-- ROBERTO-- HE'S TRICKED ME! HE'S NOT GOING TO PULL THE WIRE! **ROBERTO!** I'LL TEAR YOUR TONGUE OUT! **ROBERTO!**

ROBERTO! LET ME OUT! HELP! PLEASE! I'M CHOKING! AGHHH! ROBERTO!

ROBERTO!
AGHHH!

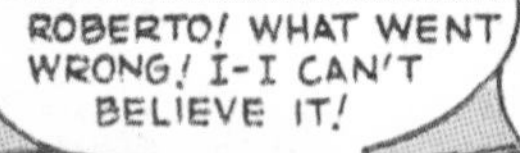
THEY RAISED THE WOODEN BOX AND OPENED IT TO LET IN THE FRESH AIR! BUT NOTHING STIRRED-- LEONARDO, THE GREAT, HAD MET HIS MASTER!

ROBERTO! WHAT WENT WRONG! I-I CAN'T BELIEVE IT!
HE HAD A **GADGET HE** WAS SUPPOSED TO PULL! IT MUST HAVE JAMMED!

SO ROBERTO TOOK OVER THE GREAT LEONARDO'S ACT AND EVEN OUTDID HIS PREDECESSOR!
--AND NOW THE DOVE SHALL BECOME TWO-- THREE--WHOOSH--PUFF--SO!
CLAP
CLAP
CLAP
BRAVO
3

OH, MY DEAREST-- YOU WERE WONDERFUL!
I SHOULD BE! I LEARNED LONG AND SERVED HARD UNDER LEONARDO!
AND NOW I HAVE HIS GIRL AS WELL! FORTUNE SMILED UPON ME THE MOMENT THE FOOL DIED!

BUT NOW DESTINY TOOK A HAND IN THE EVENTS THAT WERE TO FOLLOW. IT WAS MIDNIGHT AT THE GRAVEYARD--AND TWO DIGGERS WERE PREPARING A NEW GRAVE--,
BAH! THEY MUST ALWAYS GIVE US THE NIGHT TASKS AT THE LAST MOMENT!
DON'T COMPLAIN, SIMON! WE HAVE A GOOD JOB! THERE ISN'T ANYONE ELSE WHO WORKS IN SUCH PEACE AND QUIET! HA! HA!

OHHH! LET ME OUT! I MUST GET OUT! I MUST RETURN TO ROBERTO!
AGHH! WHAT HORROR HAVE WE DUG UP FROM THE EARTH?

I MUST KEEP MY PROMISE! ROBERTO! ROBERTO! YOU MUST JERK THAT WIRE! ROBERTO! WHERE ARE YOU? I AM COMING FOR YOU, ROBERTO!
YAAAH! HELP! YAAH!

EVERYTHING SEEMS HAZY! IT IS NIGHT! THERE IS NO ONE HERE! YET THIS--THIS UNBELIEVABLE PAIN! OOH! I CANNOT BREATHE! I DO NOT WANT TO BREATHE! I MUST FINISH MY TASK! YES, QUICKLY! QUICKLY!
4

MOMENTS LATER
BEFORE I HAD NOTHING! NOW-- EVERYTHING IS MINE! EVERYTHING! W-WHAT WAS THAT?
KNOCK KNOCK

WHY DID YOU NOT DO AS I SAID, ROBERTO? WHY? YOU HAVE MADE ME SUFFER THE TORTURES OF THE DAMNED! BUT I HAVE RETURNED FOR YOU ROBERTO!
NO! IT CANNOT BE! LEONARDO IS NOT ALIVE! LEAVE ME ALONE! DON'T TOUCH ME!

IT WON'T HURT ONE BIT, MY FAITHFUL SERVANT! JUST ONE SMALL TOUCH! JUST ONE YEARNING CARESS OVER THE FLESH OF LIFE! AND THEN YOU SHALL BE AS I! UGHH!
NO! GET AWAY! I-I'M DUE TO RETURN FOR THE SECOND ACT! THERE! YOU'LL SHATTER UNDER MY BLOW!

COME BACK, ROBERTO! THERE IS MUCH TO SHOW YOU IN THE BEYOND! YOU SHALL NEVER ESCAPE! NEVER! NEVER!
--GOT TO KEEP--MOVING--GOT TO--MUSTN'T LOSE MY SANITY!

ROBERTO WAS AGAIN ON STAGE! AGAIN HE PERFORMED HIS BAG OF TRICKS--THIS TIME WITH THE FRENZIED DESPERATION OF A MADMAN! AND SLOWLY, INEXORABLY, THE CHANGE OCCURRED!

NOW, I SHALL MIX THESE CARDS--AND--OHH--MY FACE FEELS SO FUNNY--GETTING NUMB!

EEEE

HIS FLESH IS MELTING OFF!

BUT THE CALL FROM THE BEYOND COULD NOT GO UNANSWERED! ROBERTO COULD NOT TURN AWAY FROM HIS MASTER'S VOICE AND HIS ROTTING BODY MADE A GRUESOME ANSWER!
NO, MASTER! DON'T CALL ME! PLEASE! I--I--DON'T WANT TO COME! PLEASE!
YAAAHH!
LOOK! LOOK! HE'S DEAD!
THE END

WE DARE YOU TO READ THESE TALES OF TERROR and SUSPENSE
NOW PUBLISHED MONTHLY
THE BEST IN SHOCK MYSTERY
GET THEM EVERY MONTH
TALES OF TERROR AND SUSPENSE!
CHAMBER OF CHILLS
WE DARE YOU
WITCHES TALES
STRANGEST TALES of FEAR and SUPERSTITION!
BLACK CAT MYSTERY
TALES BEYOND BELIEF AND IMAGINATION
TOMB OF TERROR
THE MARRIAGE OF THE MONSTERS!

BLOOD GHOST

More than seventy-five years ago there stood on the New England coast a huge inn with a spacious dining room, and a special room called The Mariners' Club. The choice brotherhood of skippers and mates who sailed the seas from the New England ports met here every week. For their benefit, the landlord served the kind of dinner that New England made famous.

But about seventy-five years ago, the Mariners Club disbanded. They never met again in the inn. It was sudden; and it was not their fault.

One of the Mariners Club members was Captain Sam Blood who ran a coastwise brig. Since his trips were short, he was always on hand for the Mariners Club dinner. He had in his small farm, two miles inland, an old and feeble mother, a brood of unkempt children, and a sick wife who from her threadbare couch complained again and again how her husband deserted her to go to the Mariners Club and wasted money she needed.

One day as the Mariners Club met, there was a sudden crash, followed by the crash of breaking bottles, dishware, falling kettles and boiling pots, frying pans and squashing food. The old salts and the landlord darted to the kitchen adjoining the Mariners Club room. They saw a slender young man in a sailor's outfit dashing out. They gave chase and caught him.

The sailor turned out to be, Mrs. Sam Blood in her husband's clothes!

Captain Blood growled darkly, "I'll settle for this dinner."

They let Mrs. Blood go.

There followed talk in the village how Mrs. Blood had been sick and pent up in her lonely couch. Surely a change of air would do her much good.

So on his next voyage, Captain Sam Blood took his wife along.

Mrs. Blood did not fare well, and at Savannah, Ga., she was just as sick as ever. So Captain Blood decided to take a cruise to South America. Since his New England sailors did not want the long voyage, he shipped them home and took a creole crew aboard.

Soon afterwards, Captain Blood returned to his New England home port a sombre, mourning widower. He said that Mrs. Blood had died at sea off Jamaica and was buried.

There followed for Captain Blood the period of mourning after which he returned to the Mariners Club. For his honor, the landlord prepared a big dinner and laid it out on the Club table.

Hardly had the old salts sat down, when the dishware and cooking utensils began a barrage of sounds. The mariners and the landlord ran to the adjoining kitchen and beheld a wreckage similar to the one Mrs. Blood had caused on her raid. This time nobody was caught in the act, although the landlord suspected an ill tempered servant he had fired.

The next week, the Mariners Club met again, and as they sat down, they were startled by crashing dishware and utensils. Everyone looked silently and ominously at Captain Sam Blood, whose face was calm but whose hands shook terribly. The implication was plain.

The Mariners Club disbanded. The landlord was stubborn and nailed the tables to prevent their being upset. He served the Mariners Club meals.

And every time he did, they were swept aside by invisible hands.

The mariners and the New England town never forgave Captain Sam Blood. For he had left with a wife and returned with a ghost.

THREE WEEKS AND $1 MADE "SAD SLIM JIM" HEP!

I CAN'T BELIEVE THAT ONLY THREE WEEKS AGO I TURNED YOU DOWN WHEN YOU ASKED FOR AN AFTER-SCHOOL JOB!

THANKS BOSS. THAT DOLLAR I INVESTED WITH JOE BONOMO SURE HAS COME BACK A THOUSAND TIMES!

REVOLUTIONARY... REVELATIONARY...

ONLY **$1** FOR MY NEW THREE WEEK **SPEED COURSE**

PLUS MY **FREE** FEATS OF STRENGTH

LISTEN YOU! CUT OUT WISHING!

NOW — Have a Wallop-Packed BODY OF SUPER STRENGTH,

Dynamic Energy and Greater Health

JOE BONOMO STARTS YOU ON YOUR WAY TOWARDS ALL THREE—IN JUST THREE WEEKS!

JOE BONOMO Is Not A Mythical Figure • Winner of the "Daily News" Modern Apollo contest. Star of Universal Pictures . . . who billed him as the world's Strongest Man. Millions of people have seen the Herculean JOE BONOMO in Action on the Screen, Stage and T.V. Let this international authority on health and strength . . . **TELL YOU HOW!...**

SHOW YOU HOW!...

Easy To Read—Easy To Do And Easy To Follow For A Man-Sized "Power-Plus Body

FOR BOYS & MEN OF ALL AGES

STARTS YOU IN JUST A SHORT **3 WEEKS**

Bernarr McFadden says: "As an instructor in muscle-building, you should stand at the head of the list. Many of your pupils already attest to your ability in building better bodies. I can recommend you most highly. Here's wishing you all possible success!"

Jack Dempsey says: "I consider your "Power - Plus" Course tops for all-around physical development — power, strength — endurance. The secrets and short cuts you reveal with your system of body development are miraculous & I cannot endorse your course too highly."

FREE FEATS OF STRENGTH

FAMOUS Strongmen's Manual

FREE • FREE • FREE

WHEN YOU ORDER NOW!

32 - Picture - Packed Pages on Strength Feats Strongmen are Famous For . . . All Yours! Do you know how to (1) Break A Spike With Your Teeth? (2) Tear A Phone Book In Half? (3) Hold 4 Persons In The Air? (4) Drive A Spike-Thru a Thick Board? (5) Break A Rock With Your Fist? See how these—plus many more—can be done.

VALUE VALUE VALUE

© Copyright MCMLII

Fellows of all ages . . . who want to make a real success out of themselves . . . a New Life, Bigger and Stronger . . . HERE IT IS! Joe Bonomo's New and Complete 3 WEEKS SPEED COURSE is priced to give you real Value. Think of it? ONE DOLLAR AND 10 MINUTES A DAY IS ALL THAT YOU NEED. Your Speed Course is written in plain, blunt, locker room language . Can Give You amazing results. Contains (1) Body Facts Lectures (2) Muscle Charts (3) Training Table Talks . GIVES YOU "Psycho-Power", "Rhythmic Progression" "Vibro-Pressure", "Tonic Relaxation" . The Big Four. Also Physical Development Quotient (PDQ) . . PLUS Inspirational Strongmen's Pictures to help wake up the Body of Yours

Yes, for less than 5c a day . . . plus 10 minutes daily . . . you, too, can find out about POWER — STRENGTH — GLOWING HEALTH — ABUNDANT VIGOR — DYNAMIC ENERGY. Get a Two-Fisted, All-'Round Thrill in becoming a Real Man in Three Weeks. Wake Up! Tone Up! Build Up! Follow Mighty Joe Bonomo and make your start toward becoming a "Super Strongman!"

YOU WILL BEGIN TO ENJOY THE THRILL AND ADMIRATION OF YOUR MAN-SIZED NEW BODY THE FIRST DAY YOU START — SO HURRY, DON'T DELAY! WRITE TODAY!

7 Day "Money-Back" Offer!

IMAGINE! Only THREE WEEKS and the amazing NEW LOW PRICE of ONE DOLLAR may actually give you MORE AMBITION—SUCCESS ENERGY and a Full Rich Life of POPULARITY!

In 7-Days Your Money Back if not Satisfied!

STRONGMEN'S CLUB OF AMERICA, Joe Bonomo, Director
1841 Broadway • New York 23, New York

MAIL THIS "NO RISK" COUPON RIGHT NOW!

ACT NOW FOR FREE OFFER

STRONGMEN'S CLUB OF AMERICA Dept.WH9
JOE BONOMO, Director
1841 BROADWAY • NEW YORK CITY 23

Okay, Joe. Send me your Famous Three Week 'SPEED COURSE' for the special price of $1. I am acting fast so be sure to include your free gift of the Strongmen's Manual "Feats of Strength." If I am not thrilled and satisfied in every way, I may return these in 7 days for a full one dollar refund.

Name ....
(Print Plainly)

Address ....

City .... Zone .... State ....

$1 enclosed ☐ Check ☐ Money Order ☐ Cash

MIDNIGHT IN A LAND OF RUIN AND HORROR-- AND SUDDENLY THE THROBBING DRUMS HERALD THE ARRIVAL OF THE DEAD, WHOSE RAVAGED FACES AND FESTERING BODIES BEAR THE MARK OF THE...
VOLCANO DOOM!
LET THE LAVA DEVOUR YOU ALL!! YOU MUST LEARN THE PRICE OF DISOBEDIENCE!!
SOMEWHERE IN THE BLACK HEART OF AFRICA, A SMALL VILLAGE SUDDENLY EXPERIENCES THE SHOCK AND THE CHAOS OF A VIOLENT AND TERRIBLE EARTHQUAKE!....
NO! N--- AARGH-H-H!!!
YAAAH-H-H! THE WORLD IS ENDED!
THE TEMPLE!! THE TEM--- YAIEEE-EEE!!
WHEN WILL IT STOP??
CRASH
THE HEAT!! THE HEAT!! AIEEE-E-E!!
MALA, FREE US FROM YOUR CURSE!! WE SHALL NEVER DEFY YOU AGAIN!!
1

OUR FALSE GOD MALA HAS BETRAYED US! HE HAS WREAKED THIS HORROR UPON US WHEN WE ARE INNOCENT OF EVIL!!
AND THESE ARE HIS AGENTS OF DESTRUCTION, OUR CHIEF AND OUR HIGH PRIEST!! IF MALA IS OUR GOD NO LONGER, THEY MUST DIE!!
BIND THE PRIEST TO THE STAKE--- WE SHALL DEAL FIRST WITH OUR WRETCHED LEADER!!
WHAT ARE YOU GOING TO DO WITH ME? MALA SHALL MAKE YOU PAY FOR THIS!
NO! NO! NOT THE VOLCANO! YOU CANNOT SACRIFICE ME TO THE VOLCANO!!
HURRY! IT IS GROWING DARK!!

I AM YOUR LEADER! YOU CANNOT DO THIS!
SEE HOW IT BOILS AND BUBBLES!! SEE HOW EAGER IT IS TO WELCOME YOU! AND NOW YOU MUST---

ONE BRIEF BUT VIOLENT THRUST-- AND THE CHIEF OF THE TRIBE HURTLES WILDLY TO A FIERY DOOM...
DIE!!
YAAGH-H-H-H!

COME! WE MUST BURY OUR DEAD BEFORE THE NIGHT IS DONE!!
AND IN THE MORNING OUR PRIEST SHALL MEET HIS DESERVED FATE!!
2

LATE THAT EVENING, AFTER THE VICTIMS OF THE EARTHQUAKE HAVE FOUND THEIR GRAVES, THE DOOMED PRIEST STRUGGLES DESPERATELY TO FREE HIMSELF--AND SUCCEEDS...
AHHH! THE BONDS ARE BROKEN! NOW THESE SLEEPING FOOLS SHALL FEEL THE POWER OF MALA'S WRATH!! I SHALL GO TO THE VOLCANO!!
O MALA WHO DWELLS IN THE DEPTHS OF THE FLAMES--HEAR ME!! RESTORE MY MASTER FROM THE BOILING LAVA... SO THAT HE MIGHT STRIKE TERROR AT THE HEARTS OF HIS MURDERERS!!!
AS THE PRIEST SHRIEKS HIS INCANTATION, A FIGURE EMERGES FROM THE VOLCANO--A RAVAGED RUIN TO MAKE THE VIEWER GASP WITH UNSPEAKABLE LOATHING!...
MY MASTER!
YOU HAVE SERVED ME WELL, TANI!! TOGETHER WE SHALL INFEST MY PEOPLE WITH THE AGONY OF DEATH!!
MALA MUST HELP US TO AVENGE OURSELVES ON THE VILLAGE!
HE SHALL HELP US! YOU MUST FOLLOW ME TO THE BURIAL GROUND WHERE OUR DEAD LIE IN RESTLESS SLEEP!!
IN THE FORBIDDING STILLNESS OF THE TROPICAL EVENING, THE FIGURE OF THE PRIEST STANDS IN THE STRANGE MOONLIGHT, UTTERING A PAGAN INCANTATION THAT FALLS UPON THE AIR LIKE A CRY OF HORROR!!
RISE FROM YOUR GRAVES, O DEAD ONES!! I SHALL GUIDE YOU BACK TO YOUR GRIEVING PEOPLE!! BAROUNDA CAVALO!!!
AND SOON THE STIRRING OF THE GRAVES BRINGS FORTH AN APPALLING SIGHT, AS THE DEAD RETURN FROM THE GATES OF HELL TO WANDER THE EARTH ONCE MORE!!...
OHH-H-H-H!!! WHAT DO YOU WISH WITH US???
ONLY THAT YOU RETURN AT ONCE TO THE VILLAGE OF YOUR BIRTH!!
3

THERE IS SOMETHING MOVING IN THE BRUSH! SEE WHAT IT IS!!
NO, NO!! I AM AFRAID!! THERE IS BLOOD ON THE MOON TONIGHT!!
SUDDENLY--TO THE STARTLED GAZE OF THE VILLAGERS--A DREADFUL CONGREGATION COMES OUT OF THE DARKNESS--LIKE MONSTROUS CREATURES FROM THE FLAMING PIT OF THE DAMNED!...
YAAAH-H-H!!! AIEEEE-E-E!!! IT CANNOT BE!
THE CURSE OF YOUR CRIME IS UPON YOU!! THE DEAD SHALL ROAM YOUR STREETS FOREVER!!
NO! NO! TAKE THEM AWAY!!
WE CANNOT LIVE IN PEACE WHILE OUR DEAD WANDER THE EARTH! THEY MUST GO BACK TO THEIR GRAVES!!
AS THE VILLAGERS STARE IN HORROR AT THEIR UNBIDDEN GUESTS, A VIOLENT FLASH OF LIGHTNING BRINGS YET ANOTHER ARRIVAL FROM THE WORLD BEYOND...
YOU HAVE CALLED ME FALSE--AND DESTROYED MY AGENT AMONG YOU! FOR THAT YOU ARE CURSED WITH THE SPIRITS OF THOSE WHO FESTER IN THEIR GRAVES!!
WE BEG YOUR FORGIVENESS, O MALA! TELL US WHAT WE MUST DO TO END THIS PLAGUE OF HORROR!!
THIS IS MY COMMAND--TWELVE OF YOU MUST BE GIVEN UP TO THE BOILING LAVA OF THE VOLCANO! ONLY THEN WILL THE CURSE BE ENDED!!
OH-H-H-H-H!!! WE ARE FORCED TO OBEY YOU, MALA!! TWELVE OF US MUST DIE AT THE VOLCANO OF DOOM!!
4

OVERWHELMED WITH FEAR AND HORROR, THE VILLAGERS STRUGGLE TO THE MOUTH OF THE VOLCANO, KNOWING THAT SOME MUST MEET A FIENDISH DEATH IN THE HUNGRY, STEAMING LAVA!!...
OHH-H-H-H!! I DO NOT WISH TO DIE!!
YET MALA MUST BE APPEASED-- OR OUR PEOPLE SHALL WALK IN ETERNAL BLACKNESS!!

FOR MY PEOPLE!! AIEEE-EE-EE!!
ARGH-H-H-H-H!!

AS THE SACRIFICE CONTINUES, NEW BODIES ARE OFFERED UP TO THE INSATIABLE GREED OF THE VOLCANO!!...
NO! NO! DON'T--- YAAAH-H-H-H!!
YOU ARE THE LAST TO GO!!...

IT IS DONE, O ALL-POWERFUL MALA!! THE CURSE UPON US MUST BE ENDED AND OUR DEAD RETURN TO ETERNAL SLEEP!!
SEE!! THE DEAD HAVE GONE! BUT OUR PRIEST AND OUR CHIEF REMAIN!!
WHAT MORE CAN MALA DEMAND OF US??
LISTEN AND OBEY! IT HAS BEEN ORDAINED BY MALA THAT THE LEADER BEFORE YOU--WHO FELT THE AGONY OF THE VOLCANO--SHOULD RULE YOU FOREVER!!
NO! NO!! THIS CANNOT BE!!

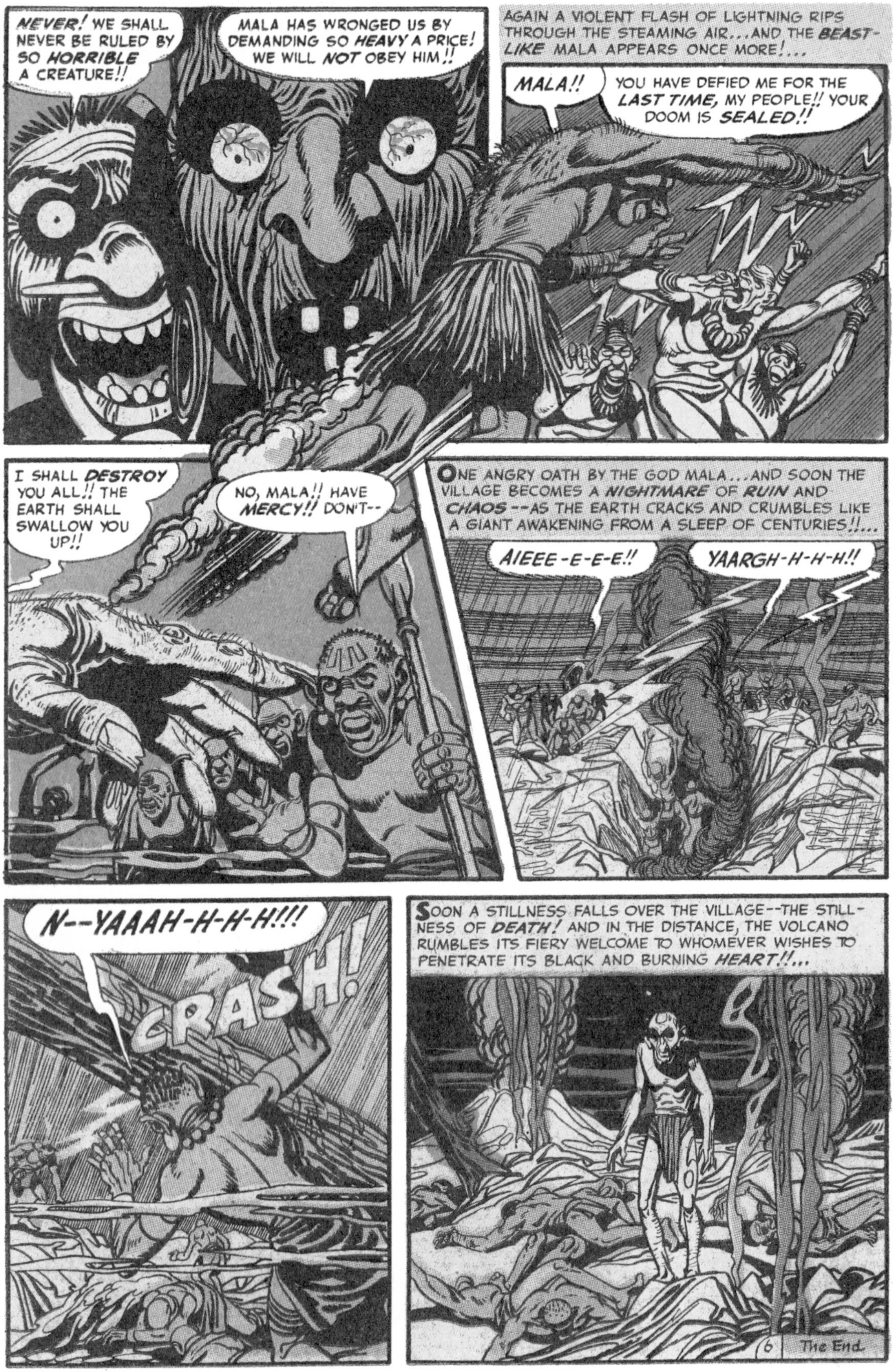

NEVER! WE SHALL NEVER BE RULED BY SO HORRIBLE A CREATURE!!
MALA HAS WRONGED US BY DEMANDING SO HEAVY A PRICE! WE WILL NOT OBEY HIM!!

AGAIN A VIOLENT FLASH OF LIGHTNING RIPS THROUGH THE STEAMING AIR...AND THE BEAST-LIKE MALA APPEARS ONCE MORE!...
MALA!!
YOU HAVE DEFIED ME FOR THE LAST TIME, MY PEOPLE!! YOUR DOOM IS SEALED!!

I SHALL DESTROY YOU ALL!! THE EARTH SHALL SWALLOW YOU UP!!
NO, MALA!! HAVE MERCY!! DON'T--

ONE ANGRY OATH BY THE GOD MALA...AND SOON THE VILLAGE BECOMES A NIGHTMARE OF RUIN AND CHAOS--AS THE EARTH CRACKS AND CRUMBLES LIKE A GIANT AWAKENING FROM A SLEEP OF CENTURIES!!...
AIEEE-E-E-E!!
YAARGH-H-H-H!!

DOOMED TO DIE

I've tried to tell them . . . I've tried and tried. But they won't listen. They won't understand. Sometimes they laugh. Sometimes they pat me on the hand and say, "Sure! Sure! We know!"—as though I were some kind of village idiot. Most of the time they just ignore me completely . . . even the ones who say they're my friends.

It's absolutely maddening. The whole thing would be so clear to them if only they'd listen to me. There wouldn't be all this fuss and bother. After all, *I* understand it now, and I'm just an ordinary, rational man. Oh, I admit it was difficult to believe at first. I never gave much thought to second sight myself. I, too, rather tended to laugh at crackpots who claimed they could see into the future. Just like *they* do.

But the weight of the evidence was overwhelming. After all, I saw and heard and felt the whole thing with my own five senses. In fact, I'm the only living person who knows just exactly what *did* happen. And I'm convinced. I really don't see why *they* all insist on being so stupidly pig-headed about it. Why, sometimes I think they actually blame *me* for it!

That's sheer nonsense, of course. I was merely the tool of fate, the instrument of destiny—and an unwilling instrument at that. Didn't I try to warn Charlie? Didn't I try to save him? Naturally, it was impossible. There's no way of altering the course of fate—although I didn't know that at the time. It's one of the things I know *now*, one of the things I try to tell *them*, one of the things *they* refuse to understand.

All they seem to be aware of are the actual *physical* facts. They know the exact date and hour I arrived at my friend Charlie Transon's hunting lodge for a week's hunting and fishing. They know the exact date and hour that I found my friend Charlie Transon's body with that 10-inch blade sticking in his heart.

But they don't know one single, solitary thing about the dreams! That's what they don't *want* to know! And yet my friend Charlie knew about them. I told him all about the first one the very first morning I was there.

"I've never believed in dreams, Charlie," I said to him, "but I believe in this one—the one I had last night. You are going to be *murdered*, Charlie!"

Of course he laughed, just as some of *them* do. He didn't laugh quite so hard the second day when I asked him, "Do you keep a hunting knife with a 10-inch blade in the top drawer of your desk, Charlie?"

"Why, yes, Roy—I do!" he answered in surprise. "But how did *you* know?"

"Because I dreamed the dream again last night, Charlie," I informed him solemnly. "And I saw the murderer take that knife out of the drawer."

I dreamed the dream on the third night, and on the fourth, and each time the details grew clearer. I knew now at just what angle the blade would descend into my friend Charlie's chest, I knew just how his last gurgle would sound as he choked on his own blood. Then, on the fifth night, I finally saw the murderer's face in the dream. And I knew I could interfere with fate no further.

I could do nothing but what I was meant to do. I had no choice but to crawl out of bed, tiptoe into my friend Charlie's room, open that desk drawer—noiselessly, oh, so noiselessly, so as not to disturb the doomed—lift out that hunting knife—how that blade shimmered in the moonlight, glowing in anticipation of its destiny-sent task—glide over to my friend Charlie's bed, and plunge that 10-inch blade into his heart—at just the right angle, of course. Even his death gurgle was letter-perfect . . .

Oh, oh! They're coming now. I can hear them. And it's about time. Just how long is an intelligent, civilized gentleman like me supposed to remain trussed up like a turkey in this ridiculous strait jacket anyhow?

Perhaps they've finally come to apologize for all these indignities. Perhaps they've finally realized that my good friend Charlie Transon was simply destined to die . . .

OUT OF THE FROZEN LAND THAT IS TIBET CAME A TERRIBLE MONSTER THAT PREYED ON HUMAN FLESH--THAT MADE NEWSPAPER HEADLINES SCREAM...

The Morning Chronicle

FOUND: THE LAIR OF THE SNOW MONSTER!!!

THE GROUP HAD BEEN DISCUSSING THE OCCULT AND THE SUPERNATURAL...
BUT YOU MUST ADMIT, GENTLEMEN--THAT SUCH PHENOMENA ARE PREPOSTEROUS!
HA, HA...OF COURSE! BUT THERE ARE MANY WHO BELIEVE SUCH THINGS!
I FOR ONE DO, GENTLEMEN--WHAT IF I WERE TO TELL YOU OF SUCH A HORROR THAT IT WOULD CURDLE THE VERY BLOOD IN YOUR VEINS? WOULD YOU THEN MOCK ME?
THAT DEPENDS--IF YOUR TALE IS SUBSTANTIATED UPON FACT--OF COURSE NOT! BUT--IF--IT'S A SUPERSTITIOUS PILE OF HOKUM--WELL...

GRANTED THEN! SETTLE BACK AND PREPARE FOR THE MOST SPINE-CHILLING ADVENTURE THAT COULD POSSIBLY HAPPEN TO ANYONE!
ALL RIGHT, MAN! BEGIN!

"MY NAME IS ARTHUR FISK! PERHAPS YOU REMEMBER THE EVENTS OF ONE YEAR AGO THAT STARTLED THE WORLD ABOUT A GIANT SNOW BEAST! IT HAS BEEN PLAYED DOWN SINCE... ANYWAY, THERE WERE FOUR OF US..."
WHAT SHALL WE DO WITH THE TRANSMITTER, COREY? WILL THE SHIP'S MEN SEND OUT A PLANE AFTERWARDS?
PROBABLY! BE PREPARED FOR A LONG STAY HERE, ARTHUR!

"WE WERE ALL PART OF THE EXPEDITION THAT HAD BEEN SUBSIDIZED TO EXPLORE THE FAR REACHES OF TIBET. CERTAIN WEATHER CONDITIONS WERE ACTING UP STRANGELY, AND WE WERE INTENSELY INTERESTED..."

WHEN WILL WE START OUR OBSERVATIONS?

AT ONCE! WILSON AND TIMKINS ARE READYING THE SLEDS NOW! THINK OF IT, ARTHUR-- TO BE THE ONLY ONES WHO HAVE COMPLETELY MAPPED TIBET!

"TIMKINS AND WILSON WERE GOOD MEN--AND EXCELLENT TOPOGRAPHISTS! BRIAN COREY WAS OUR EXPEDITION CHIEF--AND I, HIS ASSISTANT. OUR JOURNEY BEGAN..."
MUSH! MUSH!
ARF-ARF!

"WE TRAVELED FOR DAYS AND FINALLY, WHEN ALL FOUR OF US WERE HUDDLED UP TOGETHER AFTER A HARD DAY'S TRIP, WE FIRST HEARD THAT HORRIBLE SOUND..."
GENTLEMEN--WE ARE TO BE CONGRATULATED! ANOTHER DAY--AND WE'LL HAVE COMPLETED...
W-WHAT WAS THAT--?
AAAOOOEEE

PROBABLY A WOLF OF SOME SORT, WILSON! YOU CAN NEVER TELL HOW FAR NORTH SOME ANIMALS TRAVEL!
IT ISN'T A JOKING MATTER, FISK! NO WOLVES ARE KNOWN IN THIS REGION! IN THE FUTURE, WE MUST ALL BE ON GUARD--FOR ANY EMERGENCY!
2

"NOTHING WAS SAID FURTHER OF THE MATTER AS WE PROGRESSED AHEAD. IN TRUTH, WE HEARD NO MORE STRANGE SOUNDS -- AND I WAS NOW DOUBTING MY OWN EARS. THEN, ON DAWN OF THE SIXTH DAY, WE ARRIVED!"
IN ALL PROBABILITY, NO MAN HAS EVER SEEN THIS LAND! AND LOOK AT THAT MOUND!
AMAZING!

"SOON, WE WERE SETTLED, AND HAD ALREADY BEGUN OUR MAPPING PROBLEMS. BUT COREY AND I WERE NOW INTERESTED IN THE MOUND ITSELF..."
WHAT DO YOU MAKE OF THIS GIANT HILL, BRIAN? IT SEEMS TOO REGULAR-- TOO MAN-MADE!
I WAS THINKING OF THE SAME THING! INCREDIBLE!

"WE BEGAN TO EXCAVATE A SMALL PART OF THE MOUND FOR EXAMINATION. SUDDENLY..."
LOOK! GOOD HEAVENS! THERE'S METAL UNDERNEATH THIS SNOW!
DIG, MAN! FASTER! FASTER!

"WE DUG FOR WHAT SEEMED LIKE HOURS. THEN..."
IT'S AN ENTRANCE TO A BUILDING OF SOME KIND! COREY-- I'M GOING INSIDE!
NO, ARTHUR! I HAVE THE STRANGEST FEELING! LET'S CLOSE IT UP UNTIL WE CAN SEND OUT OUR NEWS OF THIS DISCOVERY!

I'M SORRY--! I DON'T AGREE WITH YOU! THIS IS THE FIND OF THE DECADE! STAY OUTSIDE IF YOU LIKE, BUT I'M GOING IN!
NO, FISK! DON'T!! COME BACK!

Y-A-A-A-A-H!
SQUISH

"I HAD HARDLY SEEN WHAT OCCURRED! ALL I KNOW IS THAT EVERY ATOM OF MY FLESH SUDDENLY REBELLED AT THE THOUGHT OF STAYING INSIDE THAT HORRIBLE TOMB ONE SECOND LONGER! I RUSHED OUT IN PANIC!
YAAAAAH! GET AWAY! GET AWAY!
WHAT IS IT? WHAT ARE YOU TALKING ABOUT?

AAAIIIIEEEEE-- GLUG--GLUGG...
SQUISSSH

KILL IT! KILL IT! WHAT HAVE I DONE?
BANG! BANG!

"CLOSER AND CLOSER THE THING PULLED POOR TIMKINS, AND THEN BEFORE OUR VERY EYES, HE WAS SWALLOWED UP LIKE SO MUCH FOOD!"
THAT'S IT! THAT'S THE SOUND WE HEARD! COREY! IT'S COMING FROM THAT MONSTER!
I'VE PUMPED IT FULL OF HOLES AND STILL IT WON'T DIE!!
AAAOOEEEE

"DESPERATELY, FRANTICALLY, GASPING WITH NUMBED FRIGHT, WE DASHED TOWARDS OUR SLEDS, FORGETTING INSTRUMENTS-- SUPPLIES--EVERYTHING IN OUR HASTE TO GET AWAY..."
MUSH! MUSH! YOU BARKING CURS! MUSH!
WILSON! WATCH OUT! WATCH OUT!
AAACOOEEEEEEEEE

AAAGGHHH!
PLOP

"WE TOOK ONE PARALYZED GLANCE -- AND THEN WE WERE FLEEING -- RUNNING PELL-MELL AWAY FROM THAT CREATURE! BUT IT ROLLED AFTER US, HUNTING, EVER HUNTING WITH A FEROCITY AND INTELLIGENCE BEYOND THAT OF MAN..."
HURRY! HURRY!!
AIIIEEE! IT'S GAINING!
AOOOEEEEEE

"DAYS AND NIGHTS WE TRAVELED -- NOT STOPPING ONCE -- NOT *DARING* TO! BUT WE WERE ONLY HUMAN. WE *HAD* TO HAVE REST! WE BOTH MUST HAVE DOZED OFF IN OUR FLIGHT, AND THAT'S WHEN IT STRUCK!"

HELP ME, ARTHUR! HELP ME... PLEASE! *PLEASE! I DON'T WANT TO DIE!* SOBB...
SQUISH!
BANG!
BANG

"BUT IT WAS USELESS, OF COURSE. COREY DISAPPEARED INTO THAT FRIGHTFUL MAW! AND *I* WAS NEXT! SUDDENLY, I WAS CRAWLING TOWARDS IT -- WHIMPERING -- HYPNOTIZED LIKE A BIRD IS IN FRONT OF A SNAKE..."

EEEE...EEEE..EE.. NO...NO...EEE..EE... SOB..SOB...

"THEN A TERRIBLE MONSOON-LIKE SNOW-STORM BORE DOWN UPON US. WITH A SOUL-SHATTERING SCREECH, THE MONSTER COLLIDED INTO ME AND VANISHED INTO THE SWIRLING MOISTURE. I COLLAPSED AS A PIERCING PAIN WENT THROUGH MY SHOULDER WITH THE BURNING PAIN OF A BESTIAL BITE!"

"HOW I REGAINED CONSCIOUSNESS -- HOW THE OTHERS IN THE TRANSPORT SHIP FOUND ME, I'LL NEVER KNOW! I BABBLED INCOHERENTLY FOR MONTHS -- AND FOR MONTHS I WAS COMMITTED INTO AN ASYLUM FOR THE INSANE..."

AHA, HA..HA, HA...AHA, HA ...IT'S STILL OUT THERE! STILL WAITING FOR ME!!! HA, HA... WAITING -- *WAITING!*

A NEWSPAPER BOUGHT MY STORY AND SYNDICATED IT I BECAME RICH, BUT I ALSO LOST MY YOUTH -- AND MY PEACE OF MIND FOR THE REST OF MY LIFE! WHAT THAT MONSTER WAS -- OR *IS* -- WE'LL NEVER KNOW! BUT IT *IS* OUT THERE -- WAITING!
GOOD HEAVENS, MAN! YOU WERE DELIRIOUS! IT WAS SHEER IMAGINATION! IT *HAS* TO BE!

IS IT? THEN HOW DO YOU EXPLAIN -- *THIS!!!?*
THE END

INDOORS! OUTDOORS!
BLACK & WHITE! FULL COLOR!
PARTIES! NEWS SHOTS!

An **AMAZING** Camera. Takes pictures **DAY or NIGHT, indoors or outdoors.** Sharp BLACK and WHITE snapshots or **FULL COLOR** photos using Kodacolor film. 12 Big pictures on 1 Roll of film. Flash attachment snaps on or off in seconds. Catch valuable news photos. **Win admiration at parties, dances.** NOW $4.95

FILM Special #620 Orthochromatic. 3 ROLLS for $1.00

PERFECT for active women and girls. Fine **JEWELLED** movement in dainty case. **GILT** hands and numbers. Smart Link Expansion Bracelet. NOW $6.98

BEST for active men and boys. **SHOCK-RESISTANT** and **ANTI-MAGNETIC!** Luminous Dial! Jewelled Movement! Red Sweep-Second! Expansion Bracelet. NOW $6.99

Ladies' **Jewelled** Watch in a smart **Gold** finish case. Dial has **12 Flashing imitation DIAMONDS and RUBIES.** Glamorous Snake Bracelet. NOW $8.49

Rich, Flashing Men's **Jewelled** Watch with **11 Sparkling imitation DIAMONDS and RUBIES.** Smart **Gold** finish case. Deluxe Basket-weave Bracelet. NOW $9.95

INITIAL RING

A **Handsome, Masculine Ring with your own INITIAL** set in Raised GOLD effect on a BRILLIANT **RUBY-RED** color stone. With 2 SPARKLING imitation **DIAMONDS** on the sides. Rich 14K R G P. NOW $2.95

FREE
NO-RISK HOME TRIAL

SEND NO MONEY! We want you to inspect and enjoy this fine quality merchandise right in your own home. **You risk nothing!** If not delighted, return for **FULL PRICE REFUND.** Every article we sell is **GUARANTEED!** Order from this famous company and be convinced.

GUARANTEED SAVINGS

BRILLIANT MEN'S WATCH

A **MAGNIFICENT** Men's Watch that you'll be **real proud of!** GUARANTEED 15 **JEWEL MOVEMENT** in a Handsome **GENUINE** 10K R G P case. Rich, brilliant GOLDEN-SPRINKLED Dial with flashing GILT NUGGET hour dots. Contrasting Jet-Black center. Genuine Alligator-grain leather strap. **TERRIFIC VALUE** NOW $12.95

"PRINCE" RING. Here's a Rich, **Massive Ring** for you. **With a Huge Flashing** imitation **DIAMOND and 6 Fiery Red** imitation **RUBIES.** 14K R G P. NOW $3.49

CLUSTER RING with your OWN **RAISED GOLD-COLOR INITIAL** on a Rich **RUBY-RED** color stone set in a circle of Blazing imitation **DIAMONDS.** 14K R G P. NOW $3.49

POWERFUL BATTERY-OPERATED *Private Line* WALL PHONES

Inter-Office | Room-to-Room | House-to-Garage | Shop-to-Storeroom

7.50 NOW 5.49 COMPLETE SET

for HOME or OFFICE USE

NOW!! Your own PRIVATE-LINE "PHONE SYSTEM" that sets up in minutes—easily—anywhere you want it. **Powerful BATTERY-OPERATED** circuit carries two-way conversations loud and clear. Signal buttons and buzzers on each phone. **SAVE TIME, SAVE STEPS—just pick up the receiver, buzz your party and make the call!** A thousand uses for this amazing instrument. All-steel construction in handsome Hammertone Enamel finish. Complete set of 2 Phones, 50 feet of Wire, Instructions and Guarantee . . . NOW $5.49

NOTE: When ordering this item, enclose $1.00 Deposit.

ROMANCE SET

Real Sparkling, Shining BEAUTY! Engagement Ring has **4 Flashing Brilliants** and a **BEAUTIFUL** imitation **DIAMOND SOLITAIRE. 7 Twinkling Brilliants** in the Wedding Ring. **12K GOLD Filled. Both** rings. NOW $3.74

DIAMOND RING for Men. 14K R G P. **REAL DIAMOND** CHIP on Gen. MOTHER-OF-PEARL face. 2 **RUBY** color side SPARKLERS. NOW $4.98

BUCKLE RING. Manly impressive style wins attention. **10K GOLD Filled.** 3 BIG imitation **DIAMONDS and RUBIES.** NOW $2.98

MAIL THIS COUPON

IDEAL CO., Dept. CS-37
Box 232 Mad. Sq. Sta., New York 10, N.Y.

SEND NO MONEY! Just cut out pictures of articles desired and attach to this coupon. Pay postman plus few cents postage and excise tax on delivery. **THEN EXAMINE IN YOUR OWN HOME. SATISFACTION IS GUARANTEED OR YOUR MONEY BACK.**

PLEASE PRINT

NAME ______________________

ADDRESS ______________________

TOWN ______________ STATE ________

(Send RING SIZES, INITIAL WANTED and your BIRTH-MONTH. If you need more room, attach a sheet of paper.)

BUY NOW & SAVE!
76 SENSATIONAL NEW GLOWING CHRISTMAS TREE ORNAMENTS ONLY $1
ACTUALLY CHARGE THEMSELVES WITH LIGHT! LIGHT UP AT NIGHT WITHOUT WIRES WITHOUT ELECTRICITY
MADE OF REVOLUTIONARY LIGHT ABSORBING PLASTIC
Now decorate your Christmas Tree with a sensational new kind of Christmas Tree Ornaments . . . these actually light up without wires or electricity . . . because they're made of safe, light absorbing plastic. They absorb the light and store it . . . then when you turn out the lights they just light up . . . it's like magic. They are durable, made of sturdy Dow STYRENE plastic and will last for years. Some up to 4½ inches high. AND . . . in daylight their colors of red, blue and white glisten with sunlit effect . . . they are beautiful by day . . . spellbinding at night.
14 BELLS LIGHT UP - SPELLING -
MERRY CHRISTMAS
NO ELECTRICITY NO WIRES
You Get ALL THESE 76 Ornaments
Every one made of solid light absorbing plastic . . . No wires, no danger. They're WIRELESS. Tested and approved by world famous testing laboratory. Just hang them on your tree. Will last a lifetime. Light up quality never wears out.
• 14 MERRY CHRISTMAS BELLS
• 10 CHURCH BELLS • 1 SANTA'S HOUSE
• 12 STARS • 10 SNOWFLAKES
• 12 ICICLES • 1 NORTH POLE
• 4 CANDY CANES • 1 SNOW MAN
• 1 SANTA CLAUS • 3 CANDLES
• 6 REINDEER • 1 CHERUB
SANTA'S WORK SHOP
NORTH POLE
Fully Guaranteed Rush Coupon
We guarantee full satisfaction or money back in ten days. Hurry coupon for guaranteed Christmas delivery. You take no risk because they have been approved by a leading testing laboratory. Your assurance of quality and value.
XMAS SPECIAL RUSH COUPON
DON'T DELAY MAIL NOW
XMAS ORNAMENTS, Dept. X-4
836 BROADWAY, N.Y. 3, N.Y.
Send your special offer of 76 all-plastic, light-up-in-the-dark Christmas Tree Ornaments by return postpaid mail. If not delighted, I'll return for refund within 10 days. I enclose one dollar for each set ordered. (Only 3 sets to each customer.) (Sorry, NO C.O.D.'s.)
Enclosed find $______for______sets
Name______
Address______

TOMB OF TERROR

TALES BEYOND BELIEF AND IMAGINATION!

TOMB OF TERROR

No. 7
JAN.

PDC

10¢

PEOPLE ONLY WHISPER ABOUT IT... EVEN THE MORBID SHUN ITS LOATHSOME MEANING... BUT NOW.. *YOU* ARE *TRAPPED*... COMPLETELY.. MERCILESSLY BY...

THE SHADOW OF DEATH!

LEE ELIAS

the SECRET of TREASURE CAVE-
How Gray Shadow Tracked Down the Mystery of Spike's Sudden Wealth.
GIVEN!
BOYS! GIRLS! LADIES! MEN!
WE GIVE YOU CASH OR PREMIUMS!
LAST WEEK HE TOOK A NEW AIR RIFLE IN THAT CAVE-
GEE! A NEW BIKE!
WHERE'S SPIKE GET THAT STUFF?
GRAY SHADOW HAS GOT TO TRAIL HIM!
I'LL BUY 2 BOXES OF WHITE CLOVERINE BRAND SALVE, SPIKE! IT'S WONDERFUL... AND THESE ART PICTURES YOU GIVE ARE LOVELY!
THANKS, MRS. JONES! THAT MAKES 10 BOXES I'VE SOLD THIS MORNING. IT'S EASY!
UGH! PALE SQUAW GIVE-UM WAMPUM!
Archery Sets, Pocket Watches, Footballs, Carving Sets (sent postage paid). Write or mail coupon to start.
ACT NOW
WE TRUST YOU!
22 Cal. Rifles 1000 Shot Daisy Air Rifles (sent postage paid). Boys—girls Bicycles (Express charges collect). Write or mail coupon to start.
HIM STOP 4 WIGWAMS-SQUAWS GIVE-UM MUCH WAMPUM-
LOOK! A REAL WATCH TOO!
MAKE HIM TALK!
I CONFESS, KIDS-I GOT ALL THESE PREMIUMS JUST FOR SELLING WHITE CLOVERINE BRAND SALVE...NEXT WEEK I'M GETTING A CAMERA. IT'S A CINCH!
BOY! I'M SENDING IN THAT COUPON RIGHT AWAY!
ME TOO! I WANT A RADIO!
OUR 57th YEAR
Corn Poppers, Speedboat Cartoon Sets, Aluminum Ware, Blankets (sent postage paid). Mail coupon for salve and pictures to start.
OUR 57th YEAR
ACT NOW!
Ukuleles, Radios, Pen & Pencil Sets, Food Choppers, Watches (sent postage paid).
WE ARE RELIABLE
Lovable fully dressed Dolls over 15" in height, Ukuleles, Alarm Clocks Write or mail coupon today
NU BRITE
ACT NOW
OUR 57th YEAR
Archery Sets, Dolls Wrist Watches, Footballs, Pencil Sharpeners School Boxes, Roller Skates, Wallets Flashlights Mail coupon for salve and pictures to start.
WE TRUST YOU!
Flashlights Footballs, Corn Poppers, Fishing Sets, Telescopes.
MAIL COUPON! YOU GET BIG CATALOG
Candid Cameras with carrying case, Telescopes, Watches (sent postage paid) SIMPLY GIVE pictures with White CLOVERINE Brand SALVE easily sold to friends, neighbors, relatives at 25c a box (with picture)
Alarm Clocks, Pen and Pencil Sets, Bibles, Billfolds, Telescopes, Roller Skates, Blankets, Aluminum Ware, Record Players Movie Machines (sent postage paid) Rush coupon to start!
WHITE CLOVERINE BRAND SALVE PRICE 25¢
OUR 57th YR.
ACT NOW!
LET'S GO!
WE TRUST YOU
OUR 57th YEAR
Pocket Watches, Carving Sets Corn Poppers Write or mail coupon to start We trust you
BE FIRST!
MAIL COUPON!
LET'S GO!
Rifles, Motion Picture Cameras with roll of film, Roller Skates, Radios. Mail coupon to start.
OUR 57th YEAR - WE ARE RELIABLE
MAIL NOW!
Wilson Chem. Co. Dept. 25-H, Tyrone, Pa. Date
Gentlemen:- Please send me on trial 14 colorful art pictures with 14 boxes of White CLOVERINE Brand SALVE to sell at 25c a box (with picture). I will remit amount asked within 30 days, select a Premium or keep Cash Commission as explained under Premium wanted in catalog sent with order, postage paid to start.
NAME AGE
ST R. D. BOX
TOWN ZONE NO STATE
PRINT LAST NAME HERE
Paste coupon on postal card or mail in envelope today

You've come through the most loathsome of roads. You have passed through the weirdest of scenes. You have arrived at the most horrible of crossways. You are at the TOMB OF TERROR!

This is the home of evil . . . this is the resting place of the supernatural . . . this is the stage for the most horrific spectacles man has ever dared to view!

Come one, come all! Look—if you dare! Read—if you dare! Understand — if you dare!

Read the amazing story that tore at the seams of the Universe! See the future at work in the interstellar masterpiece of horror that tells the story of the EYELESS ONES!

Watch the most feared creature imaginable wreak havoc upon an innocent world. Read the strangest tale ever told of the figure of evil that was the SHADOW OF DEATH!

Gasp as you see the spine-chilling saga of suspense and violence that signalled horror unlimited with the BEAM OF TERROR!

And visit the most loathsome site of all . . . the Hades that existed on Earth . . . the inferno of torture and torment . . . the place of eternal mayhem . . . the COLONY OF HORROR!

This is what lies ahead in the magazine of mystery and shocking impact that is the . . .

TOMB OF TERROR!

TOMB OF TERROR, January, 1953, Vol. 1, No. 7, is published every other month by HARVEY PUBLICATIONS, INC., at 420 DeSoto Avenue, St Louis 7, Mo. Editorial, Advertising and Executive offices, 1860 Broadway, New York 23, N. Y. President Alfred Harvey; Vice-President and Editor, Leon Harvey; Vice-President and Business Manager Robert B. Harvey. Entered as second-class matter at the Post Office at St. Louis, Mo., under the Act of March 3, 1879. Single copies, 10c. Subscription rates, 10 issues for $1.00 in the U. S. and possessions, elsewhere $1.50. All names in this periodical are entirely fictitious and no identification with actual persons is intended. Printed in the U. S. A.

CHEW "SPECIAL FORMULA"
CHEWING GUM!
Reduce
UP TO 5 lbs. A WEEK WITH DOCTOR'S PLAN!
NOW—at last—a new, scientific idea which guarantees you can lose as much weight as you wish—or you DON'T PAY A PENNY! The wonderful part is that it is so simple . . . so very easy and safe to lose those ugly, fatty bulges on hips, abdomen, chin, neck, bust, arms, thighs, legs, etc. The results of lost weight by normally overweight men and women are really amazing. No hardship, no exhausting exercises, drugs or laxatives. Here's the new, modern way to reduce . . . to acquire an improved figure and the slimmer, exciting, more graceful silhouette you've dreamed about. Simply chew Special Formula Chewing Gum and follow the Doctor's Plan. This tasty wholesome Chewing Gum possesses Sorbitol, is sugar-free, and reduces appetite. Sorbitol is a new discovery and contains no fat and no available carbohydrates. Just chew this delicious gum and reduce with the Doctor's Plan. If your heart's desire is a slender, beautiful attractive figure—if you want more popularity, friends, romance—then start today! Doctor's Plan will amaze you. Try it for only 10 days, then step on the scale. You will hardly believe your eyes. The important thing is to start . . . so MAIL COUPON BELOW TODAY!
FREE A full 12-day supply package will be given FREE with each order of 24-day supply for $2.00.
100% MONEY BACK GUARANTEE
Let your scale prove you can lose weight and acquire a slimmer attractive figure. A 10-day trial must convince you OR NO COST.
12-DAY SUPPLY ONLY $1
MAIL THIS COUPON
DOCTOR'S PLAN, DEPT. H-40
400 Madison Avenue N. Y. 17
Save postage. Doctor's Plan pays postage if you enclose payment now. (If c.o.d., postage and mailing charges extra.)
☐ I enclose $2 cash, check, or money order. Please rush the full 24-day supply PLUS the FREE 12-day package.
☐ I enclose $1. Please rush full 12-day package.
Please Print Clearly
NAME
ADDRESS
CITY STATE
ORDER TODAY—MAIL COUPON NOW!

CAN ANYONE ACTUALLY FORETELL WHAT AWAITS MAN IN THE FASCINATING, YET FEARSOME FUTURE? COME WITH US INTO THE NEXT CENTURY AND MEET...

THE EYELESS ONES

IN A FUTURAMIC CITY, A GREAT EVENT IS ABOUT TO TAKE PLACE!
AND SO WE TAKE OFF FOR THE UNKNOWN PLANET ON WHICH WE HAVE REASON TO BELIEVE LIFE EXISTS! WISH US LUCK!
BRAVO! GOOD LUCK!

WE'LL SOON SEE IF OUR CALCULATIONS ARE CORRECT, MYRNA!
HERE'S HOPING, CLAUDE!

THEY ARE! LOOK THERE!
YOU'RE RIGHT, PROFESSOR! STAND BY FOR A LANDING! ALERT THE OTHERS!

THE AIR IS BREATHABLE BUT THERE'S NOT A SIGN OF LIFE ANYWHERE!
STRANGE! IT'S HARD TO BELIEVE WE COULD HAVE BEEN SO WRONG ABOUT IT!

JOCK! TAKE THREE MEN AND MAKE PRELIMINARY EXPLORATIONS! REPORT BACK HERE BEFORE DARK! I DON'T WANT YOU OUT THERE AT NIGHT!
RIGHT, CLAUDE! WE'LL START NOW!

THE QUARTETTE SEARCH FRUITLESSLY FOR HOURS ON THE SURFACE OF THE BARREN PLANET! THEN SUDDENLY...
JOCK, ARE YOU SURE...!
I'M POSITIVE! I SAW SOMETHING DART INTO THIS HOLE! C'MON!

FANTASTIC! ENDLESS CATACOMBS AND TUNNELS!
PERHAPS FROM AN ANCIENT UNDERGROUND CIVILIZATION!

BUT AS THE GROUP INSPECTS THE CAVERN IN AWE, THEIR PRESENCE IS DETECTED AND RESENTED BY A GROTESQUE BAND OF ITS HIDEOUS RESIDENTS!
THIS PLACE IS ...WHA...A...! LOOK OUT!
MONSTERS! AND THEY HAVE NO EYES!
GRMFF!

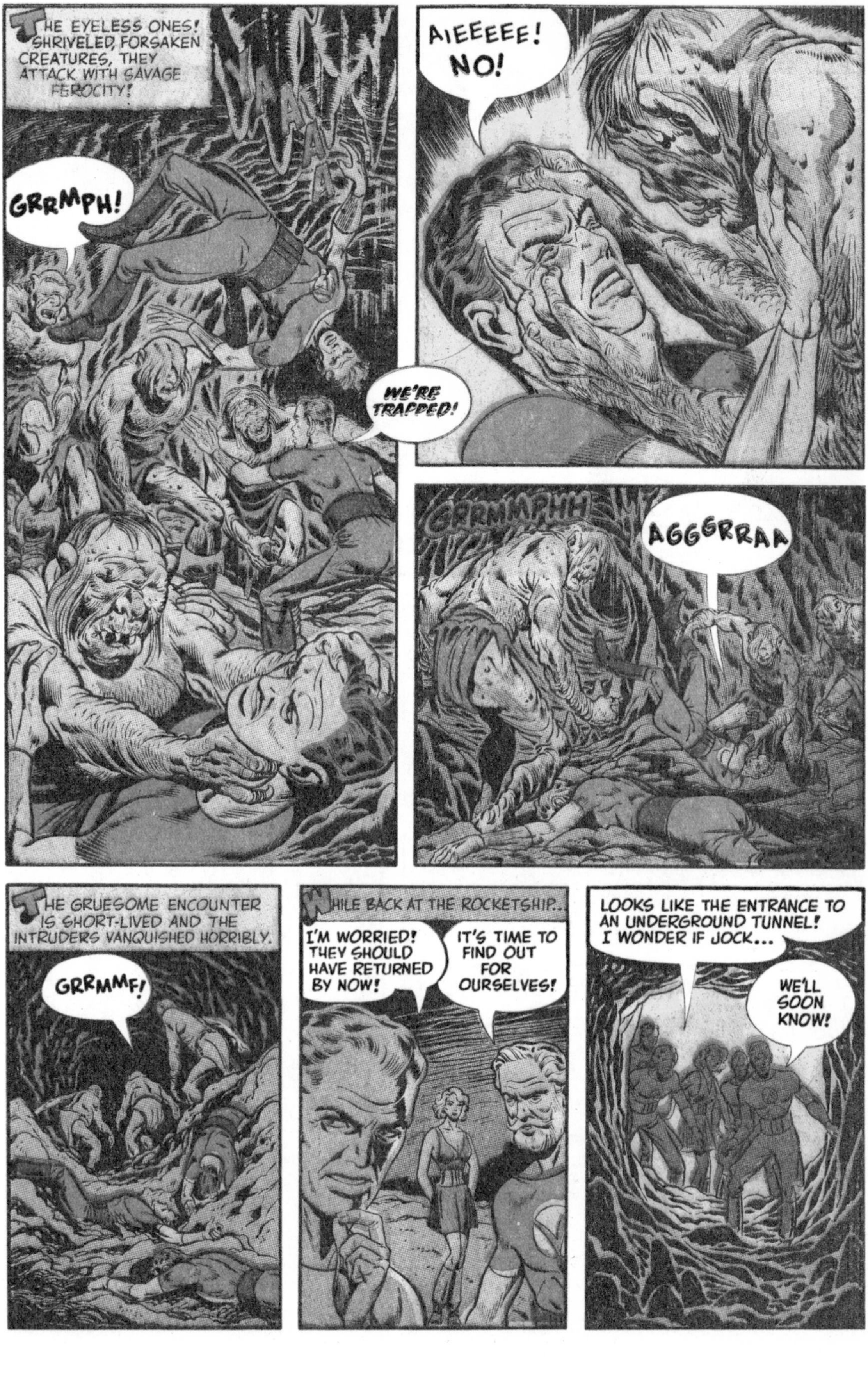

THE EYELESS ONES! SHRIVELED, FORSAKEN CREATURES, THEY ATTACK WITH SAVAGE FEROCITY!
GRRMPH!
WE'RE TRAPPED!
AIEEEEE! NO!
GRRRMMPHH
AGGGRRAA

UPON ENTERING THE CAVERN, CLAUDE'S PARTY LEARNS THE LURID TRUTH!
OH, NO!
DEAD! SLAUGHTERED! BUT HOW! BY WHAT!

THE GHASTLY ANSWER IS SOON FORTHCOMING!
LOOK!
THEY'RE MONSTERS!
EEEEK!

GRRMPH!
RUN! IT'S OUR ONLY CHANCE!
FASTER, MYRNA!

AIEEEE! A BLANK WALL!
THEY'RE GAINING ON US!

TRAPPED! THIS LOOKS LIKE GOOD BYE!
GRRRMPH!
NO!... AEEEK!

GRRMPH!
AGGRRAAA!

THE SAVAGE CREATURES ATTACK WITH UNBRIDLED FURY! BUT AS THEY DO, A SECOND BAND OF EYELESS ONES INTERCEPTS THEM!
GRMMPH!
LOOK! MORE OF THEM! THEY SEEM TO BE ON OUR SIDE!
LUCKY FOR US!

A BRIEF BUT HORRIBLE BATTLE FOLLOWS... AND SOON THE FIRST BAND OF MONSTERS ARE CUT TO RIBBONS...
ARRGGH
GRMPH

THE SECOND BAND DOES VANQUISH THE FIRST, AND ITS APPARENT LEADER APPREHENSIVELY ATTEMPTS TO COMMUNICATE WITH THE HUMANS!
I THINK HE WANTS US TO FOLLOW HIM!
NO!
WE'D BETTER! BESIDES THEY DON'T SEEM HOSTILE TO US!
GRMPH!

I WONDER WHERE THEY'RE TAKING US!
WITHOUT EYES! HOW DO THEY KNOW WHERE THEY'RE GOING!

WELL! LOOKS TO ME LIKE A COURTROOM OR SOME-THING!
IT'S EVIDENT THAT THEY HAVE THEIR OWN PRIMITIVE CIVILIZATION!

WHAT'S HE TRYING TO SAY?
GRMPH.
THEY MAKE SOUNDS LIKE CREATURES WHO WERE ONCE CAPABLE OF SPEECH! STRANGE!

I THINK I CAN READ HIS SIGNS! HE'S TELLING US THAT THIS IS THE GOVERNMENT OF THE EYELESS PEOPLE! AND THAT THOSE WHO ATTACKED US WERE OUTLAWS. NOW HE WANTS US TO LEAVE THE PLANET!
GLADLY!

THE MONSTERS PROVIDE THEIR UNWELCOME GUEST WITH SAFE CONDUCT BACK TO THEIR ROCKET SHIP...
FRANKLY, I'LL BE GLAD TO LEAVE THIS PLANET, MYSELF!
THOSE HIDEOUS MONSTERS! MURDERERS!

STILL, CLAUDE, I'VE SEEN ENOUGH TO CONVINCE ME THAT AT ONE TIME A MORE COMPLEX CIVILIZATION DID EXIST ON THIS PLANET!

LOOK! THE REMAINS OF A STRANGE STATUE OR MONUMENT!
YOU WERE RIGHT, PROFESSOR! I GUESS THIS PROVES THERE WAS A CIVILIZATION OF SOME SORT HERE AT ONE TIME!

YES! CENTURIES OLD, I'M CERTAIN! WAIT UNTIL WE TELL THEM OF THIS BACK HOME ON MARS!

SO THE **EYELESS ONES** ARE THE ONLY REMAINS OF OUR CIVILIZATION AS WE KNOW IT TODAY! IS THAT THE DESTINY ACTUALLY IN STORE FOR THE EARTH? FORTUNATELY, OUR GENERATION WILL NEVER KNOW THE ANSWER!

THE END.

SHADOW of DEATH

EEEEEE!

MY NAME IS WALTER FARNO. AS A WRITER OF SOME RENOWN, I AM ALSO A VERY INTENSE TRAVELER. COME WITH ME AS I TELL YOU MY STORY... I FIRST ARRIVED AT BELNOW IN THE PYRENEES DURING THE SPRING MONTHS. THE TOWN MAYOR GREETED ME WITH GUSTO...
AH, MONSIEUR FARNO! WELCOME! WELCOME TO OUR SMALL VILLAGE! I HOPE YOU WILL FIND YOUR STAY AN ENJOYABLE ONE!
I'M SURE I WILL, MONSIEUR MAYOR!

HERE YOU!! CAREFUL WITH THAT BOX, OAFS!
IT IS YOURS, MONSIEUR?
CRASH

UH--YES! YOU SEE, SIR... I'M NOT ONLY HERE ON A VACATION, BUT ALSO TO-- UH--COLLECT THINGS! I AM AN AVID COLLECTOR! THAT BOX HOLDS MY--COLLECTION!
SO! BIEN! BELNOW HAS EVERYTHING AT YOUR DISPOSAL! NOW FOLLOW ME, MONSIEUR!

BELNOW GREETED ME WITH OPEN ARMS! IT WASN'T OFTEN THAT A FAMOUS WRITER CAME TO VISIT THEM. BUT MY PURPOSE WAS NOT FOR A REST. YOU SEE, I HAD ONLY TOLD THE MAYOR HALF THE TRUTH. THAT NIGHT AT MY INN, I MET THE VILLAGERS...

OOOOH! AH! YOUNG PAUL IS A HERCULES, IS HE NOT, MONSIEUR?
THAT HE IS! WHAT MAGNIFICENT STRENGTH!

ALL RIGHT, MY FRIENDS! THAT IS ENOUGH FOR TONIGHT! NOW I MUST GO BACK TO MY BLACKSMITH'S SHOP TO WORK! SEE YOU TOMORROW!
GOOD NIGHT, PAUL! WE'LL HAVE ALL THE WINE YOU WANT NEXT TIME! HA HA!

OH, PAUL! MAY I WALK ALONG WITH YOU? I WOULD LIKE A BIT OF FRESH AIR!

COME ALONG, MONSIEUR FARNO! IT IS A PRIVELEGE! AH, THERE IS NOTHING LIKE THE SPRING AIR, EH? HA, HA...

WE WALKED ALONG TOGETHER FOR QUITE A WHILE. THEN WHEN THE FOREST BECAME DENSE--AND THE FULL MOON REACHED ITS PEAK, I STOPPED...
WHY DO YOU STOP, MONSIEUR? ARE YOU TIRED PERHAPS?
NO, PAUL! NOT TIRED AT ALL-- JUST--HUNGRY!!

THEN--OF COURSE--I COULDN'T HELP MYSELF! THERE WAS NO USE DENYING THE INEVITABLE...
MONSIEUR--Y-YOU'RE CHANGING! LET ME OUT OF HERE!
I CAN'T, PAUL! TO TELL YOU THE TRUTH-- I'M FAMISHED!
2

HE MADE A FUTILE ATTEMPT TO ELUDE ME, BUT OF COURSE I WAS SO MUCH STRONGER! EVEN THIS GIANT COULDN'T STOP A VAMPIRE!
WHAT WARM, SWEET BLOOD, PAUL! IT HEARTENS ME GREATLY! HA, HA...

AND THE NEXT AFTERNOON, I MET MAYOR LAFARGE IN THE INN-SALOON. HE WAS VERY DISTURBED.
PAUL HAS BEEN KILLED, MONSIEUR FARNO! YOU WERE SEEN WITH HIM LAST! CAN YOU TELL ME THE CIRCUMSTANCES?
INDEED NOT, SIR! I LEFT HIM IMMEDIATELY! HOW COULD SUCH A YOUNG GIANT BE OVERPOWERED AND KILLED?

THAT IS WHAT ALSO PUZZLES ME! AND THAT IS WHY YOU HAVE BEEN ABSOLVED OF ALL GUILT! FORGIVE ME, BUT WE ARE SUSPICIOUS OF EVERYONE! OH-- I WANT YOU TO MEET MY DAUGHTER, DESIRÉ!
CHARMED!

IT IS A HORRIBLE THING, IS IT NOT, MONSIEUR? I KNEW PAUL VERY WELL! WHO WOULD WANT TO DO SUCH A THING? HIS NECK WAS--- IT WAS AWFUL!
PLEASE DON'T LET IT MAKE YOU OVERWROUGHT, DESIRÉ! A PRETTY GIRL LIKE YOU NEEDS PLENTY OF LAUGHTER AND GAIETY!

AND IN THE DAYS THAT FOLLOWED, I CULTIVATED THIS WONDERFUL GIRL'S FRIENDSHIP. PICNICS, DAYS ON THE BEACH, DANCING.

CONTRARY TO POPULAR BELIEF, VAMPIRES ARE LIKE ORDINARY PEOPLE--THAT IS TO SAY, THEY CAN GO OUT DURING THE DAYTIME. BUT, OF COURSE, THEY DO HAVE ABNORMAL APPETITES. AND MINE WAS GROWING AGAIN...
PARDON ME OLD MAN! CAN YOU TELL ME WHERE THE ROAD TO BELNOW IS? I SEEM TO BE LOST!
IT IS NOT FAR FROM HERE! YOU JUST...
3

YOU GO THREE KILOMETERS TOWARDS RUE CHAMPLAIN -- T-THEN ... YOU --
YES? GO ON--! SOMETHING WRONG, OLD MAN?

HA, HA, HA...
MONSIEUR! YOUR HANDS! YAAAAAHHHHHH!

I WENT HOME, MY GAIETY BUBBLING OVER! THE NEXT MORNING, OVER THE BREAKFAST TABLE...
I JUST HEARD THE NEWS! THIS IS TERRIBLE! SOMETHING MUST BE DONE!
IT WAS MY GRANPERE, WALTER! DO YOU UNDERSTAND? I-I LOVED HIM! SOB-- SOB!

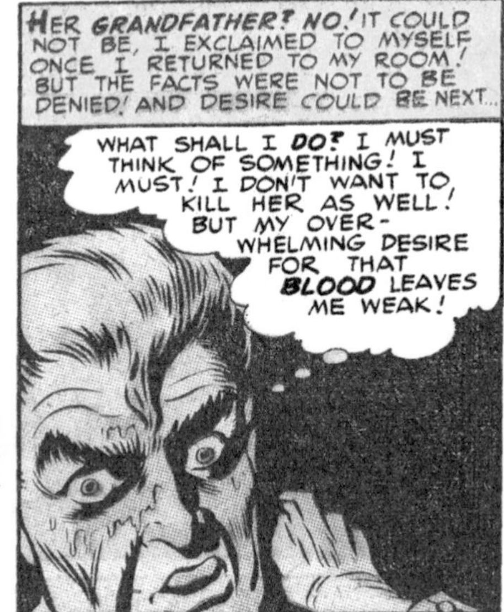
HER GRANDFATHER? NO! IT COULD NOT BE, I EXCLAIMED TO MYSELF ONCE I RETURNED TO MY ROOM! BUT THE FACTS WERE NOT TO BE DENIED! AND DESIRE COULD BE NEXT...
WHAT SHALL I DO? I MUST THINK OF SOMETHING! I MUST! I DON'T WANT TO KILL HER AS WELL! BUT MY OVER-WHELMING DESIRE FOR THAT BLOOD LEAVES ME WEAK!

NEVERTHELESS, I HAD TO KEEP UP A PRETENSE. I ORGANIZED A SEARCH PARTY TO CAPTURE THE "MURDERER", AND THE POOR SIMPLE PEASANTS FELL ALONG WITH MY PLANS...
COME! WE MUST FIND THIS MAN! HE IS PROBABLY HIDING IN THE FOREST!
YES! WE WILL HANG HIM ONCE WE CATCH HIM!

WE'LL SPLIT UP SO THAT WE MAY SEARCH MORE EASILY! THE MAYOR AND I WILL TAKE THE CENTER ROUTE.
BIEN! WE WILL GO TO THE RIGHT AND LEFT OF YOU, MONSIEUR!

MOMENTS LATER...
LOOK **THERE**, MONSIEUR LE MAYOR! **QUICKLY!**
EH? **WHERE?**

OH.. I'M AFRAID YOU **MISSED** HIM! HE WAS A LITTLE TOO **FAST** FOR YOU!
NONSENSE! I THINK I SEE SOMETHING..!

AAIIIIEEEEE!
THE ONLY THING YOU SAW WAS YOUR **IMAGINATION!** NOW YOU SHALL **REALLY** SEE HIM!! HA, HA...

I ATTENDED TO MY BUSINESS QUICKLY. THEN, WITHOUT WASTING ANOTHER MOMENT, I SLASHED MY FACE, TORE MY CLOTHES SUFFICIENTLY -- AND RAN BACK TOWARD THE MAIN BODY...

OHHH.. HELP! HELP! THE **MAYOR!** HE'S BEEN ATTACKED BY -- BY A **VAMPIRE!** I SAW IT WITH MY **OWN EYES!** I BARELY ESCAPED DEATH!! **HURRY!**
IT'S MONSIEUR FARNO! SACRE BLEU! WE **MUST** FIND THE CREATURE!

OH — WALTER — WALTER, MY DARLING!! YOU-- YOU ARE **ALIVE!!** I HEARD THE MEN'S SHOUTS! FATHER IS --IS--?
YES, DEAR! THIS IS A HORRIBLE NIGHTMARE! WE MUST LEAVE THIS ACCURSED PLACE! COME! I'LL TAKE YOU **HOME!**

AFTERWARDS, IN MY OWN ROOM, I SHOULD HAVE **EXULTED** OVER MY CUNNING, BUT I WAS **TORN** BY THE BITTER ANGUISH OF MY **EVIL!** DESIRE NOW MEANT MORE TO ME THAN **LIFE** ITSELF! BUT SHE WAS THE ONLY ONE LEFT OF THAT PRECIOUS BLOOD!

NO! NO! WHAT AM I THINKING ABOUT? I—I WOULD RATHER **KILL** MYSELF FIRST! I'LL FIND ANOTHER VICTIM! YES -- **THAT'S IT!**

SO THAT VERY NEXT NIGHT I STALKED A PRETTY YOUNG THING WHO LIVED NEAR THE OUTSKIRTS OF THE VILLAGE--TO BLOT OUT THE TEMPTATION OF KILLING DESIRE...

DON'T BE ALARMED, MY CHILD! IT WILL HURT BUT A MOMENT!

EEEEEE!!

I SAW THE SHEER FRIGHT IN THE MORTAL'S EYES. THEN I KNEW I HAD BEEN FOUND OUT! MANY ALTERNATIVES WERE OPEN TO ME--BUT I THOUGHT OF DESIRÉ--AND OUR LOVE. I OPENED HER NOTE!

"DARLING--TAKE ME AWAY FROM BELNOW! I LOVE YOU! WE CAN BE MARRIED BY THE VILLAGE PRELATE--AND BE TOGETHER FOREVER! I WAIT FOR YOUR ANSWER--DESIRÉ...

THEN I KNEW WHAT TO DO! ALREADY, THE INN-PORTER WOULD BE SUMMONING HIS FELLOW BUMPKINS FROM EVERY HOUSE IN THE VILLAGE--AND MY HEART WAITED DOWN BELOW. I WAS AT THE WINDOW INSTANTLY...

DESIRÉ--COME UP QUICKLY! I'VE *CAUGHT* THE VAMPIRE! DO EXACTLY AS I SAY. TAKE A LARGE WOODEN STAKE FROM THE STOVE. *YOU* MUST KILL IT AS IT LIES IN ITS COFFIN!

Y-YES...

I EXERTED EVERY OUNCE OF MY POWER TO HYPNOTIZE HER--FOR SHE WOULD NEVER DO IT OF HER OWN FREE WILL--REALIZING WHO AND WHAT I WAS BEFORE SHE COULD KILL ME. I HEARD THE DOOR OPEN...

WE DARE YOU TO READ THESE TALES OF TERROR and SUSPENSE
NOW PUBLISHED MONTHLY
THE BEST IN SHOCK MYSTERY
GET THEM EVERY MONTH
TALES OF TERROR AND SUSPENSE!
CHAMBER OF CHILLS
WE DARE YOU
WITCHES TALES
WEIRD YARNS OF UNSEEN TERROR
STRANGEST TALES of FEAR and SUPERSTITION!
BLACK CAT MYSTERY
TOMB OF TERROR
THE MARRIAGE OF THE MONSTERS!

MEDICAL SUPERSTITIONS

Medicine and pharmacy began as specialized forms of magic. Savage man did not know the causes of diseases and death, and naturally believed they were the work of evil spirits and demons, sometimes summoned by enemies. To rid their bodies of such malignant spirits, sick savages hired shamans and medicine men.

This belief grew into the conviction that there was a strong tie between anything cast off by the body and disease and death. That was why savages were so careful to collect spilt blood, sputum, nails, and hair and bury them out of harm. For if an enemy could get hold of them, he would hire a witch-doctor to work a spell on them, and the former owner would fall sick and die.

In Australia, aborigines believe that if an enemy sticks a nail, quartz, or glass into his footprints, he will be lame until the offending nail or glass is removed.

Australian aborigines knock out one or two front teeth of boys about to become men. These teeth are carefully preserved, for if possessed by an enemy, the boy would suffer whatever harm would be done to them.

For ages, it was believed that treating a weapon causing a wound, would heal the wound; and likewise, putting the weapon into fire would cause the wound to inflame and fester. This superstition was universal through the Revolutionary War, and, in many places, it is still regarded as a fact!

For instance, if a German peasant's pig breaks his leg, the peasant binds the leg of a chair with splints and lets no one sit on that chair until the pig's leg heals.

In general, the arrow, sword, or dagger that caused the wound was annointed with oil and grease to soothe the wound and let it heal. If the weapon was not available, a piece of iron, shaped like the offending weapon, was stuck into the wound so that blood flowed on it. Then the substitute was annointed in place of the original weapon.

The idea went much farther. If a man wounded an enemy or hurt him, and was sorry afterwards, he only had to spit into the hand that did the injury and the other fellow's wound would heal.

In a similar way, mothers were very careful of their children's milk teeth. They believed that their children's new permanent teeth would take the form of the animal which first stepped upon the cast-away teeth. For instance, dropping teeth into a pig trough by accident would give the child permanent pig-like teeth. To insure strong teeth, mothers cast milk teeth into mice and rat nests for mice and rats had the strongest and sharpest teeth they knew.

To be sick in the ancient times was a misfortune. Primitive doctors believed that the body was composed of four humors and the humor having an upper hand would have to be counteracted with a medicine of opposite properties. As an example, for fever, a medicine known to be chilling, and for chills, a burning type of medicine.

In general, the belief was that the nastier the medicine, the stronger its healing effect. One prescription called for chopped unborn puppies mixed with lizards and boar fat, and all boiled to a thick jelly.

It was fortunate that a worse concotion was applied to the weapon causing injury, or cast away hair, sputum, or blood rather than drunk. But superstition exacted its toll since people died more from the horrible brews than disease itself.

Nowadays we know that lunacy and epilepsy are diseases. Not so the ancients of the Near East, especially Egypt and Arabia. They believed that a lunatic was a sacred saint, and whatever he did, was due to the fact that his mind was not in this world but in the other.

Such habits still persist to this day; people buy barbiturates—drug poisons—and belladonna —again poison—to treat themselves without benefit of doctors.

HOW 'MINI-GYM' TURNS PLANT "DRIP" INTO SUCCESS DYNAMO
SURE, TOM, YOU'VE GOT THE BRAINS AND MORE FOR THAT SUPERVISOR'S JOB --- BUT YOU'D NEVER BE ABLE TO KEEP THOSE TOUGH HOMBRES IN THE SHOP IN LINE!
WELL, MAYBE YOU'RE RIGHT, BOSS!
TOM'D LOVE TO DATE YOU, BETTY! WHY DON'T YOU GIVE HIM A BREAK?
OH, TOM'S A NICE GUY, JANE --- BUT YOU KNOW HOW IT IS --- I LIKE A MAN WHO CAN DISH IT OUT AS WELL AS TAKE IT!
IT'S NO USE, SAM --- I'M MOVING ON! I'M WORSE THAN A WASH-OUT IN THIS PLANT! I CAN'T GET PROMOTIONS LIKE YOU!
TAKE IT EASY, TOM! ALL YOU NEED IS A DAILY, 10-MINUTE WORK-OUT WITH 'MINI-GYM' AND YOU'LL SOON BE GIVING ME A RUN FOR MY MONEY! HERE, LOOK AT THIS AD!
GOSH, SAM, I'M A NEW MAN! AM I GLAD YOU MADE ME CLIP THAT 'MINI-GYM' COUPON! WATCH ME DO JOE BONOMO'S TRICKY EXERCISE 10 AGAIN! IT'S A KILLER-DILLER!
GO TO IT, KID! I ALWAYS KNEW YOU HAD THE STUFF, BUT IT TAKES 'MINI-GYM' TO GIVE A MAN TOP TRAINING!
NEXT TIME, FELLER, YOU'D BETTER THINK FIRST BEFORE YOU START SHOOTING OFF YOUR MOUTH AT ME!
OH, TOM, YOU'RE WONDERFUL!
HONEST, TOM, I-I DIDN'T MEAN NOTHING!
TWO MONTHS LATER...
THAT SUPERVISOR'S JOB IS YOURS, TOM! AND I DON'T HAVE TO WISH YOU LUCK! YOU'VE MADE YOURSELF INTO A REAL "COMER" WHO MAKES HIS OWN LUCK!
THANKS, BOSS! I'LL MAKE GOOD... AND HOW!
AMBITIOUS MEN OF ALL AGES!
TO GET WHAT YOU WANT OUT OF LIFE GET FIT WITH JOE BONOMO'S MAGIC DE-LUXE 'MINI-GYM'!
Our special Price Only
3.95 complete
Packs All The Punch Of A Big, Expensive Gym, Including . . .
• Rowing Machine • Wall Exerciser • Tension Pulls • Bicycle
Why let the other fellow walk away with the job . . . and girl that should be yours? Life's prizes go to the smart man who keeps himself in "prize" physical condition. It's easy with the sensational new 'MINI-GYM'. For with this new wonder exerciser, you can . . .
Enjoy Real Fun Out Of Keeping Fit
Man alive, you haven't really lived 'til you get your eager hands (Yes, and feet, too) into Joe Bonomo's fun-packed exerciser, the unique, new 'MINI-GYM'! Even though you hated exercise before, with superb 'MINI-GYM' and Joe Bonomo's big, new personal instruction book . . . you'll eat it up! Find yourself having real fun . . . and loving it!
See How Fast 'MINI-GYM' Helps Get You into 'A-1 Shape!
You bet, almost before you know it, a daily 10 minutes with 'MINI-GYM' builds you into the kind of real "he man" material bosses want most . . . and girls go for fastest! Can't help but be, for this new "miracle" 'MINI-GYM' is an all-round, all-over body conditioner . . meaning it does a 100% job of building YOU! Toning, strengthening and pepping up every muscle in your whole body!
'MINI-GYM'S' Perfected By The Famous JOE BONOMO!
World-famous, professional strong man himself, Joe Bonomo knows what it takes to build the physically perfect man! (Yes, and woman, too!) And he's put all his first-hand knowledge into the design of this terrific, new exerciser! So in 'MINI-GYM' you've got everything it takes for genuine, professional body-building!
Great For Women, Too! Builds Pep, Personality!
Though 'MINI-GYM' is plenty tough for the professional athlete, it's easy enough to be handled . . . and enjoyed . . . by any teen-age girl or small woman. How come? Because Joe Bonomo designed 'MINI-GYM' for girls and women, too! Especially those who want to develop real pep, alluring curves and a super gorgeous figure! No wonder gals everywhere go for 'MINI-GYM' in a big, BIG way!
"MINI-GYM"
FREE Joe Bonomo's Personal Instruction Book
Every thrill-packed page written for you by Joe Bonomo, this big, 64-page book printed in 2 colors, gives you a complete 'MINI-GYM' health course. Far more than an instruction manual, it's an all-round, all-over Body Conditioner Course! Complete with 90 especially posed photos, charts, and fun-to-follow text. Size: 5½" x 8½". YOURS FREE with your 'MINI-GYM'!
You Can't Be Too Old For 'MINI-GYM!'
Thirteen or 30, 18 or 80, once you see 'MINI-GYM', you can't wait to try it! Why? Because 'MINI-GYM' adapts instantly to the exercise needs . . . and thrills . . . of any age and all physical conditions from the weakest to the strongest!
POSITIVE MONEY-BACK GUARANTEE!
Yes, it means just that! Order your 'MINI-GYM' today. Then test it in every way possible . . . exercise with it and enjoy it for 10 exciting days. If you are not satisfied in every way . . . in fact, delighted . . . just return 'MINI-GYM', and your money will be instantly refunded! Fair enough, isn't it?
'MINI-GYM' CORP. Dept. HC78
1841 Broadway, New York 23, N.Y.
MAIL "NO RISK" COUPON NOW!
Order Your 'MINI-GYM' by MODEL S, M or L.
MODEL S
☐ If you are under 5 ft. tall
MODEL M
☐ if you are 5 ft. to 5 ft. 10 in. tall
MODEL L
☐ If you are over 5 ft. 10 in. tall
'MINI-GYM' CORP. Dept. HC78
1841 Broadway, New York 23, N. Y.
RUSH ME one complete 'MINI-GYM', MODEL ...., with 64-page Joe Bonomo Course Book. I will deposit $3.95, plus postage, with postman. If I am not satisfied in every way, I may return 'MINI-GYM' and Book within 10 days for full refund.
I enclose $3.95, You pay postage. Same money-back guarantee.
NAME ....
Print Plainly Please
STREET ....
CITY .... ZONE .... STATE ....
I enclose $3.95. You pay postage. Same money-back guarantee.
(Canadian and Foreign Orders, $4.95. Cash with orders.)

A SPARKLING POOL... WHITE COTTAGES... A GAY AMUSEMENT HALL... ALL THE TRAPPINGS OF A PLEASANT SUMMER RESORT! YET WHAT IS THE UNSPEAKABLE EVIL, THE UNNATURAL DREAD THAT TRANSFORMED THIS PEACEFUL SCENE INTO A GRISLY...

COLONY OF HORROR!

COME!! WHY DO YOU *DELAY*?? WE NEED MORE PERFORMERS -- AND THE SPOTLIGHT IS ON *YOU*!!

YAAAGH-H-H!!! *STOP!* PLEASE *STOP!!*

WHAT ARE YOU GOING TO DO WITH MY WIFE???

A QUIET WARM SUMMER AFTERNOON -- AND JIM AND MARY TURNER, WITH MARY'S FATHER, ENJOY A CHEERFUL DRIVE IN THE COUNTRY...
THAT MUST BE THE PILGRIM'S CHURCH, FATHER! LOOK HOW OLD IT IS!!
IT'S BEEN DESERTED EVER SINCE THE LAST WITCH WAS BURNED THERE -- OVER TWO HUNDRED YEARS AGO! -- SAY, JIM, IS THE CAR STALLING??

OUT OF GAS! AND THE LAST STATION IS TEN MILES BACK!
THAT SEEMS TO BE A SUMMER COLONY OVER THERE, JIM! MAYBE THEY CAN HELP US!

A SHORT WALK TO THE COLONY --AND THE THREE ARE SUDDENLY CONFRONTED BY FACES PALE WITH THE CAST OF... DEATH-- AND EYES SHINING WITH A FLAME OF EVIL!...
YOU HAVE A FAR WALK TO THE NEXT STATION --WHY NOT SPEND THE NIGHT WITH US? WE CAN MAKE YOU... COMFORTABLE!
TH-THANKS! IT SEEMS WE HAVE NO CHOICE!!

PERHAPS YOU WOULD CARE FOR A SHORT SWIM IN OUR POOL BEFORE SUPPER. IT'S STILL EARLY!
FINE! THAT WILL BE JUST WHAT WE NEED!

I DON'T LIKE THIS PLACE! DID YOU SEE THE LOOKS IN THEIR EYES-- LIKE BIRDS OF PREY WAITING TO DEVOUR THEIR VICTIMS!!
NONSENSE, JIM! THEY'RE GOOD-HEARTED PEOPLE!

AS MARY'S FATHER PREPARES TO LEAP INTO THE POOL, THE PEOPLE OF THE COLONY GATHER ABOUT SMILING--BUT IN THEIR SMILES IS A STRANGE AND EAGER LUST THAT FREEZES THE BLOOD...
HAVE A GOOD SWIM!!
THERE'S SOMETHING EVIL AND FETID IN THE AIR!! I CAN FEEL IT!

COME ON IN! THE WATER'S FINE!
FATHER!! BEHIND YOU!! THERE'S SOMETHING-- SOMETHING HORRIBLE--!

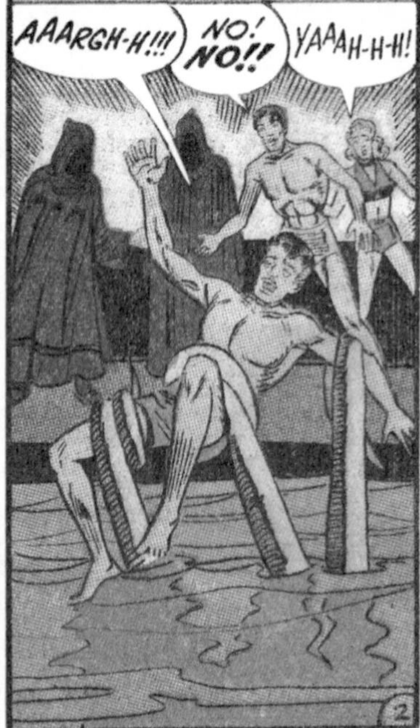
SUDDENLY, OUT OF THE SLIMY WATER EMERGES A GHASTLY CREATURE--UNLIKE ANY THAT EVER EXISTED ON LAND OR SEA--A MONSTER THAT CRUSHES ITS VICTIMS WITH THE SAVAGE FURY OF A COBRA!!...
AAARGH-H!!!
NO! NO!!
YAAAH-H-H!
2

FEED WELL, MY PRETTY ONE! FEED WELL!!
M-M-MGHH-.

MY FATHER! WHAT HAVE YOU DONE TO MY FATHER???
WHAT MONSTROUS PLACE IS THIS?? WHO ARE YOU??
IT IS TIME YOU KNEW THE TRUTH!!

WE ARE PEOPLE OF DARKNESS--OF THE REGIONS OF FLAME AND DEATH--AND THIS IS WHERE WE SPEND OUR SUMMERS--FOR SPORT...AND ENTERTAINMENT... AS YOU SHALL DISCOVER!!...

YOU'RE WITCHES!!

DRAGGED TO A RAT-INFESTED COTTAGE BY THEIR UNEARTHLY CAPTORS, THE TWO WAIT IN NUMBING TERROR FOR THE DOOM THAT HOVERS OVER THEM LIKE A GREEDY VULTURE!...
WHAT'S GOING TO HAPPEN TO US? AND WHAT DID THEY MEAN BY ENTERTAINMENT??
I THINK I HEAR ONE OF THOSE LOATHSOME CREATURES COMING!

THE AMUSEMENT HALL IS OPEN--AND THE PERFORMANCE HAS BEGUN!! STUDY IT CAREFULLY--FOR TOMORROW YOU SHALL PERFORM FOR US!!
WHY DON'T YOU KILL US AND BE DONE WITH IT? WHY MUST YOU PLAY WITH US???

WITH THE SOUND OF WILD LAUGHTER AND LOUD APPLAUSE SOUNDING IN THEIR EARS, THE COUPLE IS LED TO A SCENE WHICH MAKES A DREADFUL MOCKERY OF THE LAUGHTER... AND A FIENDISH LUST OF THE APPLAUSE!!...
HOW DO YOU LIKE OUR ENTERTAINMENT? VERY AMUSING--IS IT NOT??
OH, NO! NO!
AIEEE!!

COME! COME!! WHY DO YOU SHRINK FROM HER LOVING EMBRACE??
LET ME GO!! LET ME GO!!!

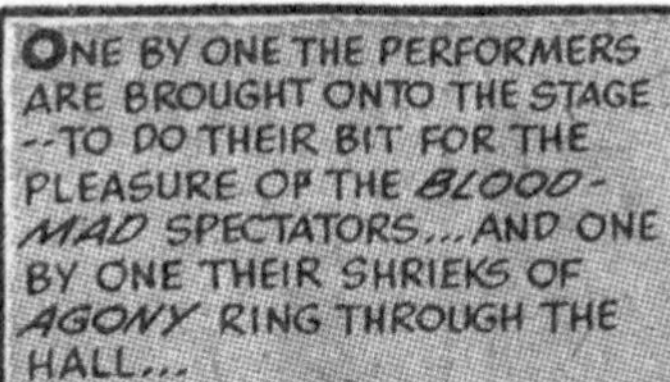
ONE BY ONE THE PERFORMERS ARE BROUGHT ONTO THE STAGE --TO DO THEIR BIT FOR THE PLEASURE OF THE BLOOD-MAD SPECTATORS... AND ONE BY ONE THEIR SHRIEKS OF AGONY RING THROUGH THE HALL...

YAAAGH-H-H!!!

ENCORE! ENCORE!
WE WANT MORE! MORE!!
STOP!! STOP!! YAAH-H
MORE! MORE!
ENCORE!

FINALLY, THE LAST SCREAMS REND THE NIGHT AIR--AND THE AUDIENCE OF FIENDS EMERGE FROM THEIR "ENTERTAINMENT" HALL, WITH THE PROMISE OF NEW VICTIMS LIGHTING THEIR RAVAGED FACES!!...
SLEEP WELL, MY FRIENDS... FOR REMEMBER, YOU SHALL PERFORM FOR US TOMORROW NIGHT!!
TAKE US BACK TO THE COTTAGE--I CAN'T BEAR TO GAZE AT YOUR HIDEOUS BEINGS!!

WHAT CAN WE DO, JIM? WHAT CAN WE DO??
WE MUST ESCAPE!! THERE'S GOT TO BE A WAY OUT-- MARY!! I HAVE IT!!--THE MISSION!!

THE MISSION WE PASSED IS JUST A SHORT DISTANCE AWAY-- AND WITCHES CANNOT LIVE UNDER THE SOUND OF CHURCH BELLS! IF I COULD GET TO THOSE BELLS---
WE WOULD BE SAVED!! BUT HOW-- THEY'VE PLACED A GUARD OUTSIDE THE DOOR!!

GUARD--COME QUICKLY!! M-MY WIFE'S GONE OUT OF HER MIND!! SHE'S TRYING TO KILL ME!!
WHAT'S THE MATTER???

AS THE GUARD STEPS INTO THE COTTAGE, TWO STRONG AND DETERMINED HANDS REACH OUT TO CRUSH THE LIFE FROM HIS THROAT!...
AAARGH-H-H!

HURRY, MARY-- WE HAVE NO TIME TO LOSE!!
NO, JIM--I--I'M TOO EXHAUSTED!! I'D ONLY GET US BOTH CAUGHT! YOU GO ALONE--- QUICKLY!!

WHILE THE MONSTROUS CREATURE IN THE POOL WATCHES ITS MASTERS PERFORM THEIR FRENZIED RITES OF EVIL, A GRIM AND SILENT FIGURE SLIPS AWAY INTO THE NIGHT!...
GOT TO HURRY--BEFORE THEY FIND MARY-- BEFORE IT'S TOO LATE!!

BUT AS MARY WAITS IN THE DARKNESS FOR THE SOUND OF HOPE, THE WITCHES COME IN SEARCH OF THE MISSING GUARD AND BRING WITH THEM THE APPALLING CHILL OF VIOLENT DEATH!....
THE MAN HAS ESCAPED--AND KILLED THE GUARD!! BUT WE STILL HAVE HER---ONE FRESH LIVING MORSEL OF FOOD FOR OUR HUNGRY PET!!
WH-WHAT ARE YOU GOING TO DO?

THROW HER IN! THROW HER IN!!
NO!! DON'T!!
5

WHAT WAS THAT SOUND??? IT-- IT COULDN'T BE---
IT'S JIM! HE-- HE'S REACHED THE CHURCH IN TIME!!!
CLANG!
CLANG!
CLANG!

AS THE SOUND OF THE BELLS RING IN THE WARM SUMMER AIR, THE DEMONS OF DARKNESS CROUCH LIKE WOUNDED ANIMALS --LIKE BEINGS WHO HEAR THEIR DOOM APPROACH LIKE A WINGED BAT!!...
AIEEE! THE BELLS!! THE CHURCH BELLS!!
WE ARE DOOMED! DOOMED--TO DIE IN FLAME!!
CLANG!
CLANG!
CLANG!

THE FLAMES! THE FLAMES!! YAAAAH-H-H!!!
AAARGH-H-H!

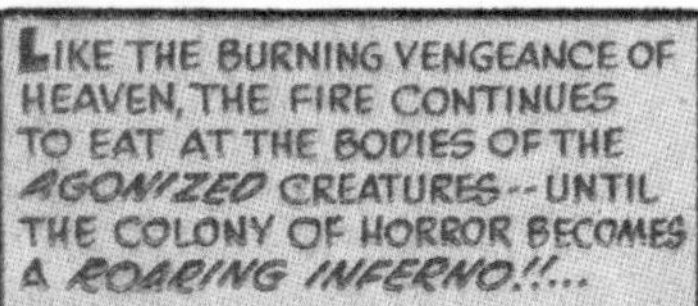

LIKE THE BURNING VENGEANCE OF HEAVEN, THE FIRE CONTINUES TO EAT AT THE BODIES OF THE AGONIZED CREATURES--UNTIL THE COLONY OF HORROR BECOMES A ROARING INFERNO!!...

YAAAGH-H-H!!!
AHHH-H-H-H!!!

JIM! JIM, DARLING!! WHERE ARE YOU??

SOON JIM AND MARY TURNER-- THE GHASTLY EVENTS OF THE CAY SEARED IN THEIR MINDS-- WATCH THE COLONY BEING DEVOURED IN FLAMES, LEAVING THE MONSTER IN THE POOL STILL HUNGRY... STILL WAITING... FOR FOOD!!...

IT'S HORRIBLE, JIM!! I--I CAN'T BEAR TO LOOK!!
THEY DIE AS THEY DESERVE TO DIE, MARY-- IN FIRE!!
THE END
6

WORLD'S *Greatest* LEGEND

The world's greatest legend is the familiar story of King Arthur and the Round Table. It has appeared in slightly different forms in almost every country. Like all legends, the story is a mixture of history and fancy.

King Arthur was an unusually brave and highly successful king of the Celtic Britons, whom he led against Saxon invaders. He fought twelve battles and won them all. This much is strict history.

The Arthurian legends which come to us in various forms from the Welsh *Mabinogian* to the German *Parsifal* make him the leader of chivalry and heroism.

Arthur was the son of King Uther of Britain and Queen Igerne. At that time, a chief king was elected for life by lesser kings and knights, and when Uther died, there was a contest. Merlin the mighty magician had a sword stuck in a stone, and said that the one young prince who could pull the sword out of stone, was the king to lead Britain to glory.

All princes and knights tried, but none of them could pull the sword out of stone. Prince Arthur entered at the dramatic moment. Walking boldly to the stone, he pulled the sword out effortlessly, and was thereby elected chief king of Britain.

In one of his battles, the sword was shattered. He needed a new one. Merlin the magician took him to a lake from which an arm clothed in white protruded holding a sword.

The Lady of the Lake approached King Arthur and he asked her if he could have the sword. She told him that it was hers, but he might have it. Arthur rowed out and took the sword from the hand. This was Excalibur, one of the most famous swords in history and legend.

King Arthur married Guinevere, daughter of King Leodegrance. As a wedding gift, Leodegrance gave Arthur the famous Round Table with seats for 150 knights. One of these seats was the Siege Perilous—which could be occupied only by the one knight who was to find the Holy Grail, the cup which Christ drank on his Last Supper.

Almost every knight of the Round Table sought the Holy Grail, each going through dangerous adventures. The most famous and most heroic of the knights, Sir Lancelot of the Lake, knew that he would never see it because his love for Queen Guinevere was sinful.

His son, Sir Galahad, was a better man and a truer knight, and he found the Holy Grail. He guarded it for the rest of his life, and when he died his spirit carried the Holy Grail out of sight of mankind forever.

Then the Round Table disintegrated. Knights who swore to chivalry fell to quarrelling among themselves. They began to fight, and a civil war resulted.

Arthur's nephew, Modred, who wanted the kingdom for himself, made well of the opportunity. He led the rebellious knights against Arthur's loyal forces.

The resulting battle was the greatest Britain had ever seen. Knights fought knights and many fell. Of King Arthur's men, only Sir Lucan and Sir Bevidere remained alive.

As Arthur was dying, he called Sir Bevidere and told him to take Excalibur to the lake. He was to throw it as far as he could into the lake.

An arm, covered with white cloth rose from the lake and seized the flying sword. It shook the sword three times, and drew it deep inside the lake forever.

Bevidere then carried Arthur to the lake and laid him on the bank. A barge manned by women in black appeared and skimmed to shore. Arthur was helped aboard, and the barge shoved off, sailing in the direction of Avalon.

The legend has it that some day Arthur will return to Britain to guide the country to greater glory.

ZACHERY JENSEN AND WILMER BLETZ OPERATED A LONELY LIGHTHOUSE TOGETHER.... BUT WHEN JENSEN KILLED BLETZ IN COLD BLOOD, THE LIGHTHOUSE'S RAY OF WARNING LIGHT BECAME THE....
BEAM OF TERROR
FOLLOW MY BEAM, ZACHERY! SURELY YOU TRUST YOUR OLD PARTNER TO GUIDE YOU! HEH-HEH!
AT A DESOLATE LIGHTHOUSE OF THE ROCKBOUND NEW ENGLAND COAST IN THE 19TH CENTURY!
THEY'RE GONNA WIDEN THE SHIPPING CHANNEL, WILMER! THE LIGHTHOUSE WON'T BE NEEDED NO MORE!
AND NEITHER WILL WE, ZACHERY! WE ALREADY GOT OUR SHIP BOUGHT... LET'S GET THAT MAP WE HID IN THE TOWER AND FIND THAT BURIED TREASURE!
YOU'RE RIGHT! WE'VE SAVED EVERY PENNY FOR OUR BOAT SINCE THAT MAP FLOATED UP IN THAT BOTTLE TWENTY YEARS AGO! IT'S NOW OR NEVER!
THEN IT'S NOW! TONIGHT AFTER DARK WE'LL GET THE MAP AND START OUT!

AND THAT NIGHT....
EASY WITH THAT LAMP, WILMER! WHAT WITH THE LIGHTHOUSE OFFICIALLY CLOSED WE'D BETTER NOT BE SEEN!
IT'S THE CHANCE WE TAKE, ZACHERY! LET'S GO IN!

WE'RE CLIMBING THIS LADDER FOR THE LAST TIME, ZACHERY!
RIGHT, WILMER! IT WON'T BE LONG NOW!

HEH-HEH! THE MAP!
LET'S GO, ZACHERY, I'VE WAITED TWENTY YEARS FOR THIS!

YOU CAN WAIT AN ETERNITY, WILMER! THE WHOLE TREASURE WILL BE MINE!
ZACHERY! WHAAA--!

ONLY A FOOL WOULD SHARE A TREASURE, WILMER! GOOD-BYE, MY FRIEND!
HA! - HA! HA!
AIEEEEEEE

YOU!!!... PAY FOR... THIS... ZACHERY.... I'LL .. SEE TO... THAT! AGGGRRAAA!!!
HEH-HEH-HEH! DIE WILMER! DIE!

ARMED WITH THE BLOOD-DRENCHED TREASURE MAP, THE DIABOLICAL JENSEN SETS SAIL FOR THE DISTANT TROPICAL ISLE, ACTING AS HIS OWN CAPTAIN!
HA-HA! MY OWN SHIP AND SOON MY OWN FORTUNE! MY WEALTH WILL BE MY POWER! AND BLETZ WILL NEVER BE FOUND IN THAT ABANDONED LIGHTHOUSE!
BUT AS THE GLOATING MURDERER TURNS, HE IS GREETED BY A HIDEOUS SIGHT... INVISIBLE TO THE OTHERS!
I.... WHAAA--! NO! IT CAN'T BE!

YOU'RE DEAD I SAY! I KILLED YOU MYSELF!
CAPTAIN'S GONE OFF HIS NUT! HE MIGHT BE DANGEROUS!
RIGHT! IT'D BE BETTER IF HE WAS BOUND AND GAGGED! FOR ALL OF US!

MAD AM I! I KILL MUTINEERS! ANYBODY ELSE CARE TO TAKE OVER MY SHIP!
NO.... SIR, CAPT'N!
AGG
BANG
BANG

THEN BACK TO POSITIONS BEFORE I TOSS YOU TO THE SHARKS! THERE'S A TREASURE TO BE HAD! BY ME! HA-HA-HA!
JENSEN'S SAVAGE BRUTALITY KEEPS THE MEN IN HAND AND THE LONG VOYAGE NEARS COMPLETION! BUT THE WEIRD AND LURID VISION CONTINUES TO PLAGUE HIM!
LAND! WE'RE NEARING THE ISLAND! WHAAAA! NO! KEEP AWAY FROM ME, BLETZ! AIEEEE!

THE GHOST OF WILMER BLETZ SLOWLY, METHODICALLY DRIVES JENSEN INSANE! BUT OBSESSED WITH HIS LUST FOR WEALTH, THE CRAZED MURDERER PLODS FORWARD FINALLY REACHING HIS FATEFUL GOAL!
THAT'S IT! WE'VE FOUND IT! WAIT! I'LL DIG IT UP!
HA-HA-HA! I'LL BE THE MOST POWERFUL MAN IN AMERICA! THE TREASURE IS MINE!
I...NO! KEEP AWAY! YOU'RE DEAD, BLETZ! DEAD!
YOUR JUST OVERTIRED, CAPT'N! HERE ....LET ME LEND YOU A HAND!
KEEP AWAY FROM THAT CHEST!
BANG
BANG
THE TREASURE IS ALL MINE I SAY! DEATH TO THOSE WHO MOVE TOO QUICKLY!
BANG
BANG
AGGGRRRAAA
NOW THE REST OF YOU--! LOAD IT ON BOARD AND REMEMBER THAT ZACHERY JENSEN IS WATCHING YOU!
YESSIR, CAPT'N!

THE RETURN VOYAGE IS UNEVENTFUL UNTIL THE MANIACAL JENSEN'S SHIP PASSES THE DESERTED LIGHTHOUSE, LAST USED AS WILMER BLETZ'S TOMB!
THE LIGHTHOUSE! STEER BY THE BEAM! RIGHT THROUGH THE CHANNEL!
BUT THE CHANNEL'S BEEN CHANGED, JENSEN! THERE ARE ROCKS THERE NOW!
DO AS I SAY! THIS SHIP IS MINE AND SO IS THE TREASURE! STEER BY THE BEAM OF LIGHT! HA-HA-HA!
BUT THE LIGHTHOUSE HASN'T BEEN USED IN OVER A YEAR! WE'LL BE RIPPED ON THE ROCKS, JENSEN!
RAVING HYSTERICALLY, THE CRAZED JENSEN HEADS HIS SHIP INTO THE EERIE BEAM FROM THE ABANDONED LIGHTHOUSE!
THIS WAY, JENSEN! STEER BY MY BEAM! HEE-HEE-HEE!
YOU HEARD HIM, MATES! STEER BY HIS LIGHT BEAM! FULL SPEED AHEAD! WE'RE COMING WILMER! HA-HA-HA!
AIEEE! HE'S MAD! WE'LL CRASH!
AIEEEE
AGGRRRAAA
THERE'S A SHARK IN THE WATER.
CRUNCH
AIEEE! GLUB..... AGGRRAAA... GULP......
HA HA HA HA-HA HA
AND AS THE LAST REMAINS OF FIENDISH ZACHERY JENSEN AND HIS VESSEL SINK SLOWLY BENEATH THE WAVES, THE STRANGE BEAM OF LIGHT FLICKERS OUT.... AS A MURDERED MAN'S REVENGE IS COMPLETE!
THE END

BUY NOW & SAVE!
76 SENSATIONAL NEW GLOWING CHRISTMAS TREE ORNAMENTS
ONLY $1
ACTUALLY CHARGE THEMSELVES WITH LIGHT! LIGHT UP AT NIGHT WITHOUT WIRES WITHOUT ELECTRICITY
MADE OF REVOLUTIONARY LIGHT ABSORBING PLASTIC
Now decorate your Christmas Tree with a sensational new kind of Christmas Tree Ornaments . . . these actually light up without wires or electricity . . . because they're made of safe, light absorbing plastic. They absorb the light and store it . . . then when you turn out the lights they just light up . . . it's like magic. They are durable, made of sturdy Dow STYRENE plastic and will last for years. Some up to 4½ inches high. AND . . . in daylight their colors of red, blue and white glisten with sunlit effect . . . they are beautiful by day . . . spellbinding at night.
14 BELLS LIGHT UP - SPELLING -
MERRY CHRISTMAS
NO ELECTRICITY NO WIRES
You Get ALL THESE 76 Ornaments
Every one made of solid light absorbing plastic . . . No wires, no danger. They're WIRELESS. Tested and approved by world famous testing laboratory. Just hang them on your tree. Will last a lifetime. Light up quality never wears out.
• 14 MERRY CHRISTMAS BELLS
• 10 CHURCH BELLS
• 12 STARS
• 12 ICICLES
• 4 CANDY CANES
• 1 SANTA CLAUS
• 6 REINDEER
• 1 SANTA'S HOUSE
• 10 SNOWFLAKES
• 1 NORTH POLE
• 1 SNOW MAN
• 3 CANDLES
• 1 CHERUB
SANTA'S WORK SHOP
NORTH POLE
Fully Guaranteed Rush Coupon
We guarantee full satisfaction or money back in ten days. Hurry coupon for guaranteed Christmas delivery. You take no risk because they have been approved by a leading testing laboratory. Your assurance of quality and value.
XMAS SPECIAL RUSH COUPON
DON'T DELAY MAIL NOW
XMAS ORNAMENTS, Dept. X-4
836 BROADWAY, N.Y. 3, N.Y.
Send your special offer of 76 all-plastic, light-up-in-the-dark Christmas Tree Ornaments by return postpaid mail. If not delighted, I'll return for refund within 10 days. I enclose one dollar for each set ordered. (Only 3 sets to each customer.) (Sorry, NO C.O.D.'s.)
Enclosed find $______for______sets
Name______
Address______

SAVE $$$...the Moto-Matic way!

LOOK

5 Day Trial—Money Back Guarantee! Compare These Prices!

Thousands sold for $2.95

NOW $1.98

2 FOR 3.75

LEOPARD *Plastic* **SEAT COVERS**

Also:
Zebra
Scotch Plaids, Stripes, Solids

Any Design 1.98 2 for 3.75

Unbelievable value! Closing out our regularly $2.95 seat covers for only 1.98 — 2 for 3.75! Made of tough, durable, plastic to simulate **LEOPARD FUR, ZEBRA, SCOTCH PLAIDS, STRIPES**, Etc. Choose your favorite design! Protects new cars against grime, dust, water. For **ALL** cars, **ALL** models. **NO** sewing needed! Just slide on or off in a jiffy. Covers front, left and right sides of seat. Mention car make, year, model; also design preferred No. 150 Out they go — one low price, 1.98 each, TWO for **3.75**

Stop Auto Thieves!

Electric Burglar Alarm

Protects car, tires, gas, accessories!

Foil auto thieves! The **NEW** Pend-Electric Burglar Alarm gives you **ALL-OUT** protection against accessory, tire, gasoline and auto thieves. Protects your **ENTIRE** car even if you leave the door open! Anyone molesting your car will get the shock of his life! The "Unseen Policeman" goes into action instantly, getting off loud, screeching horn blasts — continuing for 15 seconds after car is left alone. Even the most daring thief will run for it! Easily installed with a screwdriver. Complete with wiring, instructions, screws, on-off switch. Completely **AUTOMATIC** and ultra-sensitive. A real investment in peace of mind No. 34. Bargain price... **3.95**

The EASY way to paint Famous Burgess ELECTRIC PAINT SPRAYER

Don't paint it... **SPRAY** it the **EASY** Burgess Electric Sprayer way! No more messy brushes and back-breaking toil! Just fill mason jar with your favorite paint, enamel, lacquer, insecticide or disinfectant. Push the handy button, aim and spray. Save **TIME**, save **WORK**, save **PAINT** too! And the results are simply amazing — look like professional jobs, so uniform, and no brush marks! So handy too for insecticides, garden sprays, lubricating oils, shellac, etc. Reaches hard-to-get-at places, such as ceilings, corners; ideal for painting wicker furniture. Hundreds of uses in home, office, farm or factory! Paint walls and ceilings, cabinets, furniture, outside the house too! Spray insecticides in the home, for garden pest control, in the garden for livestock, etc.

PAINT YOUR OWN CAR! SAVE $50.00, OR MORE!

Spray it the factory way ... get wonderful **EVEN** coverage—no brush marks, no drippings or paint splashes! So clean, so easy, so satisfying! The Burgess is complete—ready to use—no extras. Has powerful, self contained 110 Volt A-C motor, 8 foot insulated cord and 8 oz mason jar. Rotary-Adjustor — gives any spray, fine, heavy or thick — up to 80 lb pressure! Guaranteed by famous Burgess factory No. 187. Look at our **LOW**, reduced price, only **7.88**

New! Made in GERMANY

ONLY $3

Hi-Power Binoscope with carrying case

3.00

3.95

PERSONAL • CARRY Hand & Body Warmer

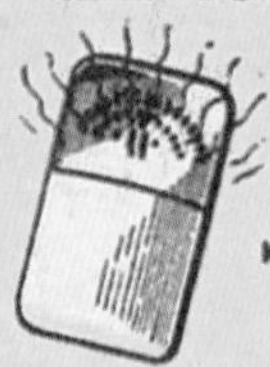

- Travels with you!
- Fits in Pocket.

NEW Hi-Heat Pocket Size Warmer is a little marvel. Gives warm as-toast heat in coldest weather! Hi-Heat has the wonder element activated by white gasoline, naphtha or alcohol. Absolutely **SAFE** — No flame — No danger. Yet it gives comforting heat up to 24 hours with only a few drops of fuel! Mirror finish metal — no moving parts to wear out. Attractive carrying case included. Ideal gift for motorists, traveling salesmen, rural dwellers. Quality construction guarantees high efficiency. **No. 21 NOW** only **2.95**

Wonder of the Age! WALKIE-TALKIES 2 WAY

No Batteries Needed!

NOW — a remarkable 2 way telephone system between house and garage, room to room, barn, workshop, etc! No batteries! No electricity! Operates at considerable distances! So useful! Fun too, for all! Complete with 2 power phones and wiring — ready for use **No. 17.** Our low price.... **3.90**

WIPE OFF RUST QUICK-EASY

NEW! AMAZING! Rust rolls off any metal surface!

Rust destroys! Save money and grief ... use **PRO-KROME** — the new wonder cream! Just apply over any metal surface, iron, chrome, steel, brass, tin, etc. Wipe and see rust roll right off before your eyes! Use on cars, tools, machinery, typewriters, kitchenware, lawn mowers, bikes, etc. Fast! Guaranteed! **No. 33** Large Tube **1.00**
3 tubes at cut price of **2.00**

TINY MIDGET CAMERA

$1.39

TAKES "SECRET" PICTURES! Also Action Shots and Color

One of the world's smallest cameras ... yet you get beautiful 2 x 3 jumbo prints from low cost 828 film. Also Kodak **COLOR** pictures—action shots of sports, accidents, nature study, friends and family. Quality ground lens. Easily concealed in hand for taking secret, forbidden pictures! **EASY!** Just aim and click. **No. 32.** Special **1.39**
"**Granital**" Luggage Tan carrying case with straps only 61¢ with Camera Total.................. **2.00**

RUSH COUPON

SEND NO MONEY—Try without obligation!

MOTO-MATIC COMPANY, Dept. 125-B-500
129 West 33rd Street, New York 1, N. Y.

RUSH the following **C O D** plus postage, on **5 DAY TRIAL** with **GUARANTEE** of absolute satisfaction or full price back

NUMBER	ITEM	PRICE

NAME ______________________

ADDRESS ______________________

TOWN ______________ ZONE ___ STATE ________

☐ SAVE MORE! Send check, money order, or cash with this coupon and we pay all postage. Same **MONEY BACK** guarantee.

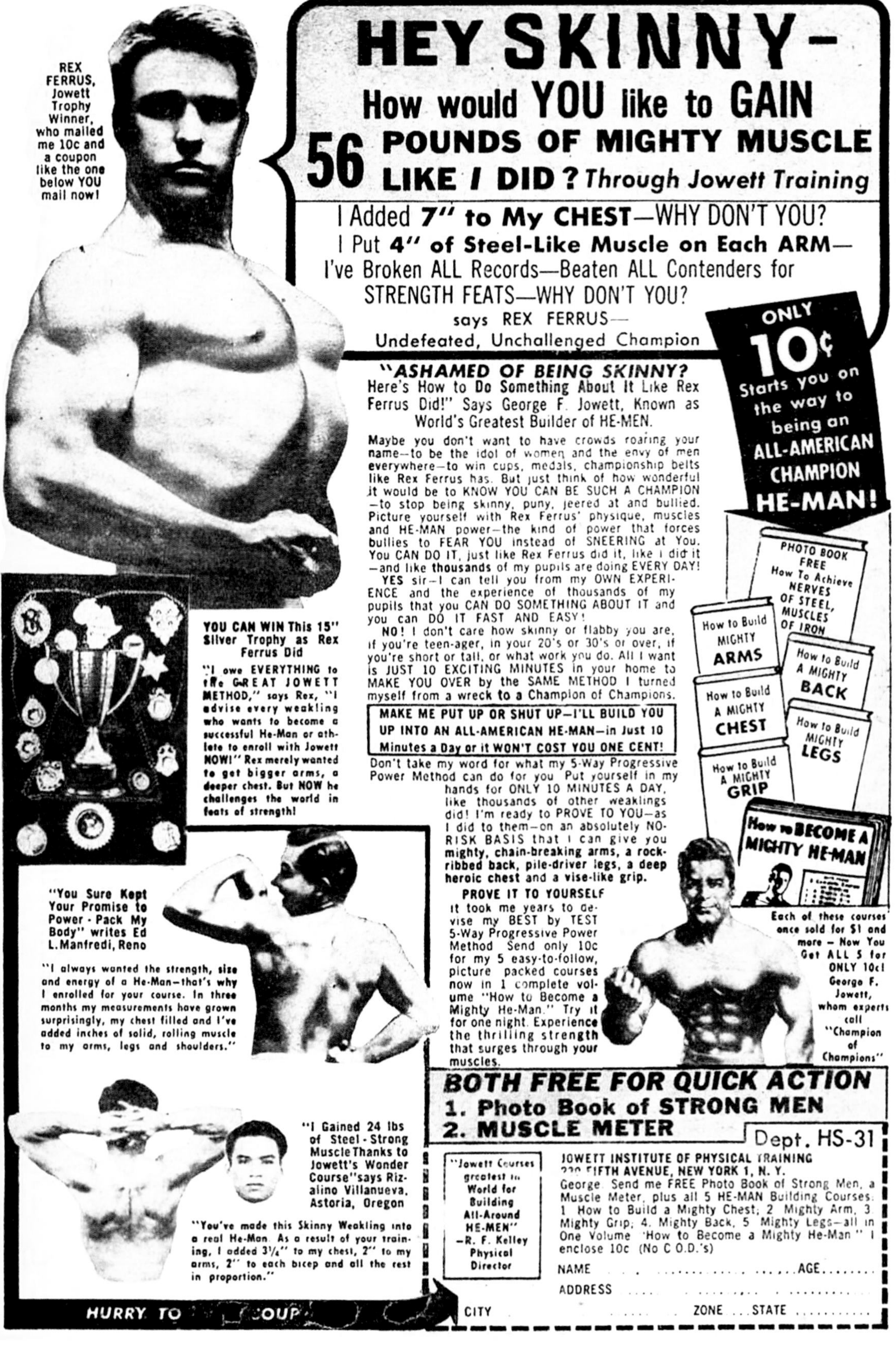
REX FERRUS, Jowett Trophy Winner, who mailed me 10c and a coupon like the one below YOU mail now!
HEY SKINNY–
How would YOU like to GAIN
56 POUNDS OF MIGHTY MUSCLE
LIKE I DID? Through Jowett Training
I Added 7" to My CHEST—WHY DON'T YOU?
I Put 4" of Steel-Like Muscle on Each ARM—
I've Broken ALL Records—Beaten ALL Contenders for STRENGTH FEATS—WHY DON'T YOU?
says REX FERRUS—
Undefeated, Unchallenged Champion
ONLY 10¢ Starts you on the way to being an ALL-AMERICAN CHAMPION HE-MAN!
"ASHAMED OF BEING SKINNY? Here's How to Do Something About It Like Rex Ferrus Did!" Says George F. Jowett, Known as World's Greatest Builder of HE-MEN.
Maybe you don't want to have crowds roaring your name—to be the idol of women and the envy of men everywhere—to win cups, medals, championship belts like Rex Ferrus has. But just think of how wonderful it would be to KNOW YOU CAN BE SUCH A CHAMPION—to stop being skinny, puny, jeered at and bullied. Picture yourself with Rex Ferrus' physique, muscles and HE-MAN power—the kind of power that forces bullies to FEAR YOU instead of SNEERING at You. You CAN DO IT, just like Rex Ferrus did it, like I did it—and like thousands of my pupils are doing EVERY DAY!
YES sir—I can tell you from my OWN EXPERIENCE and the experience of thousands of my pupils that you CAN DO SOMETHING ABOUT IT and you can DO IT FAST AND EASY!
NO! I don't care how skinny or flabby you are, if you're teen-ager, in your 20's or 30's or over, if you're short or tall, or what work you do. All I want is JUST 10 EXCITING MINUTES in your home to MAKE YOU OVER by the SAME METHOD I turned myself from a wreck to a Champion of Champions.
MAKE ME PUT UP OR SHUT UP—I'LL BUILD YOU UP INTO AN ALL-AMERICAN HE-MAN—in Just 10 Minutes a Day or it WON'T COST YOU ONE CENT!
Don't take my word for what my 5-Way Progressive Power Method can do for you. Put yourself in my hands for ONLY 10 MINUTES A DAY, like thousands of other weaklings did! I'm ready to PROVE TO YOU—as I did to them—on an absolutely NO-RISK BASIS that I can give you mighty, chain-breaking arms, a rock-ribbed back, pile-driver legs, a deep heroic chest and a vise-like grip.
PROVE IT TO YOURSELF
It took me years to devise my BEST by TEST 5-Way Progressive Power Method. Send only 10c for my 5 easy-to-follow, picture packed courses now in 1 complete volume "How to Become a Mighty He-Man." Try it for one night. Experience the thrilling strength that surges through your muscles.
PHOTO BOOK FREE How To Achieve NERVES OF STEEL, MUSCLES OF IRON
How to Build MIGHTY ARMS
How to Build A MIGHTY BACK
How to Build A MIGHTY CHEST
How to Build MIGHTY LEGS
How to Build A MIGHTY GRIP
How to BECOME A MIGHTY HE-MAN
Each of these courses once sold for $1 and more — Now You Get ALL 5 for ONLY 10c! George F. Jowett, whom experts call "Champion of Champions"
YOU CAN WIN This 15" Silver Trophy as Rex Ferrus Did
"I owe EVERYTHING to the GREAT JOWETT METHOD," says Rex, "I advise every weakling who wants to become a successful He-Man or athlete to enroll with Jowett NOW!" Rex merely wanted to get bigger arms, a deeper chest. But NOW he challenges the world in feats of strength!
"You Sure Kept Your Promise to Power-Pack My Body" writes Ed L. Manfredi, Reno
"I always wanted the strength, size and energy of a He-Man—that's why I enrolled for your course. In three months my measurements have grown surprisingly, my chest filled and I've added inches of solid, rolling muscle to my arms, legs and shoulders."
"I Gained 24 lbs of Steel-Strong Muscle Thanks to Jowett's Wonder Course" says Rizalino Villanueva, Astoria, Oregon
"You've made this Skinny Weakling into a real He-Man. As a result of your training, I added 3¼" to my chest, 2" to my arms, 2" to each bicep and all the rest in proportion."
BOTH FREE FOR QUICK ACTION
1. Photo Book of STRONG MEN
2. MUSCLE METER
Dept. HS-31
"Jowett Courses greatest in World for Building All-Around HE-MEN" —R. F. Kelley Physical Director
JOWETT INSTITUTE OF PHYSICAL TRAINING
220 FIFTH AVENUE, NEW YORK 1, N. Y.
George: Send me FREE Photo Book of Strong Men, a Muscle Meter, plus all 5 HE-MAN Building Courses: 1. How to Build a Mighty Chest; 2. Mighty Arm; 3. Mighty Grip; 4. Mighty Back; 5. Mighty Legs—all in One Volume "How to Become a Mighty He-Man." I enclose 10c (No C.O.D.'s)
NAME .... AGE ....
ADDRESS ....
CITY .... ZONE ... STATE ....
HURRY TO ... COUP...

SOLDIERS
SAILORS
WACS
MORTARS
MARINES
PT BOATS
HOWITZERS
TRUCKS
CANNONS
BOMBERS
TANKS
CRUISERS
BATTLESHIPS
PT BOATS
MARINES
WAVES
WACS
SAILORS
SOLDIERS
SOLDIERS
SAILORS
WACS
WAVES
MARINES
PT BOATS
BATTLESHIPS
CRUISERS
JETS
MACHINE GUNS
BAZOOKAS
RIFLEMEN
50 COMBAT ACTION PLASTIC TOYS
$1 POSTPAID
Your Own TASK FORCE
Now you can be Commander in Chief of this complete task force. Have pitched battles, gunnery drills, deploy your troops for attack and defense. Here's a complete army 50 pieces in all including soldiers, sailors, marines, PT boat, Howitzers, tanks, planes, and ships. You'll be thrilled and delighted with this complete task force Nothing else like it!
LOOK WHAT YOU GET. SOLDIERS SAILORS · MARINES · WACS · TANKS JEEPS · PT BOATS · BATTLESHIPS · JET PLANES · BOMBERS · MACHINE GUNNERS HOWITZERS · TRUCKS · BAZOOKA MEN RIFLEMEN
Here's a great collection of military toys yours for just a single dollar bill. You'll have hours of fun and pleasure with this wonderful set Every piece made of plastic in realistic scale. Precision formed of Styrene...nothing like it has ever been offered at this price Rush your order now. 6" long die cut cannon that shoots harmless bombs included in your order NOW!
FREE 6" LONG DIE CUT SHOOTING CANNON!
Supplies Limited! Don't delay. Rush name and address and $1 for each set. Your complete 50-piece task force will be shipped by return mail. Sorry no COD's. Rush your dollar today.
FIGHTING FORCE Dept. 11
1860 Broadway
New York 23, N.Y.
I enclose ________ at $1 per set.
Rush your 50-piece Fighting Force set prepaid.
Name ________ Age ____
Address ________
City ________ State ________

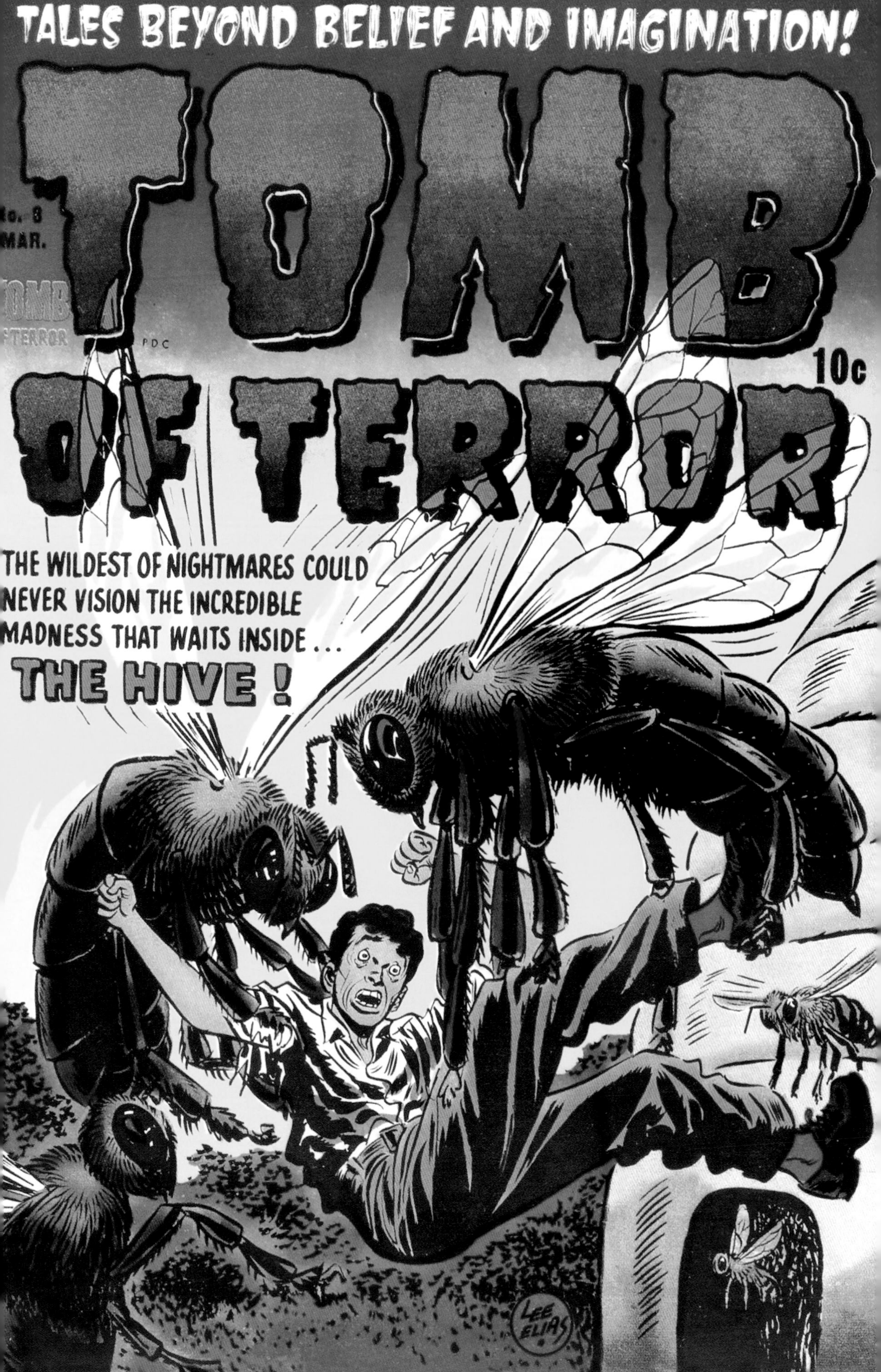
TALES BEYOND BELIEF AND IMAGINATION!
TOMB OF TERROR
MAR.
PDC
10c
THE WILDEST OF NIGHTMARES COULD NEVER VISION THE INCREDIBLE MADNESS THAT WAITS INSIDE...
THE HIVE!
LEE ELIAS

the SECRET of TREASURE CAVE-
How Gray Shadow Tracked Down the Mystery of Spike's Sudden Wealth-
GIVEN!
BOYS! GIRLS! LADIES! MEN!
WE GIVE YOU CASH OR PREMIUMS!
LAST WEEK HE TOOK A NEW AIR RIFLE IN THAT CAVE-
GEE! A NEW BIKE!
WHERE'S SPIKE GET THAT STUFF?
GRAY SHADOW HAS GOT TO TRAIL HIM!
I'LL BUY 2 BOXES OF WHITE CLOVERINE BRAND SALVE, SPIKE! IT'S WONDERFUL... AND THESE ART PICTURES YOU GIVE ARE LOVELY!
THANKS, MRS. JONES! THAT MAKES 10 BOXES I'VE SOLD THIS MORNING. IT'S EASY!
UGH! PALE SQUAW GIVE-UM WAMPUM!
Archery Sets, Pocket Watches, Footballs, Carving Sets (sent postage paid). Write or mail coupon to start.
ACT NOW
WE TRUST YOU!
22 Cal. Rifles 1000 Shot Daisy Air Rifles (sent postage paid). Boys—girls Bicycles (Express charges collect). Write or mail coupon to start.
HIM STOP 4 WIGWAMS-SQUAWS GIVE-UM MUCH WAMPUM-
LOOK! A REAL WATCH TOO!
MAKE HIM TALK!
I CONFESS, KIDS- I GOT ALL THESE PREMIUMS JUST FOR SELLING WHITE CLOVERINE BRAND SALVE... NEXT WEEK I'M GETTING A CAMERA. IT'S A CINCH!
BOY! I'M SENDING IN THAT COUPON RIGHT AWAY!
ME TOO! I WANT A RADIO!
OUR 57th YEAR
OUR 57th YEAR
ACT NOW!
Corn Poppers, Speedball Cartoon Sets, Aluminum Ware, Blankets (sent postage paid). Mail coupon for salve and pictures to start.
Ukuleles, Radios, Pen & Pencil Sets, Food Choppers, Watches (sent postage paid).
WE ARE RELIABLE
Lovable fully dressed Dolls over 15" in height, Ukuleles, Alarm Clocks Write or mail coupon today
ACT NOW
OUR 57th YEAR
NU BRITE
MAIL COUPON! YOU GET BIG CATALOG
Candid Cameras with carrying case, Telescopes, Watches (sent postage paid)
SIMPLY GIVE pictures with White CLOVERINE Brand SALVE easily sold to friends, neighbors, relatives at 25c a box (with picture)
WHITE CLOVERINE BRAND SALVE PRICE 25¢
OUR 57th YR.
ACT NOW!
LET'S GO!
Alarm Clocks, Pen and Pencil Sets, Bibles, Billfolds, Telescopes, Roller Skates, Blankets, Aluminum Ware, Record Players Movie Machines (sent postage paid) Rush coupon to start!
Archery Sets, Dolls Wrist Watches, Footballs, Pencil Sharpeners School Boxes, Roller Skates, Wallets Flashlights Mail coupon for salve and pictures to start.
WE TRUST YOU!
Flashlights Footballs, Corn Poppers, Fishing Sets, Telescopes.
WE TRUST YOU
OUR 57th YEAR
MAIL NOW!
Wilson Chem. Co. Dept. 25-H, Tyrone, Pa. Date
Gentlemen:- Please send me on trial 14 colorful art pictures with 14 boxes of White CLOVERINE Brand SALVE to sell at 25c a box (with picture). I will remit amount asked within 30 days, select a Premium or keep Cash Commission as explained under Premium wanted in catalog sent with order, postage paid to start.
NAME AGE
ST. R. D. BOX
TOWN ZONE NO STATE
PRINT LAST NAME HERE
Paste coupon on postal card or mail in envelope today
Pocket Watches, Carving Sets Corn Poppers Write or mail coupon to start We trust you
BE FIRST!
MAIL COUPON!
LET'S GO!
Rifles, Motion Picture Cameras with roll of film, Roller Skates, Radios. Mail coupon to start.
OUR 57th YEAR - WE ARE RELIABLE

You've given us the skeleton key to your hearts, and welcome us with pangs of joy! You've let us run up and down your spine, in and out of your nervous track -- and in four colors too!

Yes, you've made the TOMB OF TERROR your choice in terror!

Still we're working high midnight to high midnight on improving the quality and impact of the stories, and we think we're doing one chilling of a job.

But we want to know what you think, which story you like best, what kind of stories you'd like to see in our pages!

So take out a few seconds and scribble this department a note. Let us know which of this issue's stories you rate best...which the least!

Is THE HIVE a honey, or does it buzz a bore? Does THE SEARCH really pay off? Can you see the EYES OF MARCH? And does THE VISION IN BRONZE have real mettle?

We want to know how you find it, so we can find out how you want it!

Scribble down the verdict and send it to the...

TOMB OF TERROR
1860 Broadway
New York 23, N.Y.

TOMB OF TERROR, March, 1953, Vol. 1, No. 8, is published every other month by HARVEY PUBLICATIONS, INC., at 420 DeSoto Avenue, St. Louis 7, Mo. Editorial, Advertising and Executive offices, 1860 Broadway, New York 23, N. Y. President Alfred Harvey; Vice-President and Editor, Leon Harvey; Vice-President and Business Manager Robert B. Harvey. Entered as second-class matter at the Post Office at St. Louis, Mo., under the Act of March 3, 1879. Single copies, 10c. Subscription rates, 10 issues for $1.00 in the U. S. and possessions, elsewhere $1.50. All names in this periodical are entirely fictitious and no identification with actual persons is intended.

Magic Dutch
Rock Garden
Grows in 4 DAYS
only $1.00
Grows in 4 Days
Lasts for months in any season
Winter-Summer, Spring or Fall
Grow grasses green and flowers tall.
Boys & girls, here's exciting news. News about something entirely different! Now, you can grow a real garden of your very own—right in your own home. Yes, here's an amazing magic garden you set up and plant yourself in a few minutes. Grow real grass and flowers in just a few days! You'll thrill to the magic of Mother Nature as you watch the grass sprout and the flowers take root and grow right before your eyes. In no time at all you'll have a colorful, healthy garden—and what a kick you'll get playing gardener, cutting the grass, watering the plants, and tending the lovely sweet-smelling flowers. You can even clip a beautiful bunch of flowers for mom, or friend. All your friends will wonder how you were able to make things grow—They'll all want you to show them how!
EVERYTHING YOU NEED
You get all these items —you don't need anything else. Plenty of Magic grass seeds . . . Magic soil. Lovely flower seeds . . . Practical, attractive container . . . Bright colored metal butterflies. Little Dutch boy and girl . . . American Flag . . . Parasol that opens and closes . . . simulated rocks. Cute ceramic dog . . . Many other exciting features.
Over a hundred square inches of garden — Special wishing pool in the center — An American flag and pole — Two attractive butterflies that look like they're flying — Your own container. Just look at the list!
For Boys and Girls of All Ages
Here's a beautiful garden all your own for just a single dollar bill. You'll have hours of fun. You'll surprise your family and friends with what you know and what you can do!
10 Day Trial FREE
If you are not 100% delighted with this Garden just send it back. We will refund the full purchase price at once. Rush Coupon now!
RUSH COUPON NOW!
HONOR HOUSE PRODUCTS CORP. Dept. 309
1860 Broadway, N.Y. 23, N.Y.
Rush my Magic Dutch Rock Gardens on approval for only $1.00. If I am not completely satisfied I may return it for prompt refund of full purchase price.
Name
Address
☐ Send C.O.D. I'll pay postman $1 plus a few cents postage.
☐ I enclose $1.00 for my garden. You pay postage. Same money back guarantee.

YOUR NAME IS CHARLIE PATCH... AN ORDINARY NAME AND YOU'RE AN ORDINARY GUY. BUT YOU HAD DREAMS OF SOMETHING *MORE*! THAT WAS YOUR TROUBLE... YOU DIDN'T FIGURE ON THE...

HIVE!

Z-Z-Z

Z-Z-Z

HELP! PUT ME DOWN! *AIIEEEE!!*

THIS WAS YOU AT ONE TIME... WITH YOUR BEES AND THE BEE-HIVES TO WORK WITH, NOT A CARE IN THE WORLD!
COME OUT, YOU LITTLE RASCALS! YOU KNOW YOUR FRIEND, DON'T YOU! *HA HA!*

AND HERE COMES YOUR EMPLOYER... A WEALTHY WOMAN, A REPUTED WOMAN...
HEY, CHARLIE! H'YAR COMES MISS CAROL! GET TIDIED UP! WE CAN'T BE IN RAGS WHEN SHE SEES US!
YEAH... OKAY, JOE! JUST LET ME FINISH THIS HERE HONEY-GATHERING...

AND CAROL LEIGHTON WAS A BEAUTIFUL WOMAN, TOO!
HELLO, BOYS! HOW IS EVERYTHING GOING?
HOWDY, MISS CAROL! JUST FINE!!

AND REMEMBER HOW PROUD YOU WERE, CHARLIE, WHEN SHE TOOK AN INTEREST IN YOU!
--AND YOU, CHARLIE! ARE THE BEE-HIVES IN GOOD CONDITION? I STILL REMEMBER THAT DELICIOUS HONEY YOU SENT ME LAST MONTH!
--IN TOP CONDITION, MA'AM! LOOK-- I'LL SHOW YOU!

HEAR THEIR DEEP BUZZIN'? THAT MEANS THEY'RE STRONG AN' HEALTHY! BEES ARE JUST LIKE PEOPLE, MISS CAROL! THEY KNOW WHEN YOU LIKE THEM OR NOT!
UH--YES! WELL! I'M GLAD YOU'RE TAKING SUCH GOOD CARE OF THEM! WE'RE KNOWN FOR OUR BEST HONEY ALL OVER THIS PART OF THE COUNTY, YOU KNOW!

IN GENERAL, I FIND EVERYTHING WELL-TENDED! I'M VERY PLEASED, BOYS! YOU'LL ALL FIND A BONUS IN YOUR PAY-CHECKS AT THE END OF THIS MONTH!
THAT'S SURE DECENT OF YOU, MISS CAROL!

THEN WHEN SHE SINGLED YOU OUT AGAIN, CHARLIE, YOUR HEART ALMOST STOPPED BEATING!
WELL--GOODBYE, BOYS! I'LL BE OVER AGAIN NEXT SATURDAY! TAKE SPECIAL CARE OF THOSE BEES OF YOURS, CHARLIE!
I WILL, MISS CAROL! AND I'LL SEND YOU THE FIRST HONEY O' THE SEASON! SOON'S MY LITTLE FRIENDS START MAKIN' IT!

THERE GOES A FINE PERSON! ONLY WOMAN I'VE LIKED WORKING FOR! SHE TREATS ALL O' US FAIR AN' SQUARE!
SHE SURE DOES!
2

THAT NIGHT, YOU FELT PRETTY PECULIAR, DIDN'T YOU? HER BEAUTY HAD AFFECTED YOU MORE THAN YOU CARED TO ADMIT...
SHE SURE IS NICE! OH-- IF ONLY I WERE ATTRACTIVE TO HER! WE COULD MARRY--AN' I COULD TAKE CARE O' A DOZEN BEE-HIVES....

WHAT WAS THAT? NOW HOW D'YA SUPPOSE ANY O' MY BEES GOT INSIDE MY SHACK?
BUZZ-Z-Z-Z

THEN IT HAPPENED, CHARLIE! THEN IT HAPPENED!
T-THEY'RE GROWIN'! --MUST BE MY IMAGINATION! IT'S GOTTA BE!
BUZZZZZ

IT WAS CRAZY... FANTASTIC! BUT YOU WERE LIVING IT!
YOU WILL COME WITH US, CHARLIE PATCH! YOU HAVE BEEN SUMMONED BY OUR QUEEN!
G-GET AWAY FROM ME! I-- I'M CRAZY TO THINK I'M SEEING THINGS LIKE THIS! N-NO! DON'T!

WE CANNOT DELAY AN INSTANT! WE MUST HURRY!
L-LET ME DOWN! HELP!! HELP!! AAIIIEE!!

THEY TOOK YOU THROUGH THE GATES OF THEIR CITY... TO A BUZZING, THROBBING BABEL OF A MADHOUSE... A HIVE THAT WAS A METROPOLIS FOR GIANT BEES!
IT- IT'S INCREDIBLE. WHAT'S HAPPENING TO ME!?
3

THEY LED YOU THROUGH MAZE AFTER MAZE --- PASSAGEWAY AFTER PASSAGEWAY -- UNTIL YOU STOOD BEFORE THE MOST BEAUTIFUL CREATURE YOU HAD EVER SEEN!
KNEEL BEFORE OUR QUEEN!
WELCOME, CHARLIE PATCH! IN RETURN FOR YOUR LIFE-LONG SERVICES, YOU SHALL BECOME MY MATE!

B-BUT -- I -- THIS IS INSANE! I'M ONLY A WORKER -- A -- A DRONE, YOU MIGHT SAY! AND YOU'RE A -- QUEEN!
YOU DO US GREAT INJUSTICE, MAJESTY! YOU SINGLE OUT AN INSIGNIFICANT DRONE! BZZZZZ!
SILENCE! I HAVE SPOKEN! PREPARE HIM FOR THE CORONATION!!

SO, IN A FEW MOMENTS, YOU WERE USHERED OUT OF THAT GREAT HALL AND TAKEN TO A SPECIAL CHAMBER WHERE YOU WERE TO BE DRESSED FOR THE CEREMONY...
THESE WORKER BEES DON'T MIND ME AT ALL ... BUT THE DRONES ... THEY'RE ...
BUZZZZZZ

IT IS NOT RIGHT FOR YOU TO BE THE QUEEN'S MATE! SHE HAS CHOSEN YOU OVER US! WE WILL NOT PERMIT THIS SACRILEGE!
NO! IT -- IT WASN'T MY DOING! I'LL ADMIT SHE'S VERY BEAUTIFUL, BUT -- AAAAAGHH!

YOU SHALL NOT LIVE! SURROUND HIM, BROTHERS! STIFLE HIM WITH OUR WINGS! STING HIM TO DEATH!
AAAIEEEEE!!
BUZZZ

ONE BY ONE, THE HUGE FURRY STINGERS PLUNGED INTO YOUR BODY, FILLING YOU WITH THEIR VENOM! THE DARKNESS CLOSED IN --- YOU WERE FALLING -- FALLING ...

NO -- DON'T!! Y -- A -- AAHH! W-WHA --? WHERE AM I? OHHH ... I -- I MUST HAVE BEEN DREAMING! BRRR...! OF ALL THE CRAZY, FANTASTIC NIGHTMARES!

NEVER IN ALL MY YEARS HAVE I GOTTEN SUCH A WHOPPER! IMAGINE GIANT BEES STINGIN' ME TO DEATH!! AND --WHERE WOULD A FELLA LIKE ME HAVE HALF A CHANCE WITH MISS CAROL?

THAT WAS QUITE A RELIEF FOR YOU, WASN'T IT? BUT THAT VERY NEXT MORNING, YOU GOT A MESSAGE FROM THE MANSION --AND THE OTHER WORKERS NOTICED IT, DIDN'T THEY?

YOU SURE SHE WANTS ME TO COME UP THERE? I--I'M KINDA DIRTY RIGHT NOW! CAN SHE WAIT WHILE I PUT ON SOME DECENT THINGS?
YEAH, CHARLIE! SHE'D LIKE THAT! SHE KEEPS MENTIONIN' YOUR NAME! HA, HA...

YOU FELT GOOD TO BE CLEAN... YOU WERE HAPPY TO BE DRESSED NICELY... AND YOU RAVISHED IN THE IDEA OF BEING WITH CAROL LEIGHTON!

SO THAT'S WHY I ASKED YOU UP HERE, CHARLIE! THE FAIR IS A VERY IMPORTANT ONE TO ME-BOTH IN PRESTIGE AND IN MONEY TO BE WON!

DON'T WORRY, MISS CAROL! MY BEE-HIVES'LL BE THE BEST IN THE COUNTY!

--AND, CHARLIE--ALWAYS DRESS LIKE THAT! YOU'RE NOT BAD-LOOKING, YOU KNOW! AND I NEED A BODY-GUARD AROUND THE HOUSE--YOU MIGHT FIT THE BILL--!
THANK Y'KINDLY, MA'AM! I'D LIKE THAT!

SO YOU WALKED OUT OF THE BIG MANSION, LIGHT IN HEART, FLOATING ON THE CLOUDS--SWIMMING IN THE THOUGHT OF CAROL LEIGHTON!

WHO EVER SAID DREAMS DON'T COME TRUE? MAYBE SHE'LL FALL IN LOVE WITH ME--AN' WE'LL BE MARRIED!
HELLO, YOU POOR RANNIES! WORK YOUR HEADS OFF! I GOT ME A BETTER JOB --IN THERE!

YOU KNOW, RUFE! SEEMS CHARLIE IS GETTING TOO BIG FER HIS BRITCHES! HE GOT NO RIGHT TO HOBNOB WITH MISS CAROL! SHE'LL BE PAYIN' ALL HER ATTENTION TO HIM--AN' WE'LL GET NO MORE PAY-RAISES!
YEAH! CALL THE BOYS T'GETHER! HE AIN'T GOIN' TO BE WITH US FER LONG!

AAAIEEE!

YES, CHARLIE...YOUR DREAM DID COME TRUE!

THE END

ABOMINABLE SNOWMAN

"And to think that two months ago we thought those headlines were crazy!"

"I'm still not sure of it, Steve. I still have a suspicion that the Abominable Snowman is as much alive as an igloo!"

Prof. Thad Summers answered his young assistant, Steve Jansen, and then pulled out a map from his vest-pocket.

"But still, Steve, we owe it to ourselves to follow the map—and see if the rotten beasts do exist!"

"That's what I came here for, Thad. And I'm not going to be surprised at all if we find them!"

Night was now crawling in, and the Himalayan Mountains of Tibet gave off an eerie touch of the unknown. The whole scene suggested Shangri-la, the Asian land of mystery.

"We'd better get an early bed," suggested Prof. Summers, "if we're going to start out in the morning."

"You took the words right out of my mouth," yawned Jansen. "I'll be raring to go," he smiled.

The night went swiftly for the little cabin on the edge of the mountain. And in the morning two figures started out against the biting wind.

WHISSHHHH!

"Ouch, Thad, but this is terrific!"

"Just be happy that we haven't faced an avalanche!"

"How much further do we have to go?"

They were shouting, fighting the impact and cacophony of the thunderous wind.

"Don't think we've much further to go. . . not more than a few miles!"

On they went . . . through the freezing snow . . . every step a possible downfall from this top of the world!

WHISSHHHH!

"I hope that villager was right, Thad!"

"He said that Kuwon was the spot . . . the lair of the Snowman . . . and brother, we're going to find out!"

WHISSHHH!

"Steve, I-I-I'm f-f-finding it hard to breathe!"

"M-m-me too, Thadddd. This wind is l-l-like a whirlpoooooool!"

WHISSSHHH!

And then it came! The wind gathered the snow in heaps and threw it at the figures . . . the wind itself twirled round and round and spun the two men in mad circles.

"Thad . . ."

"Steve . . ."

But the voices grew further apart . . . they faded . . . and finally everything was silent.

Steve Jansen found himself smashed to the ground, a veritable snowman himself. His eyes were blinded by the burning sun and the horrible whiteness of the never-ending snow. His eyes saw only white . . . and then . . .

"What's that? What man or beast is that?"

From the distance it came slowly, but ever-moving. First he could tell nothing but a spot on the horizon. But then it took shape—horrible, loathsome . . . abominable!

"I-i-it's the Abominable Snowman! Just as they've described him!"

It was moving still closer. The missing link . . . the half-man, half-ape . . . the weird conglomeration of man and beast that is the ruler of the North!

"No! Keep back! Keep back!"

But it was no use . . . the Snowman was on a mission of death!

"Thad! Thad, where are you? Help me! Aieeeeee!"

But Thad Summers could not hear him. The wind had carried him, toppled him and mashed him. At that moment he lay unconscious at the foot of a snow drift.

When he'd find the dead body of his assistant, he'd blame it on the snow and the wind! And he'd leave Tibet forever . . . convinced that the Abominable Snowman was as alive as an igloo!

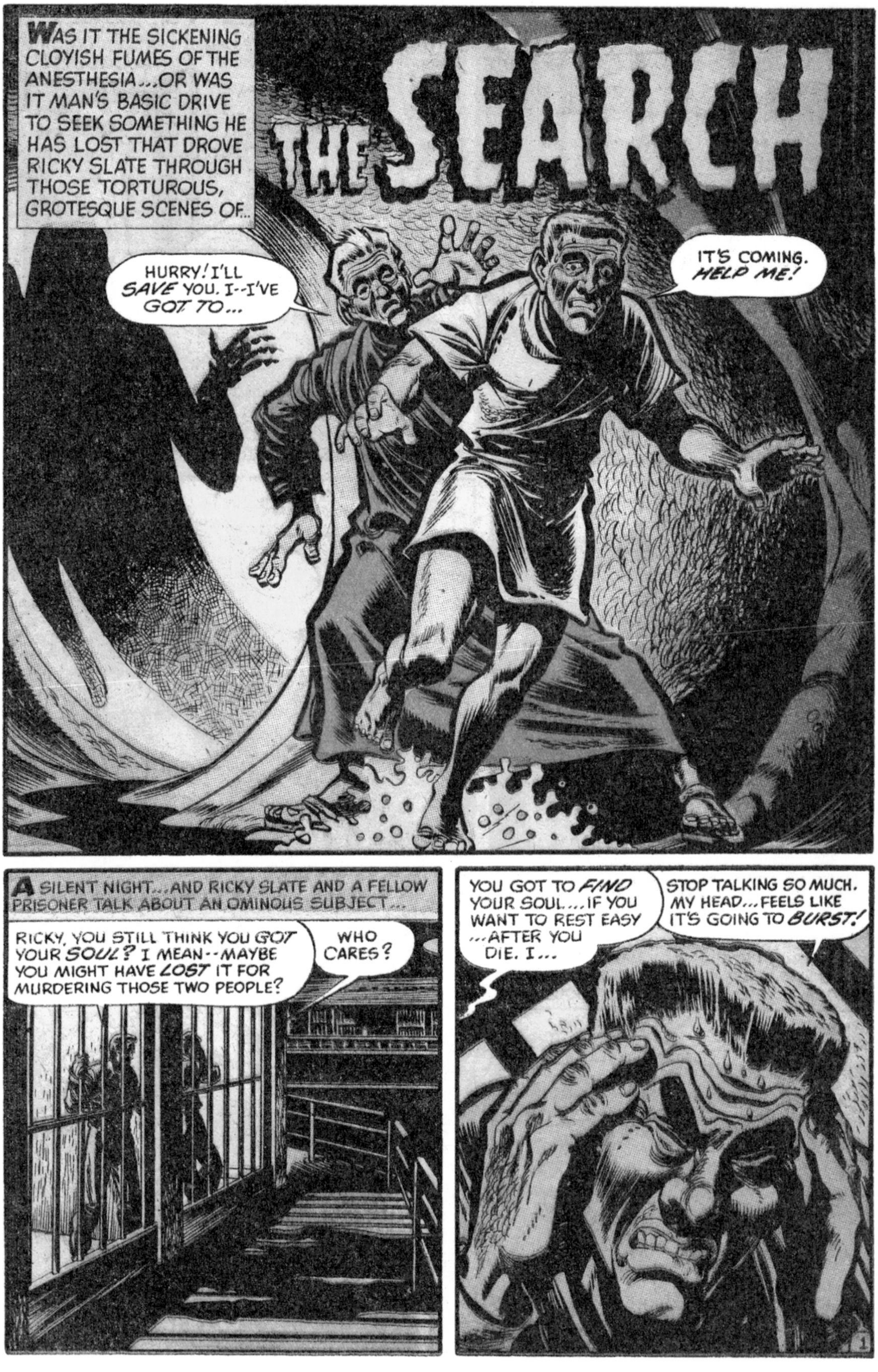

WAS IT THE SICKENING CLOYISH FUMES OF THE ANESTHESIA...OR WAS IT MAN'S BASIC DRIVE TO SEEK SOMETHING HE HAS LOST THAT DROVE RICKY SLATE THROUGH THOSE TORTUROUS, GROTESQUE SCENES OF..

THE SEARCH

HURRY! I'LL *SAVE* YOU. I--I'VE *GOT TO*...

IT'S COMING. *HELP ME!*

RICKEY SLATE'S BRAIN FELT AS IF BARBED HOOKS HAD GRIPPED IT... A HORRIBLE, CLAWING PAIN THAT NEEDED PROMPT MEDICAL ATTENTION..

THE HYPNOTIC TORPOR OF SLEEP FADED INTO MISTY NOTHINGNESS. THEN, SLATE FOUND HIMSELF IN ANOTHER WORLD, BOTH INCOMPREHENSIVE AND FANTASTIC!
WH--WHERE AM I? WHY AM I HERE?

AND...THAT MAN... COMING TOWARDS ME...

D--DON'T COME NEAR ME! STAY AWAY!
HELLO, SLATE. DON'T BE AFRAID!

THE WORDS WERE KINDLY, QUIET...A WELCOMING BALM THAT SOOTHED SLATE. AND, AS HE LOOKED UP...
WHAT DO YOU WANT?
DON'T YOU KNOW? I'M HERE TO KEEP YOU ALIVE...SO THAT YOU CAN FIND YOUR SOUL!

OH! THAT'S WHY I'M HERE...TO LOOK FOR MY SOUL.
YES! BUT BE CAREFUL! DANGER LURKS BEHIND EVERY CORNER. FOLLOW ME CLOSELY!

SLATE SOON FOUND HIMSELF AT A SLOW-MOVING, COZY RIVULET THAT SEEMED TO COME FROM SHEER BLACKNESS...
BE DEATHLY STILL...
WHERE ARE WE? I--I'M SCARED! I FEEL LIKE SOME-ONE'S WATCHING ME...
3

A BONY, CLUTCHING HAND, DEVOID OF LIFE BUT SEEMINGLY ALIVE, RAVENOUSLY REACHED OUT FOR SLATE... BUT THE OLD MAN'S CRACKLING WARNING ECHOED IN THE ABYSS...

WHO..? NO! NO! IT COULDN'T BE...
YES, IT'S US! THE MEN YOU *MURDERED*...
THAT'S WHY YOU *LOST* YOUR SOUL, RICKY!

SUDDENLY, SLATE FOUND HIMSELF IN THE GRIP OF COLD DEATH...
COME ON, RICKY! YOU'RE GOING TO THE SOULLESS DEPTHS!
NO-OOO!
WHAT?!!

THE OLD MAN ENTERED INTO THE SPECTRAL FRACAS, SEEMING TO DRAW UPON THE STRENGTH OF HIS YEARS TO FREE SLATE...

YOU'RE *LOOSE,* RICKY, *RUN!*
BUT...*WHERE..?*

GOT TO... RUN. THERE... GO THROUGH *THERE*...

SWIFTLY, FEVERISHLY, SLATE CLIMBED HIGHER, MAKING HIS BID FOR SAFETY...AND HE HEARD THE COARSE VOICE OF THE OLD MAN...
WAIT! WAIT!
NO! I'M NOT WAITING...

I'M SCRAMMING! *RIGHT NOW!*

RICKY SLATE SQUIRMED THROUGH THE NARROW APERTURE TO ITS OTHER SIDE...ONLY TO FACE BUBBLING QUAGMIRES THAT EXUDED FETID ROT... AND AN OMINOUSLY FAMILIAR BLACK FIGURE...
SA... NO! NO!
SLATE, YOU HAVE REACHED THE REALM OF THE SOULLESS DEPTHS! THERE IS YOUR DESTINY!

YOUR SOUL IS LOST TO YOU FOREVER. GO! GO!
DON'T... DON'T ...AIEEEE!

AS SLATE WAS SUCKED UNDER BY THE REEKING CAULDRONS OF QUICKSAND, A KINDLY WRINKLED FACE RUSHED TOWARD HIM...
HELP! HELLLL...
I TRIED TO TELL YOU...TRIED TO...OHHH, MY LORD...

IT'S ALL OVER...ALL OVER...ALL OVER...

SUDDENLY, MYSTICALLY, THE BLACKNESS OF DEATH FADED ...AND IN ITS STEAD CAME THE PURE WHITE OF THE OPERATING ROOM...AND REALITY...
IT'S ALL OVER, DOCTOR!
I KNOW... I KNOW...

DURING THE OPERATION, I--I FELT THAT SLATE WAS LOOKING FOR SOMETHING...AND I WAS HELPING HIM FIND IT. I TRIED SO HARD... BUT HE GOT AWAY FROM ME, SOMEHOW...
I DON'T THINK IT WAS YOUR FAULT, DOCTOR!
THE END
6

MOST AMAZING EXPOITS EVER TOLD
THE RAGE IN SUSPENSE
TOPS IN SHOCK MYSTERY
WE DARE YOU
WITCHES TALES
STRANGEST TALES OF FEAR AND SUPERSTITION!
BLACK CAT MYSTERY
TALES OF TERROR AND SUSPENSE!
CHAMBER OF CHILLS
TOMB OF TERROR
THE HIVE!
FROM THE WORLD OF THE SUPERNATURAL...FROM THE NETHERLAND OF ENDLESS EVIL...FROM THE DEEPEST BOWELS OF GREED-HUNGRY SOULS COME THESE FRANTIC ACCOUNTS OF SUSPENSEFUL, REALISTIC TALES OF TERROR!
Get them NOW at your nearest newsstand!

ADVERTISEMENT

MOST AMAZING SPACE KIT IN THE UNIVERSE!

Hey Kids, here's a complete Space Patrol Kit for you to lead. You can be squadron leader and direct SPACE BATTLES . . . deploy your rocket ships . . . send them into SPACE.

Now you can try to pioneer unexplored planets using your solar-powered spacemobile. You can try setting up interplanetary observatories, laboratories and radar detecting units . . . Imagine using your cosmic ray neutralizer as protection against deadly cosmic rays . . . Imagine talking to other planets hundreds of light years away. Chase flying saucers and flying discs. Track down Martian spies and rescue 4 Astra Space Beauties. You get a complete squadron . . . 2 spaceport hangars with rocket launchers that you can actually launch 19 rockets into space with — an interplanetary refueler, giant rocket ships, smaller rocket ships, Rocket Men — Mars Men — Beautiful Astra Girls. Every piece is perfectly scaled and is made of long life VINYL.

FREE!

PLASTIC ROCKET GUN! 6 inches long. Sends code with real trigger. Yours Free For Promptness! Hurry! Mail Coupon TODAY!

2 Rocket Launchers • 4 Martian Spies • 16 Space Men • 4 Astra Beauties • 2 Space Transports • 2 Refueling Stations • 1 Spacemobile • 2 Moon Rockets • 1 Flying Saucer • 1 Flying Disc • 2 Rocket Ships • 1 Set Fuel Tanks • 1 Space Badge • 2 Observatories • 2 Radar Detectors • 1 Searchlight • 1 Ray Gun • 1 Nuclear Laboratory • 1 Ray Neutralizer • 1 Mystery Planet • 1 Transmitter • 19 Rockets

SPACE SQUADRON 15th Floor • 1860 Broadway, New York 23, N.Y.

MAIL THIS COUPON NOW!

SPACE SQUADRON, 15th FLOOR
1860 BROADWAY, NEW YORK 23, N.Y.
Send .... set(s) of 70 Interplanetary Spacemen, Rocket Ships and Scientific Equipment postpaid. Include FREE GIFT as advertised. Enclosed is $............ Send .... sets. If dissatisfied, I'll return for refund within 10 days but keep the Free Gift.
Name..
Address..
City.......................... Zone........ State...........
MONEY BACK IF NOT DELIGHTED

NOW YOU CAN FLY A REAL
JET PLANE!

JETEX JAVELIN

SPECIAL OFFER

If bought in the store, the JETEX #50 engine alone would cost $1.95; the JETEX JAVELIN, $.75, a total cost of $2.70. Rush the coupon and you get both the JETEX JAVELIN and the JETEX #50 jet engine for only $1.98! (plus postage and handling charges, C.O.D.).

$1.98

Includes fuel supply.

Guaranteed to give you Fun-filled Flights!

You'll thrill and amaze your friends, be the envy of your neighborhood with this real JET airplane. The JETEX JAVELIN is a colorful, sleek-looking 14 inches of greased lightning. It will fly 1,000 feet! Go at a scale speed of 600 miles per hour! It takes off under its own power, loops, circles, stunts and then goes into a long glide and comes to a beautiful landing.

The JETEX JAVELIN is a cinch to build. Comes complete with the famous JETEX #50 jet engine and all parts already cut out. Nothing more to buy! Just follow the easy instructions, glue the parts together and you're ready for thrills! This amazing jet airplane uses the modern stressed skin construction which gives more strength and durability for its weight than any other type of construction. With ordinary care, it will make hundreds of fun filled flights.

It's fun to assemble, thrilling to fly. So don't delay—SEND NO MONEY—rush your order today to be sure of prompt delivery.

Designed by Commander Wallis Rigby

Yes, Commander Rigby, world famous designer, is the inventor of the JETEX JAVELIN. The Commander says, "I have created thousands of models, but the JETEX JAVELIN is the finest thing I have ever done"!

GUARANTEED TO FLY!

The JETEX JAVELIN is unconditionally guaranteed to fly if all instructions have been faithfully followed. If the JETEX JAVELIN does not fly, return the plane and the JETEX #50 engine within 10 days and your money will be refunded.

AMAZING JETEX #50
JET ENGINE

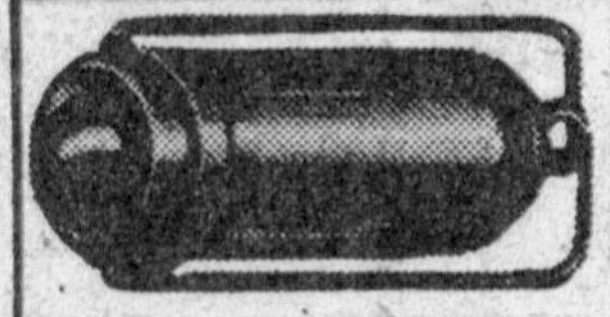

The world's smallest jet engine and the most powerful engine of its size ever sold! It runs on solid fuel, starts every time, completely reliable. NO MOVING PARTS TO BREAK OR WEAR OUT. Can be used to power model airplanes, racing cars and boats.

MAIL THIS COUPON NOW!

JETEX JAVELIN **RUSH!**

1860 Broadway, N.Y.23, N.Y.

Please rush the JETEX JAVELIN and JETEX #50 jet engine. I will pay postman only $1.98 plus C.O.D. charges on arrival.

Name..

(*please print*)

Address...

City.............................Zone........State...................

☐ I enclose $2.00 in cash, check or money order to save on C.O.D. charges. If the airplane does not fly, I may return it in 10 days for full refund of purchase price.

SEEMINGLY, THEY SAW ALL... CASTING A STRANGE, HORRIBLE SPELL OVER EVERYONE CAUGHT IN THEIR WEB. BUT BEHIND THESE TWIN ORBS GORGED IN ENDLESS BLACK DEPTH WAS HELD THE SINISTER SECRET OF...

THE EYES OF MARCH!

HE'S *DEAD*... BUT YET HIS *EYES* KEEP LOOKING AT ME. I... I'VE GOT TO FIND OUT IF THEY'RE *CLOSED!*

THE QUIET PALL OF SILENCE THAT HAD PERVADED NICHOLAS MARCH'S HOME WAS BROKEN BY LAURA DUNCAN... HER BITTER WORDS SHARP AND CRACKLING...
I LOVE SOMEONE ELSE. IT'S *ALL OVER*, NICHOLAS!
I DO NOT THINK SO.

WE HAVE KNOWN EACH OTHER TOO LONG, MY DEAR LAURA. YOU KNOW WHAT I AM LIKE. DO YOU THINK YOU CAN TREAT *ME... NICHOLAS MARCH...* LIKE THAT?

I WILL NEVER STAND FOR THIS! NEVER!
I--I'M SORRY, NICHOLAS. G...GOOD-BYE!

SO LATER, IN A WOODED GLEN BATHED IN A SICKLY YELLOW MOONLIGHT, LAURA ENIGMATICALLY FELT THE CLAWING SENSATION OF FEAR. SHE SOUGHT PROTECTION IN JOHNNY FRANKLIN'S ARMS...
I...I'M AFRAID, JOHNNY. I DON'T KNOW WHY, BUT I'M SCARED OF HIM...
EASY, DARLING. WHAT CAN ME DO?

I DON'T KNOW. I...I FEEL AS THOUGH THOSE EYES OF HIS ARE LOOKING AT ME RIGHT NOW! OHH, THOSE TWO EYES...
HIS EYES? BUT, DARLING, THAT'S SILLY.

JOHNNY FRANKLIN SCOFFED...BUT THIS WAS NO LAUGHING MATTER TO A MAN WHOSE EYES BLAZED LIKE CAULDRONS OF LIVID BRIMSTONE!
IF I CAN'T HAVE LAURA... NO ONE CAN! SHE MUST DIE. AND I KNOW JUST THE WAY. IT'LL BE IRONIC... SHE WAS ALWAYS AFRAID OF MY EYES...

LATER...
I RECEIVED YOUR MESSAGE, NICHOLAS. WHAT DO YOU WANT?
I WANTED YOU TO...

...LOOK INTO MY EYES...
NO! LET ME ALOOOONE! I...I...AM UNDER YOUR POWER. I... WILL...DO... ANYTHING...

I COMMAND YOU TO GO TO THE CLIFF!
I... HEAR... YOU...

THE IMAGE OF NICHOLAS MARCH'S EYES STILL ETCHED IN HER BRAIN, LAURA DUNCAN WALKED OUT INTO THE NIGHT... THE SOLITARY VOICE OF DEATH CALLING TO HER FROM THE YAWNING DEPTHS BENEATH HER NEXT STEP...
GO... TO... THE... CLIFF...

THE CLIFF! THE CLIFF CLIFF..CLIFF.. CLIFF...

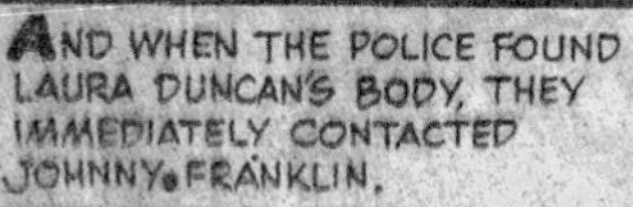

AND WHEN THE POLICE FOUND LAURA DUNCAN'S BODY, THEY IMMEDIATELY CONTACTED JOHNNY FRANKLIN.

WE FOUND YOUR NAME IN HER PURSE, MR. FRANKLIN. WE THOUGHT YOU MIGHT BE ABLE TO HELP US.
I--I DON'T KNOW WHAT HAPPENED. UNLESS...?

UNLESS ...WHAT?
I REMEMBER NOW. SHE SAID SOMETHING ABOUT THOSE EYES! COULD IT...? I'M GOING TO FIND OUT!

FRANKLIN'S MEMORY REELED DIZZILY FROM LAURA'S LAST WORDS... THOSE WORDS THAT WERE GRIPPED BY THE BLOODLESS TALONS OF FEAR... AN AWESOME DREAD CAUSED BY THE MAN WITH THE SEEMINGLY OMNISCIENT EYES. SO...
MARCH! WHERE ARE YOU?
YES. WHO IS IT?

I'M JOHN... UGH! THOSE EYES! LAURA WAS RIGHT. THEY ARE HORRIBLE!
YOU KNOW ABOUT LAURA'S FEAR. WELL THEN... LOOK INTO MY EYES AND SEE WHAT LAURA SAW!

NO. YOUR EYES KILLED LAURA. AND... I'M SHUTTING THEM!
YOU CANNOT. MY EYES WILL HOUND YOU! ARGGHHH!

I'VE KILLED HIM... BUT HIS EYES ARE STILL LOOKING AT ME! I BETTER GET OUT OF HERE!

AS THE DAYS PASSED, JOHNNY FRANKLIN TRIED TO REJECT THE TORTURING IMPRESSION OF MARCH'S BLACK, IGNOMINIOUS EYES FROM HIS MIND. HE THOUGHT HE WAS SUCCEEDING... UNTIL...
I NEED THAT COFFEE. I...OHHH. THE EYES...

SOON... HIS BLEAK THOUGHTS WERE EVEN REFLECTED IN A MIRROR...
A SHAVE WILL... NOO-O! THE EYES AGAIN... OPENED... STARING! BUT... MARCH IS DEAD! AM I DREAMING? I'VE GOT TO FIND OUT!

THERE WAS ONLY ONE WAY FOR FRANKLIN TO DISCOVER WHETHER MARCH'S SEPULCHRAL EYES WERE REAL ... OR IMAGINARY...
I...I HAVE TO DIG UP HIS...COFFIN! BUT, I KNOW HIS EYES ARE CLOSED! THEY HAVE TO BE!
4

I...I'VE REACHED THE COFFIN. NOW... TO OPEN THE LID!

SLOWLY, CREAKINGLY, FRANKLIN LIFTED THE LID OF THE COFFIN. THEN HE SAW AN ALL-TOO FAMILIAR SIGHT... SOMETHING TERRIBLE... EYES THAT STARED EVEN AFTER SIGHTLESS DEATH...
I... NOOO. THEY'RE OPENED... AND... LOOKING AT ME! NO! NO!

RUN... GOT TO RUN FROM THOSE EYES! I HAVE TO ESCAPE FROM THEIR SIGHT...

BARBED FEAR COILED AROUND FRANKLIN... DISTORTING REALITY INTO GRIM, EERIE APPARITION... BECLOUDING ANYTHING BEFORE HIM...
NO! IT'S... MARCH'S EYES! AIEEE!

THUD!
SCREEEEEEEE

HE RAN RIGHT INTO THE CAR!
IT'S JOHNNY FRANKLIN. HE'S TRYING TO SAY SOMETHING!
MARCH'S EYES... KILLED LAURA... NOW ME. ALL THE TIME... LOOKING AT ME... LOOKING ...STARING...

MARCH LOOK...? THAT'S IMPOSSIBLE, FRANKLIN. NICHOLAS MARCH WAS BLIND! HE COULDN'T SEE ANYTHING!
BL...? ARGH-H.
THE END.

FINAL BLOW

"I'm not going to fight him!" Ben Lewis' voice pounded through the room.

"Whaddaya mean? Ya scared of the jerk?"

Ben whirled around and looked squarely at his manager. "I'm a fighter, see? Don't ever say I'm scared of anybody! Understand?"

"I didn't mean ta say that, Ben." Roscoe Tatum was retreating, but he knew inside that he had hit the truth. "Go home and take it easy kid. Tomorrow you'll have a clear head, and you'll see things my way."

"I'm not seeing things anybody's way but my own, Roscoe! And I said I'm not fighting Bolo Grand!"

Roscoe now was more than sure. "OK, boy—then just go home and take it easy!"

Ben Lewis didn't need any invitations. He reached for his hat, and then raced for the door.

"Remember, Roscoe . . . I'm not fighting the guy!"

"Sure, sure, sure . . ." was the manager's good-bye and it followed Ben Lewis even to his hotel room.

The fighter grabbed a cigarette and threw himself on his bed. "So what if I'm scared of him . . . so what?" He could admit it to himself . . . that was easy.

"But Roscoe knows it. And if he knows it, then everyone's going to know it!" But Ben could never admit it to anyone else. Ben was a fighter—and a fighter can't be scared!

"Got to do something . . . got to do something fast!" But Ben wasn't coming up with any solution.

He flicked the ashes of his cigarette and watched them drop nicely, easily to the floor. He looked at them for a moment, and then shut his eyes to the ashes . . . the room . . . to everything . . .

Then suddenly he saw himself fighting Bolo Grand . . . he saw himself being peltered by blow after blow after blow! His head was a throbbing glob of senseless flesh . . . the blood gushed over his face trekking a carpet of crimson . . .

"No . . . no . . . stop it . . . stop it!"

And then just as suddenly he wasn't fighting Bolo Grand anymore. Now he was walking a street . . . a dark street . . . a lonely street. Now he was walking into a hotel. Now he was entering a room. And now he was talking . . .

"Yeah, Bolo. That's right. I didn't want to fight you. And I'm not going to fight you. I've come to settle that score—right now!"

And suddenly he saw himself with a knife in his hand. *How did he get it?* He didn't know—and there was no time to think of that!

"Get back, Lewis! Don't be a fool! Get back!"

But Ben wasn't going back—he was going forward . . . closer, closer to Bolo Grand! And now he saw himself plunging his knife . . . frantically . . . mercilessly . . .

"Aghhhhhh!"

And he saw Bolo Grand topple to the floor. And he saw himself plunge his knife again . . . and again . . . and once more into the soft flesh of Bolo Grand's body!

Now he saw himself running through the streets . . . back over the black, lonely streets . . . lugging something behind him. He couldn't see what it was! And then he saw nothing at all!

"No! No!" Ben rubbed furiously at his eyes . . . and then saw where he was. "Thank the Lord, my own room . . . my own bed . . . only a dream . . . a nightmare!"

But then Ben Lewis looked at his hands . . .

"Aghhhh! Oh, no! Blood! Blood!"

And then he saw a trail of blood . . . a spreading rivulet of horror that streamed from his closet!

"No . . . no . . . no . . ." he shouted as he followed the river to its base . . . and opened the closet and saw . . .

"Bolo Grand! Bolo Grand's dead body!"

STATEMENT OF THE OWNERSHIP, MANAGEMENT AND CIRCULATION REQUIRED BY THE ACT OF CONGRESS OF AUGUST 24, 1912, AS AMENDED BY THE ACTS OF MARCH 3, 1933, AND JULY 2, 1946, OF TOMB OF TERROR published Monthly at St. Louis, Missouri for October 1, 1952.

1. The names and addresses of the publisher, editor, managing editor, and business managers are: Editor: Leon Harvey, 1860 Broadway, N. Y. C.; Managing Editor: Alfred Harvey, 1860 Broadway, N. Y. C.; Business Manager: Robert B. Harvey, 1860 Broadway, N. Y. C. Publisher: Harvey Publications, Inc. 1860 Broadway, N. Y. C.

2. The owners are Harvey Publications, Inc. 1860 Broadway, N. Y. C.; Leon Harvey, 1860 Broadway, N. Y. C.; Alfred Harvey, 1860 Broadway, N. Y. C.; Robert B. Harvey, 1860 Broadway, N. Y. C.

3. The known bondholders, mortgagees, and other security holders owning or holding 1 percent or more of total amount of bonds, mortgages, or other securities are: None.

4. Paragraphs 2 and 3 include, in cases where the stockholder or security holder appears upon the books of the company as trustee or in any other fiduciary relation, the name of the person or corporation for whom such trustee is acting; also the statements in the two paragraphs show the affiant's full knowledge and belief as to the circumstances and conditions under which stockholders and security holders who do not appear upon the books of the company as trustees, hold stock and securities in a capacity other than that of a bona fide owner.

(signed) ROBERT B. HARVEY, Business Manager

Sworn and subscribed to before me this 30th day of September, 1952.

Fred Stevens (My commission expires March 30th, 1954)

A DYING MAN'S OATH!...THE CLANKING OF AN EMPTY SUIT OF ARMOR THROUGH A MEDIEVAL CASTLE! ...A FIENDISH MURDERER HAUNTED BY A...

VISION IN BRONZE

KEEP AWAY, I SAY! KEEP AWAY!

CLANK-CLANK!

CLEZ AND DODDS, TWO WEALTHY ANTIQUE DEALERS, HAVE PURCHASED A HUGE CASTLE IN SUBURBAN ENGLAND!

A FINE LOOKING CASTLE, CLEZ! IT SHOULD HOUSE OUR WORKS HANDSOMELY!
YES, DODDS! IT SHOULD SERVE US WELL! VERY WELL!

WITH THEIR POSSESSIONS MOVED IN, THE TWO PARTNERS INSPECT THE CASTLE'S DUNGEON-LIKE BASEMENT!

NOW HERE'S AN ODD PIECE, DODDS! WORTH SOME MONEY, TOO, I'D SAY!
YES, CLEZ! PECULIAR THING! PROBABLY AN ANCIENT TORTURE INSTRUMENT...SOME MINDS CERTAINLY CREATE HORRIBLE THINGS!

ER...DODDS...WHY DON'T YOU STEP INTO IT FOR A MOMENT! YOU KNOW...JUST FOR A JOKE TO SEE WHAT IT'S LIKE!
DON'T MIND IF I DO, CLEZ! SHOULD BE INTERESTING!

BUT AS DODDS STEPS AMIABLY INTO THE STRANGE SUIT OF ARMOR, HIS EVIL PARTNER SPRINGS INTO PREMEDITATED ACTION!
GOODBYE, DODDS! GOODBYE!
CLEZ--! WHAT ARE--!
SLAM

HA-HA! NOW OUR VALUABLE ANTIQUE TREASURES ARE MINE ALONE! SORRY, DODDS!
HELP! (GASP) LET ME (GASP) OUT... CLEZ...

DIE, DODDS! HA-HA! DIE!
(...GASP) SOMEDAY...CLEZ... (GASP)...WE WILL EXCHANGE PLACES...

THE SINISTER CLEZ RETURNS UPSTAIRS LEAVING HIS DOOMED PARTNER PLEADING FOR HELP...PLEAS THAT GO UNHEARD AND UNHEEDED!
HELP!...SOMEBODY... (GASP)...PLEASE... (GASP)...WE WILL CHANGE PLACES, CLEZ...AGGRRAA...

AND DODDS' ONLY ANSWER IS DEATH!
2

BUT WITH HIS PARTNER'S DEATH, THE EVIL CLEZ EXPERIENCES A SUCCESSION OF BUSINESS REVERSALS!
BUT, MADAM!
SORRY! THIS PIECE WON'T DO!

THIS WORK LOOKS LIKE AN IMITATION, MR. CLEZ! I'LL NOT COME BACK!
BUT I ASSURE YOU...!

HIS PRICES ARE RIDICULOUS!
WE'LL LEAVE!
BUT I---!

BORDERING DANGEROUSLY UPON BANKRUPTCY, CLEZ IS FORCED TO SELL HIS ENTIRE COLLECTION AT A DEVASTATING LOSS! THEN ONE EVENING...
IT ALL STARTED WITH DODDS' DEATH! IT'S THAT SUIT OF ARMOR! I CAN'T STAND THE SIGHT OF IT! PERHAPS IF I SELL IT, MY ROTTEN LUCK WILL CHANGE!

CLEZ RACED DOWN TO THE CASTLE'S BASEMENT... DOWN TO A ROTTING ATMOSPHERE AND TO THE ARMOR ENCASING HIS PARTNER'S BONES!
HA HA! IT SHOULD BRING A FAT PRICE ON THE MARKET!

LET HIS BONES ROT!

THE DIABOLICAL ANTIQUE DEALER SELLS THE ARMOR, AND AT A GRATIFYING PRICE!
HA-HA! IT'S GONE! IT WILL PLAGUE ME NO MORE!

NOW BUSINESS WILL-- WHAT'S THAT CLANKING I HEAR!?
CLANK
CLANK!

WHAAA--! NO!
CLANK
CLANK

CLANK
NO! IT'S NOT POSSIBLE! I'VE SOLD IT! IT CAN'T MOVE BY ITSELF!
CLANK

THE NEXT MORNING, THE SHAKEN CLEZ APPREHENSIVELY RETURNS TO THE BASEMENT TO DISCOVER A BLOOD-CURDLING SIGHT!
THE ARMOR! BACK AGAIN! AND DODDS' SKELETON--GONE!

TERROR STRICKEN, CLEZ AGAIN SELLS THE WEIRD SUIT OF ARMOR!
THEN YOU'LL BUY IT!
CERTAINLY! IT'S FASCINATING!
4

GOOD RIDDANCE TO IT! THIS TIME FOR GOOD! HA-HA!

BUT THAT NIGHT TERROR WINS ITS PLACE ONCE MORE...
WHAAA---! NO! NO! IT ISN'T---!
CLANK
CLANK

I'M IMAGINING IT! AIIIEEEE!

CLANK
CLANK
KEEP AWAY! AIIIEEE!

RUNNING—AS IF FROM DEATH—CLEZ REACHES HIS ROOM AND BOLTS HIS DOOR FROM THE NIGHT'S GHASTLY HORROR!
I-I-I'VE GOT TO FIND OUT!
SLAM!

THE NEXT MORNING, CLEZ DASHES FRANTICALLY TO THE BASEMENT...
THE ARMOR AGAIN! BUT NOTHING INSIDE IT!

THAT NOISE! WHAT WAS THAT!
STOMP
STOMP

BUT IF THE WOMAN WERE LOOKING FOR A SUIT OF MEDIEVAL ARMOR, SHE WOULD HAVE DONE WELL TO LOOK IN THE BASEMENT...THERE SHE WOULD HAVE FOUND THE ARMOR--AND CLEZ! FOR DODDS WAS TRUE TO HIS DYING OATH! THE MEN HAD CHANGED PLACES!

THE END.

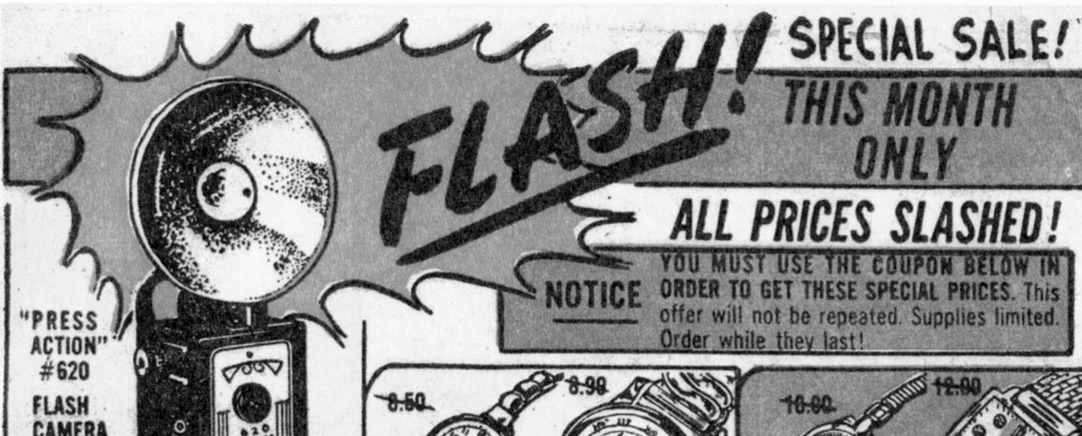

INDOORS! OUTDOORS! BLACK & WHITE! FULL COLOR! PARTIES! NEWS SHOTS!

An **AMAZING** Camera. Takes pictures **DAY** or **NIGHT, indoors or outdoors.** Sharp BLACK and WHITE snapshots or **FULL COLOR** photos, using Kodacolor film. 12 **Big pictures** on 1 Roll of film. Flash attachment snaps on or off in **seconds. Catch valuable** news photos. **Win admiration at parties, dances.** NOW $4.95

FILM Special #620 Orthochromatic. 3 **ROLLS for** $1.00

PERFECT for active women and girls. Fine **JEWELLED** movement in dainty case. **GILT** hands and numbers. Smart Link Expansion Bracelet ... NOW **$6.98**

BEST for active men and boys. **SHOCK-RESISTANT** and **ANTI-MAGNETIC!** Luminous Dial! Jewelled Movement! Red Sweep-Second! Expansion Bracelet. NOW **$6.99**

Ladies' **Jewelled** Watch in a smart **Gold** finish case. Dial has **12 Flashing imitation DIAMONDS and RUBIES.** Glamorous Snake Bracelet. NOW **$8.49**

Rich, Flashing Men's **Jewelled** Watch with **11 Sparkling imitation DIAMONDS and RUBIES.** Smart **Gold** finish case. DeLuxe Basket-weave Bracelet. NOW **$9.95**

INITIAL RING

A Handsome, Masculine Ring with **your own INITIAL** set in Raised GOLD effect on a **BRILLIANT RUBY-RED** color stone. With 2 SPARKLING imitation **DIAMONDS** on the sides. Rich 14K R.G.P. NOW **$2.95**

FREE
NO-RISK HOME TRIAL

SEND NO MONEY! We want you **to inspect** and **enjoy** this **fine quality** merchandise – right in your own home. **You risk nothing!** If not delighted, return for **FULL PRICE REFUND.** Every article we sell is **GUARANTEED!** Order from this famous company and **be convinced.**

IDEAL CO.
BOX 232, MAD. SQ. STA., N.Y. 10, N.Y.

GUARANTEED SAVINGS

BRILLIANT MEN'S WATCH

A MAGNIFICENT Men's Watch that you'll be **real proud of!** GUARANTEED **15 JEWEL MOVEMENT** in a Handsome **GENUINE** 10K R.G.P. case. Rich, brilliant **GOLDEN-SPRINKLED** Dial with flashing **GILT-NUGGET** hour dots. Contrasting Jet-Black center. Genuine Alligator-grain leather strap. **TERRIFIC VALUE.** NOW **$12.95**

"PRINCE" RING Here's a Rich, **Massive Ring** for you. With a **Huge Flashing imitation DIAMOND and 6 Fiery Red imitation RUBIES.** 14K R.G.P. NOW **$3.49**

CLUSTER RING with your OWN **RAISED GOLD-COLOR INITIAL** on a Rich **RUBY-RED** color stone set in a circle of Blazing imitation **DIAMONDS.** 14K R.G.P. NOW **$3.49**

FASCINATING! FUN!
Build EXCITING MINIATURE **OLD TIMER AUTOS**

1909 STANLEY STEAMER

- EASY
- UNIQUE
- COLORFUL
- DECORATIVE

COMPLETE *De Luxe* SET OVER **75** PARTS with CEMENT-PAINTS-BRUSH ~~8.50~~ **$4.95** for all 5 Kits

AUTHENTIC REPLICAS OF COLLECTORS ITEMS

1900 1903 1903 1910

IT'S EASY! IT'S EXCITING! Amazingly simple to assemble **–anyone can do it!** No carving, shaping or sanding necessary. Molded 3/8" scale-model parts are **realistic down to the smallest detail:** padded seats, horn, lamps, steering wheel, brake lever—**even a comical "Old-Timer" driver.** Make them for unique table lamps, book-ends, wall decorations, desk ornaments. **This De Luxe Set is COMPLETE –all 5 Model Kits with Cement, Paints, Brush, Instruction Folders and OVER 75 PARTS** ... NOW **$4.95**

NOTE: When ordering this item, enclose $1.00 Deposit.

ROMANCE SET

Real! Sparkling, Shining BEAUTY! Engagement Ring has **4 Flashing Brilliants** and a **BEAUTIFUL** imitation **DIAMOND SOLITAIRE. 7 Twinkling** Brilliants in the Wedding Ring. **12K GOLD Filled.** Both rings. NOW **$3.74**

DIAMOND RING for Men. 14K R.G.P. **REAL DIAMOND CHIP** on Gen. MOTHER-OF-PEARL face. 2 **RUBY** color side **SPARKLERS.** NOW **$4.98**

'Sun Glow' Ring. A rich simulation of a glowing Big **10 CARAT STAR RUBY** with 2 side **DIAMONDS. Deep fire!** Sterling. NOW **$2.98**

MAIL THIS COUPON

IDEAL CO., Dept. CS-55
Box 232 Mad. Sq. Sta., New York 10, N.Y.

SEND NO MONEY! Just cut out pictures of articles desired and attach to this coupon. Pay postman plus few cents postage and excise tax on delivery. THEN EXAMINE IN YOUR OWN HOME. **SATISFACTION IS GUARANTEED OR YOUR MONEY BACK.**

PLEASE PRINT

NAME ______________________

ADDRESS ______________________

TOWN ______________ STATE ______

(Send RING SIZES, INITIAL WANTED and your BIRTH-MONTH. If you need more room, attach a sheet of paper.)

ADVERTISEMENT

Look Lovely in French Waist

This Beautiful Model shows you how you can look in "French Waist." Our taffeta butterfly dress flatters every figure. Figure-magic for every woman — no matter her size! The sophisticated drape, the elegant cut, the face-framing neckline are eternally feminine, eternally enchanting! In rustling rayon taffeta in navy, black, peacock.

STYLE NO. 45493

Sizes 9-17, 10-20 .... $10.98

Sizes 40-48, 20½-28½ $11.98

10 DAY TRIAL FREE

Order today. Wear 10 days FREE. If not delighted return for refund. Waist sizes 20 to 44, $2.48. (50¢ additional for the 4 extra-length detachable and adjustable garters.)

FREE TRIAL COUPON

GUARANTEED DISTRIBUTORS CO., Dept. F868
836 Broadway, New York 3, N. Y.

Rush my new FRENCH WAIST three-in-one at once. If I am not thrillingly satisfied I will return it after 10-day FREE trial for prompt refund of full purchase price.

Size .... (waist size in inches.)

Also send .... sets of extra-length detachable and adjustable garters at only 50¢ for set of four.

☐ Send C.O.D. I will pay postman on delivery plus few cents postage.

☐ I enclose payment. The Guaranteed Distributors Co. will pay postage.

NAME....................................

ADDRESS....................................

"Scram! You SKINNY Scarecrow!
the boys shouted at me
ONLY A FEW WEEKS AGO!
"I was a SKINNY, scared, girl-shy skeleton. Now I feel and look great. Pal, do as I did, right NOW! Mail the Coupon below.
I gained 53 lbs.
of MIGHTY MUSCLE
6½ inches on my CHEST; 3 inches on each ARM. You can do it in 10 minutes a day!" —NewYork
Roger D. Hirsch
YOU CAN WIN THIS 15" TALL SILVER TROPHY AS THEY DID! 10 MINUTES OF FUN A DAY IS ALL YOU NEED!
ROGER HIRSCH was an 112 lb. 6 ft. weakling LOOK AT HIM NOW!
"They used to call me, 'SKINNY, SKINNY'
But look at me now —an All-American Jowett Champion"—says John Sill, Utah, who like millions, mailed me 10c and a coupon like the one below YOU MAIL NOW!
"NOW, I am a NEW STRONG MAN. It's wonderful! I never dreamed I could live to have a big 49 inch CHEST!! powerful 17 inch ARMS!! a small 32 inch WAIST the big 17 inch difference between my chest and waist attracts everybody's admiration at the beach."
Felipe Mendoza
—CALIFORNIA
"This is The GREAT CHANGE You made in me in 90 DAYS! From a SKINNY WEAKLING to a MIGHTY MAN. With ONE hand I can now lift overhead a boy weighing 145 pounds. I can bend a 1½ inch IRON BAR around my neck. Jowett gives you muscle quality as well as quantity." Yours,
Jobie Jackson Jr.
ARKANSAS
Jobie Jackson NOW!!!
Jobie Jackson Only 90 DAYS ago!
MAN! aren't YOU as SICK and TIRED as I and thousands of MIGHTY JOWETT HE-MEN WERE OF BEING SKINNY?
Then, Come on, Pal, do as they did! Give me 10 Pleasant Minutes a Day and I'll give YOU a NEW HE-MAN BODY for your OLD SKELETON FRAME.
NO! I don't c e how skinny or flabby you are; if you're a teen-ager, in your 20's or 30's or over; if you're short or tall, or what work you do. All I want is to MAKE YOU OVER by the SAME METHOD I turned myself from a wreck to a Champion of Champions.
YES! You'll see INCH upon INCH of MIGHTY MUSCLE added to YOUR ARMS. Your CHEST deepened. Your BACK AND SHOULDERS broadened. From head to heels, you'll gain SOLIDITY, SIZE, POWER, SPEED! You'll become an ALL-Around, ALL-American HE-MAN, a WINNER in everything you tackle—or my Training won't cost you one single cent!
Develop YOUR 520 MUSCLES
Gain Pounds, INCHES, FAST!
Friend, I've traveled the world. Made a LIFETIME STUDY of every way known to develop your body. Then I devised the BEST by TEST, my "5-WAY PROGRESSIVE POWER" the only method that builds you 5-ways fast. You save YEARS, DOLLARS like movie star Tom Tyler did. Like Champ Roger Hirsch . . . Like MANY THOUSANDS like you did. SO . . .
HURRY TO MAIL COUPON!
George F Jowett Whom experts call "Champion of Champions"
How to Build MIGHTY ARMS
How to Build A MIGHTY CHEST
How to Build A MIGHTY BACK
FREE Photo Book How to Achieve Nerves of Steel, Muscles of Iron
How to Build MIGHTY LEGS
How to Build A MIGHTY GRIP
How to BECOME A MIGHTY HE-MAN
This may be Your LAST chance to GET AMAZING NATIONAL EMERGENCY OFFER! All these 5 Picture Packed COURSES on He-Man Building for only 10¢ while supply lasts! MILLIONS have been sold for $1 & more
BOTH FREE FOR QUICK ACTION
1. Photo Book of STRONG MEN
2. MUSCLE METER
DEPT. HA-25
"Jowett Courses greatest in World for Building All-Around HE-MEN". —R.F. Kelley Physical Director
JOWETT INSTITUTE OF PHYSICAL TRAINING 230 FIFTH AVENUE, NEW YORK 1, N.Y. HA-25
George Send me FREE Photo Book of Strong Men, a Muscle Meter, plus all 5 HE-MAN Building Courses 1. How to Build a Mighty Chest; 2 Mighty Arm, 3 Mighty Grip; 4 Mighty Back, 5 Mighty Legs—all in One Volume How to Become a Mighty He-Man." I enclose 10c (No C O D's)
NAME AGE
ADDRESS
CITY ZONE STATE

EXTRA MONEY
FOR ALL THOSE "EXTRAS" YOU WANT!
Earn It Easily—
In Spare Time—With STUART Greeting Cards
Have extra money of your own . to do with as you please. Just show Stuart's new, fast-selling All-Occasion Greeting Cards in your spare time. 21-Card Assortment of Birthday, Get-Well and other folders needed the year 'round sell on sight to folks in your neighborhood. Fast $1 sales pay you up to 50c per box. Sell just 100 boxes and $50 cash is yours!
BIG LINE BOOSTS YOUR EARNINGS!
Also show sensational Humorous Cards, Gift Wraps, Imprinted Notes, Scented Stationery, other new money-makers. You can sell several boxes on each call and double or triple your earnings!
Get Your Samples TODAY!
ACT NOW! Earn extra cash for yourself or your group. Send no money. Mail coupon or postcard today for complete details and Assortments on approval. Imprint Samples FREE!
No Experience Needed
Send for Samples Today!

TOMB OF TERROR

TALES BEYOND BELIEF AND IMAGINATION!

TOMB OF TERROR

MAY No.9 10c

PDC

WHAT DID LUTHER DARK FIND AT THE END OF *THE TUNNEL!*

Hello again. We, the editors of your choice in terror, THE TOMB OF TERROR, want to welcome you to this magazine that dares to be continuously different!

We're striving for the new, the explosive, the daring -- and we want you to watch our growth! We know you've already seen it, but we want you to constantly keep tabs on us.

Match, compare... then speak up! And then be ready for an even bigger thrill when the next issue comes your way.

Look at the present line-up of startlingly different stories and let us know how they rate.

Was THE TUNNEL worth following? Is THE PRIZE worth capturing? Does the CAULDRON bubble, or does it fizzle out? And were you swept by the BACKWASH?

You'll be amazed and chilled... and perhaps even shocked by what you'll find in future issues. But let us know if we're riding the right track.

Take out a few seconds and write to the...

TOMB OF TERROR
1860 Broadway
New York 23, N. Y.

TOMB OF TERROR Contents

NO. 9

TOMB OF TERROR, May, 1953, Vol. 1, No. 9, is published every other month by HARVEY PUBLICATIONS, INC., at 420 DeSoto Avenue, St. Louis 7, Mo. Editorial, Advertising and Executive offices, 1860 Broadway, New York 23, N. Y. President Alfred Harvey; Vice-President and Editor, Leon Harvey; Vice-President and Business Manager, Robert B. Harvey. Entered as second-class matter at the Post Office at St. Louis, Mo., under the Act of March 3, 1879. Single copies, 10c. Subscription rates, 10 issues for $1.00 in the U. S. and possessions, elsewhere $1.50. All names in this periodical are entirely fictitious and no identification with actual persons is intended. Printed in the U. S. A.

THIS IS AN INSANE ASYLUM. THE MAN IS CALLED CARLO KARINE.

THE INMATES ALLOW HIM HIS PLEASURE. IT IS ALL HE HAS LEFT IN THIS WORLD.

HE STIRS AND STIRS... DAY AFTER DAY AFTER DAY...

AND SHOUTS...
BUBBLE
CAULDRON
BUBBLE!
1

THESE ARE THE MAN'S EYES. THEY TRY TO FORGET THE PAST. BUT THAT IS ALL THEY SEE! THEY CAN ONLY GO BACK -- BACK -- BACK IN TIME...

THEY STOP AT A TIME, TWENTY YEARS AGO... A TIME WHEN CARLO KARINE WAS A POOR BUT HONEST GLASS BLOWER...

I'VE GOT TO MAKE GOOD ON THIS JOB! I'VE GOT TO BLOW IT UP PERFECTLY!

GADS, CARLO! IS THAT A PILLOW?
NO... HE'S AN ARTIST! ABSTRACT, OF COURSE! HA!
B-BUT I FOLLOWED ALL THE DIRECTIONS!

THE MANAGER HAD SEEN ENOUGH. HE CALLED CARLO INTO HIS OFFICE...
I'M SORRY, CARLO. WE JUST CAN'T USE YOU ANY LONGER...
PLEASE, SIR! GIVE ME ANOTHER CHANCE! I-- I'LL STARVE! PLEASE!

NO, CARLO DIDN'T GET HIS SECOND CHANCE! HE WAS KICKED OUT INTO THE STREET, SAD AND DEJECTED -- AN OUTCAST...
WHAT CAN I DO? WHERE CAN I GO? A FEW BUCKS BETWEEN ME AND THE POOR HOUSE!

AND HE DIDN'T SPEND THOSE LAST FEW DOLLARS TOO WISELY!
W-WILL YOU -- UH -- WILL YOU DANCE WITH ME...?
WITH YOU?

LISTEN, EVERYONE! CARLO WANTS ME TO DANCE WITH HIM! HA, HA, HA...
GET YOURSELF A COW, CARLO!
YOU'RE NOT A MAN-- YOU'RE A MOUSE!

HE LEFT QUICKLY... SHAMEFULLY. EVERYONE KNEW HIS PLIGHT, AND WITHIN THE BARRIER OF HIS ROOM, HE CRIED...
I'M NO GOOD TO ANYONE! WHAT'S THE USE IF I LIVE OR DIE? IF ONLY I HAD SOMEONE TO KEEP ME COMPANY... IF ONLY...

WAIT--! THAT OLD BOOK! IT'S HERE SOMEWHERE IN THIS MESS!

HE FOUND THE BOOK--THE BLACK BOOK THAT HAD GATHERED DUST FOR SO MANY YEARS! HE OPENED ITS YELLOWED PAGES AND READ...
"--FROM SNAKE'S BLOOD, AND FROG'S GUT, DRAIN THE FLUID OF LIFE... AND COOK IT WELL IN A CAUDRON OF HELL FOR THE THING WHICH YOU MOST DESIRE!"

IF THE WORLD OF MEN REJECT ME... THEN I'LL CALL ON THE OTHER WORLD! I'LL CREATE FOR MYSELF A COMPANION OF MY OWN WHIMS... OF MY OWN DICTATES! I'LL BE THE ONE THAT LAUGHS!

HE GATHERED THE LOATHSOME INGREDIENTS, AND AS MIDNIGHT CRAWLED IN...
NOW I'LL MIX IT WELL! STIR... STIR... STIR! WHAT DOES IT MATTER IF I GROW TIRED? THERE IS MUCH WORK TO DO TONIGHT! SO I MUST STIR... STIR... STIR!
3

BOIL, CAULDRON, BOIL! BUBBLE, BUBBLE, CAULDRON! BOIL AND BUBBLE...GIVE ME THE SHAPE I SEEK! GIVE ME THE BEAUTY RIGHTFULLY MINE! GIVE ME ENCHANTMENT DIVINE! HA, HA... IT GROWS!!

COME TO ME, CARLO KARINE! YOU ARE MINE AS I AM YOURS! YOU ARE HANDSOME TO ME! KISS ME! KISS ME!
THE BOOK DIDN'T LIE! IT CRUMBLED TO PIECES IN MY HANDS... BUT IT DIDN'T LIE! THERE IS MY MASTERPIECE! YOU'RE BEAUTIFUL, MY SWEET! BEAUTIFUL, BEAUTIFUL!

THAT WAS HOW SHEILA CAME TO BE. SHEILA, THE BEAUTIFUL, A SIGHT NONE COULD BELIEVE!
W-WHO IS SHE? SHE'S GORGEOUS!
IT--IT'S CARLO WITH HER!
YES, AND SHE'S CARLOS WIFE!

THE MONTHS PASSED, AND CARLO'S REPUTATION GREW. MORE PEOPLE TALKED TO HIM... MORE PEOPLE RESPECTED HIM! AND ALL ADMIRED HIS "WIFE"! AND SUCCESS CAME TO CARLO, TOO...
YOU CAN HAVE ANY LOAN YOU WANT, CARLO!
THANK YOU, HUGO. THAT'S VERY GENEROUS OF YOU, ISN'T IT, SHEILA?
YES, MY DARLING.

THE YEARS BROUGHT EVEN GREATER SUCCESS TO CARLO. AND HE GLOATED OVER HIS CREATION...
PLEASE DANCE WITH ME, MRS. KARINE!
NO, WITH ME!
LET THEM FIGHT FOR HER ATTENTIONS, THE FOOLS! SHE IS MINE! ONLY I HAVE THE RIGHT TO ASK HER LOVE!

THEN IT HAPPENED! THE PARTY WAS OVER, AND CARLO WENT TO BED. BUT AT MIDNIGHT, A STRANGE SOUND AWAKENED HIM...
CREA-A-AK!
W-WHAT WAS THAT? SHEILA--WHERE ARE YOU? ANSWER ME!

THERE SHE IS! BUT WHAT IS SHE DOING OUTSIDE? SHE'S GOING DOWN INTO THE CRYPT! STRANGE --VERY STRANGE...

HE FOLLOWED HER DOWN--DOWN--DOWN INTO THE GLOOMY CRYPT AND OPENED THE DOOR TO THE DANK, MOIST CELLAR BELOW! AND THERE--HE SAW--!!
KISS ME, MY BELOVED! KISS ME FOR I NEED YOUR FIRM LIPS ON MINE! KISS ME AND WIPE AWAY THE THOUGHT OF CARLO KARINE... HIS UGLINESS... HIS AGEDNESS!
NO--
N-NO!!

SHE CREATED HIM OUT OF THE SWIRLING MIST OF THE CAULDRON AS I CREATED *HER!* SHE CANNOT MOCK ME THIS WAY! SHE--ABOVE ALL! SHE WHO HAS BROUGHT ME EVERYTHING IN LIFE!

I'M GOING TO KILL YOU! I'M GOING TO CRUSH YOU BOTH TO A PULP! YOU SHOULDN'T HAVE DONE IT, SHEILA! YOU SHOULDN'T! I HATE YOU NOW! *I HATE YOU!*

THEY FOUND HIM SITTING ON THE FLOOR, STILL CLUTCHING THE IRON BAR. HE LAUGHED AND THEN HE CRIED! HE MOANED AND GROANED AND SCREAMED! AND THEY COULDN'T STOP HIS ANGUISH!
W-WHY DID YOU DO IT, SHEILA? W-WHY DID YOU CREATE *HIM?* I--I LOVED YOU! YOU CHEATED ME! BUT I LOVED YOU!!... WHY? WHY?

THEY ARRESTED HIM FOR MURDER--BUT NO ONE COULD FIND THE BODY! INDEED, TWO SMALL RUBBERY MOUNDS NEXT TO THE CAULDRON MEANT NOTHING TO THEM. YET HE INSISTED HE HAD KILLED HER...

YES, I DID IT! TAKE ME AWAY! HANG ME! ELECTROCUTE ME! KILL ME! I DON'T WANT TO LIVE! HA, HA... SHE WAS MINE--SHE WAS MY OWN CREATION!!

SILENCE IN THIS COURT! THIS MAN IS *INSANE!*

YES, THEY CALLED HIM INSANE, AND THEY SENT HIM TO AN ASYLUM...
BOIL--BUBBLE, CAULDRON, BUBBLE! I'LL HAVE MY LOVE AGAIN TONIGHT! BUBBLE, CAULDRON, BUBBLE!

THAT'S THE STORY OF THOSE EYES. THAT'S THE STORY OF A MAN--AND HIS *CAULDRON!* *The End.*

The STRANGER

Yes, I guess it's not too good to be caught in an unfriendly town. And now you're caught, aren't you? A murder in town so they bring in all strangers. And there's nothing you can do when a group of vigilantes take law in their hands.

They're talking to that nice looking kid at the end of the line now . . .

"We ain't seen you hereabouts, stranger. What did you come into town for? Murder, maybe?"

The kid's shaking something awful. How you wish you could stop it.

"No, mister . . . honest. I was just passing through . . . honest, mister . . ."

"Leave the kid alone! He looks all right!" Thank the Lord for that guy. Sure, the kid is innocent.

Now they're talking to the elderly gent.

"Listen, Pop, what were you doing in this town? Strangers don't come here for nothing!"

"M-my c-car broke down . . . I was at this gentleman's garage . . ."

"Yeah, that's the truth. I seen him there!"

Now they're talking to that pretty girl.

"Listen, lady, a pretty gal like yourself doesn't come here just for kicks! What do you have to say for yourself?"

Yes, she certainly is pretty, and how they all know it.

"Well, sir, I was going to see my aunt who lives a few miles from here. And I saw the huge crowd in town, and just HAD to stop." She's sure dazzling them with those beautiful eyes. And even at a time like this, she makes use of them.

But she's still talking . . . "Now, I don't want to point any accusing finger at anyone, but I kind of think I know who did it."

"YOU know?"

"Who? Tell us!"

Gads, what's her angle?

"You see, as I was coming into town, I did see a man running like all blazes out of here. Now I don't want to say that he was the one who . . ."

"You just tell us, lady! We'll do the figuring!"

"Well, it was this gentleman right here!"

Look! Look who she's pointing at! Yes, my friend, it's YOU! I know you never saw her before . . . I know you were just coming into town when it happened! But THEY don't!

"I think the gal's got something there!"

"I ain't ever seen him before!"

"He looks like the type!"

"I'm sure he did it!"

"What do you have to say for yourself, mister?"

They're closing in on you now . . . they're breathing hard for your neck . . . your face spells murder to them, and they're almost reading it in your sweat!

"Look, he ain't saying a word!"

"Sure, 'cause there's nothing to say! He knows we got him!"

"Get the string!"

Don't just stand there and wave at them! Tell them! Tell them fast! . . . But how can you speak to say . . . you haven't the power of speech!

FOOD FOR THOUGHT
AN OLD CHINESE DELICACY IS AN EGG WHICH HAS BEEN PRESERVED IN LIME FOR GENERATIONS--SOMETIMES A HUNDRED YEARS OR MORE! THESE EGGS HAVE YOLKS AS HARD AS NUTS AND TASTE MUCH DIFFERENT FROM THE ORDINARY EGG!

PEOPLE OF SPAIN REGARD OCTOPUS AS ONE OF THE FINEST OF SEA FOODS...THEY BOIL THE OCTOPUS IN ITS OWN INKY-BLACK JUICES AND PRODUCE A STEW WHICH TO MANY TASTES MUCH LIKE A DISH OF MUSHROOMS!

NATIVES OF AFRICA LOOK UPON ELEPHANT STEAK AS A TOOTHSOME DISH, DESPITE THE FACT THAT IT IS VERY TOUGH. THE COOK BURIES THE ELEPHANT MEAT IN THE GROUND AND KEEPS A HOT FIRE OVER IT FOR A FEW DAYS. WHEN REMOVED, THE MEAT IS TENDER AND, THEY SAY, DELICIOUS!

A FAVORITE MEAL OF MANY MEXICANS IS THE EGGS OF WATER BEETLES, GATHERED ON THE LAKES NEAR MEXICO CITY. IT IS SAID THAT, WHEN FRIED, THESE MASSES OF EGGS TASTE LIKE ORDINARY FRIED CORN-MEAL MUSH!

IN THE HEART OF THE AMAZON JUNGLE IS A TREE WHICH ACTUALLY GIVES FORTH RICH, CREAMY, NOURISHING MILK! IT IS NATURALLY KNOWN AS A "COW TREE" AND IS LOOKED UPON AS SACRED BY THE NATIVES!

MANY PEOPLES REGARD BLOOD AS A DEFINITE DRINK OR FOOD. AMONG SEMI-CIVILIZED TRIBES IN MADAGASCAR, THE BLOOD OF FRESHLY KILLED CATTLE IS DRUNK TO FRIGHTEN OFF THE EVIL SPIRITS WHICH THEY FEAR SO TERRIBLY!

WHAT WAS AT THE OTHER END OF

THE TUNNEL!

HA HA! THE COPS'LL NEVER KNOW. A LITTLE BIT MORE AND... I'LL BE OUT!

A PRISON YARD, AND, YES, A CONVICT... A CONVICT WITH A REBELLIOUS SPIRIT...
LOOK WHAT I'M DOING! ME... LUTHER DARK! THEY GOT ME... GARDENING!

WELL, I'M NOT STICKING AROUND. I'LL BREA OUT... SOMEHOW. I... WAIT! THIS EARTH... SOFT! THE TROWEL CUTS RIGHT INTO IT! HMMM...
1

LUTHER DARK LOOKED AROUND... AND AN IDEA TOOK SHAPE IN HIS MIND...
AND, THE PRISON WALL...ONLY ABOUT FIFTY FEET AWAY. YEAH, THAT'S IT. I'M GOING TO DIG MY WAY OUT!

LUTHER DARK WAS A CONVICT WHO DIDN'T HAVE TIME TO WASTE! SO LATER THAT NIGHT...
IT'S A GOOD THING MY CELL IS ON THE GROUND FLOOR. NOW... I'LL REMOVE ONE OF THESE BLOCKS!

IT'S A GOOD THING I SMUGGLED THIS TROWEL IN WITH ME! IT SURE CHIPS AWAY THIS CEMENT!

SO HE CHIPPED OFF THE OLD BLOCK...
THERE... I'LL JUST LIFT... UNN-H...THIS BLOCK. THEN...I'LL BEGIN DIGGING!

HE LOWERED HIMSELF INTO THE BLACK CAVITY BENEATH THE CELL FLOOR... RIGHT INTO THE STENCH OF EARTHAL DAMPNESS! THEN HE BEGAN TO DIG...
EVERYTHING'S SO QUIET DOWN HERE. BUT, I GOT TO GET STARTED!

THE EARTH IS SOFT! WHAT A CINCH!
2

FURTHER AND FURTHER HE WENT... CLOSER AND CLOSER TO HIS FREEDOM!
WELL, I MADE A GOOD START. I BETTER GET BACK. IT'S ABOUT TIME FOR BED CHECK.

AS HE RETURNED TO THE CELL, HE SLID THE CEMENT BLOCK BACK INTO PLACE...AND A PAIR OF EYES WATCHED CLOSELY!
NOBODY'LL FIND OUT ABOUT THE TUNNEL! NOBODY!

BUT, THE NEXT DAY THE EYES SHOWED THEIR MEANING...
DARK, I WANT TO TALK WITH YOU STEP AROUND THE CORNER.
OKAY.

I KNOW WHAT YOU'RE DOING, DARK. I SAW YOU LAST NIGHT! YOU'RE DIGGING A TUNNEL...TO ESCAPE! I WANT IN. OR ELSE...?
OR ELSE... WHAT?

LUTHER DARK HAD NO ROOM FOR ONE MORE. IT WOULD BE BUT HE... AND HE ALONE!
I'LL SQUEAL! NO...NO... DON'T... ARGH-H!
YOU'RE NOT TELLING ANYONE...'CAUSE I'M SHUTTING YOU UP-- FOR GOOD!
CRACK!

HIS PROBLEM WAS SOLVED...AND NO ONE PINNED THE MURDER ON HIM. SO LUTHER DARK RETURNED TO HIS TUNNEL THAT NIGHT...
THAT CON...THINKING HE CAN BULL-DOZE ME. HA HA! THIS TUNNEL IS FOR ME... ONLY!

BUT THEN HE SAW SOMETHING...
WHAT'S THIS? WATER, EH? THAT'S PRETTY STRANGE!

AND THERE WAS MORE...
THIS WATER IS REALLY COMING. PUDDLES... ALL AROUND WHAT'S GOING ON?

AND STILL MORE!
AM I GOING THE RIGHT WAY? I CAN'T MAKE IT OUT! ANYHOW, I BETTER GET BACK!

FRANTICALLY, LUTHER DARK WENT BACK TO HIS CELL. HE REPLACED THE BLOCK AND THEN...
WARDEN SMITH! HOW NICE OF YOU TO COME WHAT'S UP?
WE'RE LOOKING OVER YOUR CELL.
JUST A ROUTINE INSPECTION, DARK.

THE WARDEN WALKED EASILY...CAREFULLY... VERY CAREFULLY!
HE'S STANDING ON THE CEMENT BLOCK... RIGHT OVER THE TUNNEL!

BUT PERHAPS NOT CAREFULLY ENOUGH!
WELL, EVERYTHING LOOKS OKAY, DARK. SORRY TO HAVE BOTHERED YOU
WHEW! THAT WAS CLOSE! I CAN'T AFFORD TO TAKE ANOTHER CHANCE LIKE THAT. I GOT TO FINISH THAT TUNNEL... TONIGHT!

SO LUTHER DARK RETURNED QUICKLY TO HIS TUNNEL...
GOT TO...DIG. I...AIEEE! SKULLS!

THE SKULLS...NOW THIS ROCK! GOT TO...THE TROWEL ...BROKE ON THE ROCK...

I'LL USE MY HANDS. TUNNEL...SEEMS...TO BE... GETTING BIGGER!

BUT THE DIRT FELL AWAY...AND A FIGURE LUNGED FROM THE DEPTHS!
YAAA-H! IT'S THE CONVICT I KILLED!

HE'S GOT ME...PULLING ME THROUGH THAT HOLE! WHERE AM I GOING? WHERE?
COME! COME!

LUTHER DARK HAD REACHED THE END OF HIS TUNNEL...THAT CEASELESS INFERNO OF RAGING FIRE...
HERE IS WHERE YOU DUG YOUR TUNNEL!
NO...NO... NOOOO!
THE END.

MR. TV OWNER!

Stop TV Interference At Once And Stop It—For Good!

An amazing no-risk challenge to every set owner who is tired of paying $5-$10-$15 for THE SAME TV REPAIRS . . . OVER AND OVER AGAIN!

Do you know that 95% of the wavy lines, streaks, zags, distortions, picture roll, flutters, and snow that ruins your TV viewing are not caused by your set at all? That they cannot be eliminated by your repairman, no matter how good he is! That they cannot be prevented by your antenna, no matter how powerful it is!

Yes, 95% of your costly television troubles are caused by electronic TV interference from the outside. And the only way to permanently remove that interference is to BLOCK IT OUT, before it even reaches your set—in exactly the same way sunlight glare is blocked out by sun glasses, before it reaches your eyes.

This is exactly what a revolutionary new TV invention—the TELERON TV WAVE TRAP (Pat. Pend.)—does for your set. This amazing "Interference Eliminator" actually eliminates the 6 most aggravating forms of interference, before they can reach your set. It actually strengthens your reception on all channels—even in poor reception areas.

WHICH OF THESE 6 TV HEADACHES DO YOU WANT TO REMOVE FOR GOOD?

WAVY LINES — Caused by airplane flying as much as 15 miles away from your home. MR. OSCAR HOLDEN of *New York City* writes: "My TELERON WAVE TRAP eliminates 95% of all wavy lines within 15 minutes after I clipped it on my set."

DISTORTION—Caused by outside telephone lines up to 11 miles away from your home . . . or by other neighborhood TV sets and antennas that compete with your set for the same channel.

TELERON WAVE TRAP eliminates 93% of all this interference BEFORE IT REACHES YOUR SET.

SNOW — Caused by constantly - running electrical appliances in your home — such as refrigerators and oil burners.

MR. M. CAINE of *Chicago, Ill.* reports: "I live in a big apartment house where there's plenty of electrical interference. But since I clipped a TELERON WAVE TRAP on my set I haven't been bothered once by snow."

BORER EFFECT — Caused by doctor's diathermy machine—or amateur radio operator as much as 3 miles away from your home.

MR. WILLIAM BENTLEY of *Los Angeles* writes "My family couldn't go through a night of TV viewing without getting terrific TV interference from a hospital about 2 miles away. Then I heard about the TELERON WAVE TRAP I tried it, And now, 6 months later I have only been bothered once by those diathermy machines in that hospital."

STREAKS — Caused by car ignitions, trucks or busses up to 2½ miles away from your home . . or by neon signs, doorbells, electric toasters, broilers, radios and phonographs within 1 mile of your home.

TELERON WAVE TRAP eliminates 98% of all this interference BEFORE IT REACHES YOUR SET

TV STATIC— Caused by atmospheric conditions up to 5 full miles away from your home.

TELERON WAVE TRAP eliminates 95% of all this irritating interference BEFORE IT REACHES YOUR SET

MOVIE-CLEAR RECEPTION 365 DAYS A YEAR!

Send for your TELERON WAVE TRAP today. Send no money. When your TELERON WAVE TRAP arrives simply clip it on the back of your set. It takes only 30 seconds — you need no special tools, no training. And it fits every set made since 1947—no matter what the brand, style or year. See for yourself how this amazing invention gives you sharp, clear pictures. How it adds new life to your picture even in fringe areas—even in weak reception zones—even on channels you could hardly pick up before.

HERE'S PROOF—TEST IT IN YOUR OWN HOME! AT OUR RISK!

If you order your TELERON TV WAVE TRAP today, you do not pay the $5 that 50,000 other TV owners paid—you deposit only $2.98 with the postman. If after you clip this amazing TELERON WAVE TRAP on your set, you are not getting perfect movie-clear reception—please return for full money back! *You try it at our risk—you do not buy it until you are 100% satisfied. ORDER TODAY AND SAVE $2!*

ORDER TODAY AND SAVE $2! MAIL COUPON NOW! Dept.
TELERON TV WAVE TRAP, 836 Broadway, New York 3 HCS-34

Please send me the TV WAVE TRAP immediately, at $2.98, plus C.O.D. postage. I understand that satisfaction is guaranteed 100%.

Name...
(Please Print)

Address...

City.............................Zone..........State.......

☐ Cash ☐ Check ☐ Money Order. SAVE MORE! Send $3.00 with coupon. We pay all postage charges. Same Money-Back Guarantee.

HARVEY PUBLICATIONS INC. New York, N.Y.

JAN 1953

SUN	MON	TUE	WED	THU	FRI	SAT
				1	2	3
4	5	6	7	8	9	10
11	12	13	14	15	16	17
18	19	20	21	22	23	24
25	26	27	28	29	30	31

FEB 1953

SUN	MON	TUE	WED	THU	FRI	SAT
1	2	3	4	5	6	7
8	9	10	11	12	13	14
15	16	17	18	19	20	21
22	23	24	25	26	27	28

MAR 1953

SUN	MON	TUE	WED	THU	FRI	SAT
1	2	3	4	5	6	7
8	9	10	11	12	13	14
15	16	17	18	19	20	21
22	23	24	25	26	27	28
29	30	31				

APR 1953

SUN	MON	TUE	WED	THU	FRI	SAT
			1	2	3	4
5	6	7	8	9	10	11
12	13	14	15	16	17	18
19	20	21	22	23	24	25
26	27	28	29	30		

MAY 1953

SUN	MON	TUE	WED	THU	FRI	SAT
					1	2
3	4	5	6	7	8	9
10	11	12	13	14	15	16
17	18	19	20	21	22	23
24/31	25	26	27	28	29	30

JUNE 1953

SUN	MON	TUE	WED	THU	FRI	SAT
	1	2	3	4	5	6
7	8	9	10	11	12	13
14	15	16	17	18	19	20
21	22	23	24	25	26	27
28	29	30				

JULY 1953

SUN	MON	TUE	WED	THU	FRI	SAT
			1	2	3	4
5	6	7	8	9	10	11
12	13	14	15	16	17	18
19	20	21	22	23	24	25
26	27	28	29	30	31	

AUG 1953

SUN	MON	TUE	WED	THU	FRI	SAT
						1
2	3	4	5	6	7	8
9	10	11	12	13	14	15
16	17	18	19	20	21	22
23/30	24/31	25	26	27	28	29

SEPT 1953

SUN	MON	TUE	WED	THU	FRI	SAT
		1	2	3	4	5
6	7	8	9	10	11	12
13	14	15	16	17	18	19
20	21	22	23	24	25	26
27	28	29	30			

OCT 1953

SUN	MON	TUE	WED	THU	FRI	SAT
				1	2	3
4	5	6	7	8	9	10
11	12	13	14	15	16	17
18	19	20	21	22	23	24
25	26	27	28	29	30	31

NOV 1953

SUN	MON	TUE	WED	THU	FRI	SAT
1	2	3	4	5	6	7
8	9	10	11	12	13	14
15	16	17	18	19	20	21
22	23	24	25	26	27	28
29	30					

DEC 1953

SUN	MON	TUE	WED	THU	FRI	SAT
		1	2	3	4	5
6	7	8	9	10	11	12
13	14	15	16	17	18	19
20	21	22	23	24	25	26
27	28	29	30	31		

HARVEY FAMOUS NAME COMICS

NOW ON SALE... GET YOUR COPY TODAY!

FROM THE WORLD OF THE SUPERNATURAL... FROM THE NETHERLAND OF ENDLESS EVIL... FROM THE DEEPEST BOWELS OF GREED-HUNGRY SOULS COME THESE FRANTIC ACCOUNTS OF SUSPENSEFUL, REALISTIC TALES OF TERROR!

Get them NOW at your nearest newsstand!

NOW! Let Indianapolis Speedway Champions Show You 106 Easy Ways To Get More "SPEED & POWER" From Your Car!

Get 42-47 Miles PER GALLON FROM YOUR CAR!

DRIVE 8,000 MILES WITHOUT OIL CHANGE!
Zoom From 0 to 60 M.P.H. in 12 Seconds!
Add 30 M.P.H. to Top Speed Of Your Car!
(MANY RESULTS PROVED IN OFFICIAL TESTING LABS.)

ANY CAR! ANY MAKE! ANY YEAR!

NEWEST SPEED & POWER MANUAL! No Experience Needed—Easy A-B-C Picture Instructions Show How To Mix, Burn Water & Gas For Amazing Speed & Economy—Resurface Cylinder Walls, Stretch Car Life Without Taking Engine Apart—Do Speed & Power Tuning With Screwdriver—Restyle '37-'47 Models to Expensive "Foreign" Look—Get Flash Starts, Top Performance, Hi Resale — Beat High Cost of Minor Repairs — SAVE HUNDREDS OF DOLLARS A YEAR!

No Guesswork — Everything You Have To Know!

Restyle, Repower Your Car! Make '37-'47 model look, run like '50!

Here for the first time is the only book of its kind ever published—a show-how, do-it-yourself SPEED & POWER MANUAL that shows you how to save 33⅓% on gas bills—80% on oil bills—90% on repair bills—*add $300 to the resale value of your car!* With sensational new discoveries of Automotive Engineers, Research Scientists and Indianapolis Mechanics, now it's easy to add new *surging* Power, Life, Mileage, Economy to your car! ... whether it's a 15 year old jalopy or a shiny new '52 model — and SAVE $75 to $300 THIS YEAR!

Clear — Simple — Complete — Easy as A-B-C with "Show-How" Pictures

Secrets Of Wizard Mechanics! Start dead-battery car with bumper jack!

This new SPEED & POWER MANUAL is so complete, so easy to follow, so FOOL-PROOF, it's like having a master Indianapolis mechanic right at your elbow! Written in plain language with simple *show-how* drawings and cutaway diagrams anyone can understand! You not only read what to do, YOU SEE HOW IT'S DONE! It's so easy when you do it the SPEED & POWER way, and right from the start you'll learn the 30 to 40 quick tricks to get flash starts, lightning pickup, 15 more horsepower, amazing fuel economy, plus hundreds of tips like using simple gas and oil mixtures to add instant power and years of driving life to your car, *even if you've never looked under a hood before!*

NEWHOUSE AUTOMOTIVE INDUSTRIES
400 MADISON AVE., N.Y. 17, N.Y.

INDIANAPOLIS: *Years ahead of the industry! Balloon Tires:* Introduced in Indianapolis 1917! Industry adopted in 1923! *Self-Starter:* Introduced in Indianapolis 1916! Industry adopted in 1928! *Ethyl Gas:* Introduced in Indianapolis . 1916! 1st sold Nationally – 1925! *Other Indianapolis Firsts:* Rear view mirror – front wheel drive—super charge—4 wheel brakes—foolproof spark plugs – demountable wheels—better springs—etc.

• Even Greenest Beginners Add 15 Horsepower With Simple Trick On Page 39!

SPEED and POWER

$1.98 ONLY
7 Day FREE Proof Money Back Guarantee

Not A Step Overlooked — For Beginner Or Expert

Learn Speed and Power Tuning! Simple adjustments for new pep.

1001 MONEY SAVING TRICKS of the master mechanics crammed into 1 great book! How to resurface cylinder walls in 10 minutes *without removing 1 part from your engine!* Stop power waste with 25¢ worth of graphite in your crankcase How to double explosive power of your engine How to fix-it-yourself, spot trouble, make emergency repairs with the tools in your car Cut engine wear: stop summer overheating. Amazing *jiffy-car-polish* tricks So complete it even has step-by-step sections showing how to rebuild, repower even junkyard Fords, Hudsons, etc., into sleek, 180 horsepower, 126 mph speedcars, with push-button doors, plastic tops, custom grillwork, exclusive redesigning with "pickup" parts, for foreign car features! It's the biggest, most complete, up-to-the-minute volume of automotive information ever published for the average car owner, yours FREE FOR A WEEK if you send TODAY!

BURN WATER SAVE GAS!

(U.S. Agricultural Department Scientists say new water-alcohol can save you money!)

HERE'S PROOF!

Ever notice how your car runs better on damp days? Engineers & Govt. testing bureaus now tell us what is actually taking place is moderate water injection, mixing with gas to give tremendous explosive power! (And test after test proves less engine wear and corrosion!) Now, at a cost of mere pennies, easy picture directions show you how to take an ordinary Mason jar and a few inches of rubber hose, attach this simple powerful "supercharger" to your carburetor, and suddenly discover sensational new power! . . . and gas savings up to 33⅓%! This is only 1 of the 106 new motor miracles any car owner can do with new SPEED & POWER MANUAL!

WHAT EVERY CAR OWNER WANTS TO KNOW!

Partial Contents:

- Water-alcohol injection systems. How they work and why.
- How to make and install a Mason-jar water injector.
- 10 ways to save on gas.
- 8 ways to save on oil.
- Special fuels, carburetion.
- Better carburetor action.
- Hi-test vs. regular gas.
- Treated gas and oil
- Air-fuel mixture adjustment
- New type carburetors
- Building your own dual manifold—dual carburetor
- Using adjustable jet screws and air-flow needles
- Supercharging your car.
- Speed and power tuning.
- Increasing top car speed.
- Increasing pickup on hills.
- Flash starts in icy weather.
- Re-working engine, ignition.
- Dual ignition systems
- Easy ways to higher horsepower.
- Eliminating tappet noise
- Eliminating carburetor flooding, fuel pump surge, motor cut-out, fuel waste.
- How to eliminate overheating.
- Engine lubrication magic: lifetime oil filters.
- 1 minute spark plug checkup.
- Hi-compression conversions.
- Sport and model changes.
- Building your own roadster.
- Hard chroming tricks.
- Customizing, restyling ideas.
- 10,000 extra tire miles.
- Touching up nicks, dents, for perfect blend and finish.
- Mounting tires on rear.
- Calif style convertible tops.
- How to preserve car finish.
- 20 ways to increase resale $.
- How to have automatic hill holder—6 forward speeds—no clutch shift in present car
- Emergency repairs made easy.
- Building a practical jet engine.
- 12 tips to A-1 car condition.

***PLUS:* Latest Information on Care, Replacement, Repair of:**

Fuel pumps—ignition, electrical systems—starter—battery—generator—body, chassis care—new silicone polishes—tires, brakes, cooling system—lubrication—oil filters—directional signals—accessories—performance boosters – lights, switches – shocks – ventilating system — transmission—rear end—engine—bearings—carburetor—speedometer cable—windshield wipers—steering wheel—etc.

. . . and much, much more!

SEND NO MONEY Mail Free Gift Coupon NOW

all 3 FREE
(even if you return book)

1. Speed and Special Equip. Catalog. 36 pages, reg. 25c value. *PLUS:* Free membership National Discount Club saves you up to 45% on auto supplies and products.

2. How To Obtain 150 Miles Per Gallon. Amazing economy secrets! Thousands of copies sold at $1.

3. Economy In Driving. Can cut your bills in half! 48 pages, reg. 50c value.

ACT NOW

Special Offer Gives You 3 Valuable Handbooks FREE!

Send TODAY and get 3 extra handbooks described here (reg. $1.75 value) yours FREE with SPEED & POWER MANUAL. Examine for 7 days. If not convinced book will pay for itself 10 times over in 1 week, save you $75-$300 in 1 year, return for money back, but *keep 3 extra handbooks as FREE GIFT!*

NEWHOUSE AUTOMOTIVE INDUSTRIES. DEPT. HCS-34
400 Madison Ave., New York 17. N. Y.

Gentlemen: Without obligation please rush me new SPEED & POWER MANUAL for NO RISK examination and trial. I agree to pay postman on arrival $1.98 plus postage. If I am not satisfied, I may return in 7 days for full money back.

Also send me ABSOLUTELY FREE, the 3 handbooks described here (reg. $1.75 value), plus my FREE MEMBERSHIP in National Discount Club. I understand these are mine FREE, whether or not I keep SPEED & POWER MANUAL.

NAME ________________

ADDRESS ________________

CITY ________ ZONE ____ STATE ______

☐ SAVE MORE! If you send $1.98 with coupon, we pay all postage charges. Same money back guarantee.

EACH SPRING THE PACIFIC OCEAN BACKWASH CAUSES A SMALL TIDAL WAVE ON SOME OF OUR WEST COAST TOWNS--MOST TIMES THE BACKWASH IS SMALL--SOMETIMES IT IS GREAT--AND SOMETIMES IT BRINGS A WAVE OF HORROR!

BACKWASH!

THE DAY OF THE ANNUAL TIDAL WAVE IS USUALLY A PLEASANT OCCASION... FOR MOST PEOPLE, THAT IS!
YOU SEE, FERGUS, THE WAVE DOES NO DAMAGE! YOUR NEW HOME ON THE COAST IS PERFECTLY SAFE!
NEVER MIND THE SALES TALK! LET'S CLOSE THE DEAL!

SO THE DEAL WAS CLOSED, AND DAN FERGUS TOOK POSSESSION OF HIS NEW HOME.
GREAT! AND ALL MINE! AND AWAY FROM THOSE STUPID FOOLS IN TOWN!

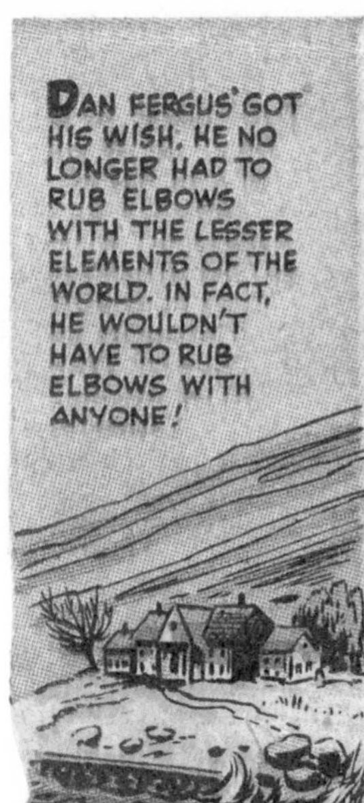
DAN FERGUS' GOT HIS WISH. HE NO LONGER HAD TO RUB ELBOWS WITH THE LESSER ELEMENTS OF THE WORLD. IN FACT, HE WOULDN'T HAVE TO RUB ELBOWS WITH ANYONE!

ALONE! ALONE AT LAST-- FREE FROM THE STUPIDITY OF MANKIND! FREE FROM FRIENDS WHO WANT TO LIVE OFF MY WEALTH!

BUT LATER, AS FERGUS INSPECTS HIS CELLAR...
WHAT ARE YOU TWO DOING DOWN THERE? THIS PLACE IS MINE!
WE MEAN NO HARM, SIR! WE HAVE NO OTHER HOME!

WE WILL WORK FOR YOU IF YOU'LL JUST LET US STAY--
GET OUT! BOTH OF YOU! THIS MINUTE!

THE FOOLS! FOR YEARS I'VE PLANNED TO BREAK WITH THE MONEY SUCKING WORLD-- AND NO ONE IS GOING TO INTERFERE WITH MY HOPES!

BUT FERGUS WAS STILL NOT ALONE, WHEN HE AGAIN RETURNED TO HIS CELLAR...
SO IT'S YOU AGAIN! I WARNED YOU!
BUT IT'S RAINING... WE'VE NO OTHER PLACE TO GO!

THIS WILL PUT A STOP TO YOUR WORRIES ABOUT THE RAIN!
BANG!
BANG!

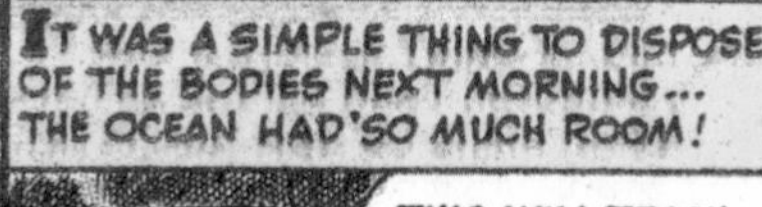

IT WAS A SIMPLE THING TO DISPOSE OF THE BODIES NEXT MORNING... THE OCEAN HAD SO MUCH ROOM!

THIS WILL TEACH YOU TO CROSS DAN FERGUS!

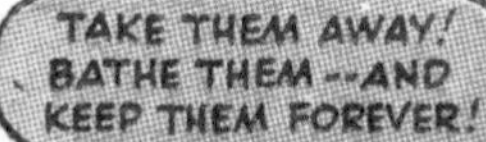

TAKE THEM AWAY! BATHE THEM --AND KEEP THEM FOREVER!

THE FOLLOWING YEAR WAS A PEACEFUL ONE FOR DAN FERGUS. HE HAD HIS PEACE. HE HAD HIS QUIET. THEN SPRING CAME AGAIN...

I COULD SWEAR I HEARD SOMETHING...

HE WALKED TO THE CELLAR DOOR -- OPENED IT!...

NO! NO! IT CAN'T BE!

HE RUSHED AWAY MADLY-- BLINDLY--SEEKING HIS SAFETY!
I'VE BOLTED MY DOOR... IT CAN'T CATCH ME HERE! IT-- WHAT AM I SAYING! I MUST HAVE *IMAGINED* IT! I'M JUST OVER-TIRED!
YES, PERHAPS HE HAD IMAGINED IT. BUT THE NEXT DAY THE TIDAL WAVE AGAIN SWEPT IN AND LEFT A *CALLING CARD* IN ITS WAKE!
IT'S...NO! NO! *NO!*

THE SEA COULDN'T BE TRUSTED...ONLY THE DEPTHS OF THE EARTH WOULD BE SILENT...
I MUST CONCEAL THE EVIDENCE! I CAN'T RISK THIS BODY TURNING UP AGAIN!

THERE YOU ARE, MY FRIEND! A RESTING PLACE AT LAST! YOU'RE THE GUEST OF DAN FERGUS!

AND DAN FERGUS HAD HIS PEACE ALSO. FOR A YEAR, THAT IS. THEN SPRING CAME AROUND ONCE MORE...
WH-WHAT'S THAT?

I...NO! NO!--IT'S THE SECOND ONE!

FERGUS MADE IT TO HIS ROOM ONCE AGAIN...
I SAW IT! HIS GHOST! I SAW IT!

AND, NEXT MORNING, HE WATCHED THE TIDE RECEDE...
THE SECOND ONE! WASHED UP BY THE RIVER! I MUST BURY HIM--IN THE SAME GRAVE WITH HIS FRIEND!

BUT THE GRAVE HAD A SURPRISE FOR DAN FERGUS...
I'LL...WHAAAA--! IT'S EMPTY! THE BODY IS GONE!
4

HE WAS NOW HYSTERICAL-- FRANTIC... HE THREW THE CORPSE INTO THE GRAVE... HE SHOVELED THE DIRT...
SO YOUR FRIEND HAS DISAPPEARED, HAS HE! WELL, YOU CAN TAKE HIS PLACE! AND YOU'LL STAY BURIED!

AND, YES, THERE WAS ANOTHER RESTFUL YEAR FOR DAN FERGUS. THEN CAME SPRING ONCE MORE!
I HEAR SOMETHING... I'M SURE I HEAR IT!
NO! YOU'RE DEAD! I BURIED YOU BOTH!
WE CAN'T REST IN THE GRAVE UNTIL YOU HAVE JOINED US, FERGUS!

HE TURNED AWAY AND RACED WILDLY TOWARD THE HALL-WAY-- HE RAN AS HE HAD NEVER RUN BEFORE!
KEEP AWAY! AIIIEEE!

I'VE KILLED YOU ONCE! I CAN DO IT AGAIN! I...AIIEEE! THE WATER!

AARRRGHH!

THE TIDAL WAVE WASHED IN --THEN WASHED AWAY... IT LEFT DAN FERGUS ON HIS OWN PRECIOUS LAND... IN THE GRAVE IN WHICH HE HAD FAILED TO KEEP HIS TWO HAPLESS VICTIMS!
The END

Flying Saucers

"I tell you I saw it!" The man's voice blasted into the telephone. The sweat inched down his forehead.

"What kind of a shape was it?" The voice on the other end was calm, even matter-of-fact.

"Like a saucer! Just like the others! I wish you people would wake up to the truth! We're not crackpots . . . we really see these things . . ."

The voice at the other end stopped him with a simple "Yes, sir." And then went on with, "We're doing all we can, sir. We're not holding back anything from the public."

The man slammed down the receiver. "How do you like those fools in the air spotters office," he said to his wife. "First they ask people to report what they see—and then they call everything optical illusions and that sort of trite!"

"Take it easy, darling," his wife said. "Perhaps there's nothing to these flying saucer reports. After all . . ."

"After all!" her husband shouted. "Don't tell me YOU don't believe me!"

"Well, dear, you're not positive you saw it . . ."

"Positive? How positive can one be! I tell you I saw a flying saucer—and if you want call me a liar!"

"Yes, dear."

This was but one incident. It could be multiplied a thousand times. In some cases the wife saw it, and the husband said, "Yes, dear." In others a little son came home with the report. Most times he was sent to bed without supper.

But the air spotters were beginning to wonder, too . . .

"Say, Tom, do you think there might be something to these flying saucers?"

"Not on your life! You must have just answered a call, huh?"

"Well, Tom, I did. This guy swore he saw it. He said we keep calling them 'crackpots,' and that we're not waking up to the truth. You know, maybe he's right."

"Now hold on, Steve! Don't tell me you're falling for it, too . . ."

"Tom! Tom!" Steve's voice shook the room. "Look out there! Look!"

Tom followed his friend's arm. His eyes peered out the huge window . . . but they wouldn't believe what they saw.

"Yes, you fool! Say it . . . say it's a flying saucer!"

"I-I-I don't know wh-what to say . . ."

Now neither of them could say anything. Their eyes were seeing too much. For now the entire expanse of the sky was lit up with countless spinning, twirling flying saucers . . . rushing madly . . . feverishly toward the ground!

Tom tore for the phone . . . he ripped at the dials . . . he waited for the end of the buzzes . . .

"Hello! Squadron C? They're real . . . the flying saucers are real! It l-looks like an invasion from Earth!"

THE LEOPARD MEN

A STRANGE CULT OF NATIVES IN AFRICA KNOWN AS *LEOPARD MEN* PROWL THROUGH THE FORESTS AT NIGHT IMITATING THE CRIES AND ACTIONS OF LEOPARDS. THEY WEAR LEOPARD SKINS AND HUGE CLAWS OF IRON!

LIKE THEIR NAMESAKES, THE LEOPARD MEN STALK THEIR HUMAN VICTIMS AND THEN SUDDENLY *LEAP* UPON THEM, SEVERING THE THROAT WITH THEIR TEETH! TO MANY AN AFRICAN NATIVE, THESE MEN ARE THE MOST DREADED CREATURES OF THE JUNGLE!

IT IS STILL NOT KNOWN HOW MANY LEOPARD MEN THERE ARE, NOR HOW A HARMLESS NATIVE IS TRANSFORMED INTO ONE. BUT IT IS BELIEVED THAT ONE WHO PARTAKES OF THE CULT'S "MEDICINE" UNWILLINGLY BECOMES A MEMBER FOR LIFE!

THE "MEDICINE" IS THE BLOOD OF ONE OF THEIR VICTIMS SERVED IN A HUMAN SKULL! IT IS ADMINISTERED SECRETLY TO THE ONE CHOSEN TO JOIN. WITHIN MINUTES, HE HAS JOINED HIS FEROCIOUS BROTHERS IN THE FOREST!

AFTER HIS INITIATION, THE NEW RECRUIT MUST HUNT AND KILL FOR HIMSELF. WHEN HE IS COMMANDED TO LURE EVEN A MEMBER OF *HIS OWN FAMILY* TO DOOM, HE MUST OBEY WITHOUT QUESTION! IF HE REFUSES, HE IS DESTROYED BY THE OTHER LEOPARD MEN!

IN MANY COMMUNITIES IN AFRICA, THE NATIVES LIVE IN DEADLY TERROR OF THE LEOPARD MEN -- AND THE TOLL OF DEATH AT THEIR HANDS IS GREAT. NO ONE DARES VENTURE FORTH AFTER NIGHTFALL FOR FEAR OF FALLING VICTIM TO THESE HIDEOUS CREATURES!

ERIC VERDIE COULD NOT LOSE! HE HAD TO HAVE...
THE PRIZE!
THERE IT IS, ERIC! NEVER BEEN SCALED! IT SEEMS TO TAUNT US!
YES, FRANZ! AND SO DOES THE $25,000 PRIZE TO THE FIRST WHO REACHES ITS PEAK!
1

I MIGHT TRY FOR THAT PRIZE, ERIC! YOU KNOW THAT I CAN MAKE IT!
YES, FRANZ! I KNOW... THAT IS, UNLESS I GET THERE FIRST!

AT LEAST, FRANZ OLGER STARTED FIRST...
UNLESS HE GETS THERE FIRST! HA! BEFORE VERDIE KNOWS I'M GONE I'LL BE WELL ON MY WAY TO THE PRIZE MONEY!

AND LATER THAT AFTERNOON, UNAWARE OF HIS RIVAL'S DEPARTURE, ERIC VERDIE AND HIS PARTY STARTED THE HAZARDOUS CLIMB!
YOU'LL ALL FOLLOW ME AND KEEP CLOSE TO ONE ANOTHER! OUR LIVES DEPEND ON IT!

AND THEIRS DEPEND ON ME! THE MONEY AND THE FAME SHALL BE MINE ALONE!

BUT ERIC VERDIE'S SATISFACTION IS SHORT LIVED!
IF I-- WHAAA! THERE'S SOMEONE ON THE PEAK! IT'S OLGER!

SO METHODICALLY... EASILY HE EXCHANGES HIS TELESCOPE FOR HIS RIFLE...

YOU'VE GONE FAR ENOUGH, OLGER! DOUBLE CROSS ME, WILL YOU?

AND FIRES!
AIEEEEE

THE FIRST OPPONENT WAS GONE... BUT THE MIGHTY MOUNTAIN STILL WAITED!
COME ON! LET'S GET STARTED AGAIN!
CAREFUL, ERIC!

SLOW ...DOWN, ERIC! LET US REST FOR A MOMENT!
YOU'LL HAVE PLENTY OF TIME FOR A REST-- WHEN WE RETURN!

PROGRESS WAS GOOD... FOR A WHILE...
THE PEAK... IT'S HIGHER THAN I THOUGHT!
NEVER MIND!...AFTER A... SHORT... REST...WE'LL CONTINUE! WE'LL MAKE IT-- OR DIE!

ERIC! ARE WE STILL ON OUR COURSE?
JUST FOLLOW ME! WE'LL MAKE OUR OWN COURSE IF WE HAVE TO!

BUT ERIC VERDIE ALMOST MADE A WRONG COURSE...
THAT WAS A CLOSE CALL, ERIC! ANOTHER FOOT AND YOU'D BE GONE!
GET ME UP! DON'T LET ME GO!

I'D BE GONE, WOULD I? WELL NOW IT'S THEIR TURN! THE PRIZE MONEY WILL BE MINE ALONE!
3

AND LATER THAT DAY, ERIC VERDIE STOOD ALONE...
GOODBYE, GENTLEMEN! THANKS FOR EVERYTHING!
THE ROPE! NO! ERIC!

AIEEE!

HA-HA! I'M ALMOST THERE! THE SUMMIT IS IN SIGHT! AND SO IS MY PRIZE!

THEN IN HIS GREATEST MOMENT OF TRIUMPH...
THE PRIZE WILL BE... WHAAA--! OLGER!

YES, OLGER STOOD WAITING... GOADING... LAUGHING! AND ERIC VERDIE CLIMBED STILL HIGHER!
YOU'RE GETTING CLOSER, ERIC!
YOU'RE DEAD! DEAD, OLGER, I SAY, DEAD!

THIS WAY, ERIC! HEE-HEE!
I... (GASP)... I'M COMING, FRANZ! (GASP) AND WHEN I GET THERE THE PRIZE MONEY IS MINE! (GASP) ... AND I'LL DEAL WITH YOU AS I DID BEFORE!

HE REACHED THE TOP! HE REACHED THE SUMMIT THAT HAD TAUNTED MAN! HE HAD CONQUERED NATURE!
VICTORY! I HAVE SCALED THE PEAK! FAME AND THE PRIZE SHALL BELONG TO ERIC VERDIE!
YOU KILLED TO GET IT, ERIC! REMEMBER?

YOU'LL MOCK ME NO MORE, OLGER! THERE MUST BE NO EVIDENCE OF YOUR DEATH!
YOU SEEM UPSET IN YOUR MOMENT OF TRIUMPH, ERIC!

BUT THE SUPERNATURAL WAS STILL TO BE BEATEN...
GOODBYE, FRANZ! HA-HA!

HE LUNGED... HE RELEASED EVERY EMOTION OF HIS BODY...
I---WHAAA! NO!

HE FORGOT THE DIFFERENCE BETWEEN MIND AND MATTER...

AND HE WON HIS PRIZE!
THE END

ADVERTISEMENT

CALLING ALL SPACE RANGERS!

OVER 70 ACTION PACKED SPACE SHIPS FLYING SAUCERS—ROCKETS—MEN FROM MARS etc. ALL FOR $1

MADE OF REALISTIC SPACE COLOR PLASTIC!

YOU CAN ACTUALLY SHOOT ROCKETS INTO SPACE WITH YOUR SPACEPORT ROCKET LAUNCHER.

Safe—Harmless

MOST AMAZING SPACE KIT IN THE UNIVERSE!

Hey Kids, here's a complete Space Patrol Kit for you to lead. You can be squadron leader and direct SPACE BATTLES . . . deploy your rocket ships . . . send them into SPACE.

Now you can try to pioneer unexplored planets using your solar-powered spacemobile. You can try setting up interplanetary observatories, laboratories and radar detecting units . . . Imagine using your cosmic ray neutralizer as protection against deadly cosmic rays . . . Imagine talking to other planets hundreds of light years away. Chase flying saucers and flying discs. Track down Martian spies and rescue 4 Astra Space Beauties. You get a complete squadron . . . 2 spaceport hangars with rocket launchers that you can actually launch 19 rockets into space with — an interplanetary refueler, giant rocket ships, smaller rocket ships, Rocket Men — Mars Men — Beautiful Astra Girls. Every piece is perfectly scaled and is made of long life VINYL.

FREE!

PLASTIC ROCKET GUN!
6 inches long. Sends code with real trigger.
Yours Free For Promptness!
Hurry! Mail Coupon TODAY!

2 Rocket Launchers • 4 Martian Spies • 16 Space Men • 4 Astra Beauties • 2 Space Transports • 2 Refueling Stations • 1 Spacemobile • 2 Moon Rockets • 1 Flying Saucer • 1 Flying Disc • 2 Rocket Ships • 1 Set Fuel Tanks • 1 Space Badge • 2 Observatories • 2 Radar Detectors • 1 Searchlight • 1 Ray Gun • 1 Nuclear Laboratory • 1 Ray Neutralizer • 1 Mystery Planet • 1 Transmitter • 19 Rockets

SPACE SQUADRON 15th Floor • 1860 Broadway, New York 23, N.Y.

MAIL THIS COUPON NOW!

SPACE SQUADRON, 15th FLOOR
1860 BROADWAY, NEW YORK 23, N.Y.
Send .... set(s) of 70 Interplanetary Spacemen, Rocket Ships and Scientific Equipment postpaid. Include FREE GIFT as advertised. Enclosed is $............ Send .... sets. If dissatisfied, I'll return for refund within 10 days but keep the Free Gift.
Name..
Address..
City...................... Zone........ State..........

MONEY BACK IF NOT DELIGHTED

GLORIFY YOUR CAR WITH THESE LEOPARD or COBRA REVERSIBLE

Design SEAT COVERS

For all cars
all makes
all models

SAVE $4.00 NOW

BUY DIRECT 2.95 EACH

NEW! 2 WAY REVERSIBLE!

- **Water & Grease Proof**
- **Fully Fire Retardant**
- **Glamorous Silky Finish**

Try in your car 5 days at MY risk!

NOW! Enjoy these beautiful seat covers for 5 days at **MY** risk! You'll be thrilled with the fine design made famous by **CADILLAC. SAVE** up to **$4.00** on each seat cover you buy! See how they beautify your car and protect the upholstery. Yes! Try them right in your own car **WITHOUT OBLIGATION**—entirely at **MY** risk! If not delighted your money comes right back—no questions asked. You have everything to gain—**NOTHING** to lose!

NEW ADJUSTOMATIC FEATURE!

Slide on . . . slide off . . . in 1 minute

So easy and fast to install! **NEW ADJUSTOMATIC** feature—simply slide on or off in **1 MINUTE FLAT!** You'll love the feel of this genuine **VYNIL** material! It's so silky-looking . . . yet **TOUGH!** Resists **flame, water, grease, grime** and soiling by babies and pets.

LEOPARD-COBRA PATTERN GIVES NEW BEAUTY TO YOUR CAR

No matter how soiled or worn out your upholstery is . . . no matter if you have a 39 Chevvy or a 53 Cadillac, these magnificent **ADJUSTOMATIC** seat covers will add new glamour to your car! Your friends will never imagine you paid so little for these quality covers!

REVERSIBLE 2 WAY PATTERN GIVES YOU DOUBLE USE!

This handsome Seat Cover can be used **TWO** ways— **INSIDE** or **OUT.** It leads 2 lives . . . change over to suit your every whim and desire. You will be delighted with the smart **LEOPARD** or **COBRA SNAKE** pattern. Well made for long satisfying service.

SPECIAL SAVINGS OFFER!

Buy your **ADJUSTOMATIC** Seat Covers by mail—**DIRECT** from the "Seat Cover King." No need to pay up to **6.95** each. Our special volume price only **2.95** each or a set of **TWO** for front and rear for only **5.00.**

You need send no money. Pay the low, low price plus postage on delivery. **SAVE MORE** by sending check, cash, or a money order, and they will be shipped **POST-PAID.**

FREE

OF EXTRA COST

Your Own CAR MONOGRAM

Handsome, GOLDEN HUED, embossed metal initial adds note of distinction to your car. No screws, no drilling. Simply press on—adheres to all metals, plastic, glass, leather, wood. Never mars car finish. GIVEN FREE of extra cost with every order for TWO seat covers. Yours to KEEP even if you return covers for refund! Mention letter desired. Price without covers—only $1.00.

YOUR MONEY BACK IF NOT SATISFIED!

When you receive your **ADJUSTOMATIC** Seat Covers, look them over carefully. Note the special construction details. Then put them in your own car. See how the rich, glamorous pattern highlights the interior of your car. Feel the Vynil material. Use them for **5 FULL DAYS.** You must be delighted **in every way.** If for any reason in the world you **are** not thrilled, return them for a **FULL REFUND** of the purchase price. Don't lose this golden opportunity! Take advantage of these low **SALE** prices! Rush the coupon **NOW!**

MOTO-MATIC COMPANY
Dept. 35-E-150
127 West 33rd Street, New York 1, N. Y.

MOTO-MATIC COMPANY, Dept. 35-E-150
127 West 33rd Street, New York 1, N. Y.

"MR. SEAT COVER KING": Rush..........sets of **REVERSIBLE SEAT COVERS,** as described below, on **5 DAY TRIAL.** I will pay low price plus postage on arrival. You are to refund full price paid if I am not satisfied in **EVERY** way! The **INITIAL** is mine to **KEEP** in any case!

☐ Send FRONT seats — 2.95 ☐ Send BACK seats — 2.95
☐ Send set FRONT & REAR at cut price of 5.00

Write Initial Desired Here

Car MODEL..........YEAR.......... Full or Split front..........
NAME..........
ADDRESS..........
TOWN..........STATE..........

☐ **SAVE MORE** by enclosing **CASH** or **MONEY ORDER** and we pay **ALL POSTAGE CHARGES.** Same **MONEY BACK GUARANTEE!**

You Can WIN
This 15" tall
SILVER TROPHY
JUST AS I DID IN
10 MINUTES
OF FUN
A DAY!
I GAINED
53 LBS. OF SHAPELY
POWER-PACKED
MUSCLES!
Which of these
2 ME'S
is YOU ?
THAT 112 LB.-6 FT.
SPINDLE-ARMED SISSY below WAS ME
A FEW SHORT WEEKS AGO
THIS MAY BE
YOUR LAST
CHANCE
TO GET ALL 5 PICTURE PACKED COURSES FOR 10¢
MILLIONS HAVE
BEEN SOLD FOR
$1 AND MORE
When I enrolled I was a skinny, sick weakling. As you can see in my "Before" Photo I looked like a child... years younger than my age. I was ashamed to take a picture in bathing trunks as I do now. I was shy with girls because I had nothing to show off. A few weeks after starting the Jowett Course my body was the best in the neighborhood. Now I get respect and admiration from every fellow and girl I meet.
Roger D. Hirsch
NEW YORK
NOW
There's that skinny scarecrow ROGER. Let's pass him by!
Roger
Hirsch
before
NO! friend you
don't have to be
SKINNY any more
just mail NOW
the FREE
coupon below
as I did. Soon
YOU can add
6½ inches to your CHEST
3 inches to each ARM
and the rest
in proportion
just as I did.
How to Build A MIGHTY CHEST
How to Build MIGHTY ARMS
How to Build MIGHTY LEGS
How to Build A MIGHTY BACK
How to Build A MIGHTY GRIP
FREE
PHOTO BOOK HOW to Achieve Nerves of Steel, Muscles of Iron
How to BECOME A MIGHTY HE-MAN
Come on, PAL, NOW
YOU GIVE ME
10 PLEASANT MINUTES A
DAY IN YOUR HOME... AND I'LL GIVE
YOU a NEW HE-MAN BODY
For Your OLD SKELETON FRAME.
says George F. Jowett World's Greatest Builder of HE-MEN
GEORGE
F. JOWETT
"Champion of
Champions"
4 times Winner
Perfect
Man Contest
ROGER HIRSCH
was a 112 lb. 6 ft. WEAKLING.
Look at him NOW—
A MOVIE-STAR HE-MAN
from Head to Toe
as YOU
can be
soon!
NO! I don't care how skinny or flabby you are; if you're a teen-ager, in your 20's or 30's or over; if you're short or tall, or what work you do. All I want is JUST 10 EXCITING MINUTES in your home to MAKE YOU OVER by the SAME METHOD I turned myself from a wreck to a Champion of Champions.
YES! You'll see INCH upon INCH of MIGHTY MUSCLE added to YOUR ARMS. Your CHEST deepened. Your BACK AND SHOULDERS broadened. From head to heels, you'll gain SOLIDITY, SIZE, POWER, SPEED! You'll become an ALL-Around, ALL-American HE-MAN, A WINNER in everything you tackle—or my Training won't cost you one solitary cent.
Develop YOUR 520 MUSCLES
Gain Pounds, INCHES, FAST!
Friend, I've traveled the world. Made a LIFETIME STUDY of every way known to develop your body. Then I devised the BEST by TEST, my "5-WAY PROGRESSIVE POWER" the only method that builds you 5-ways fast. You save YEARS, DOLLARS like movie star Tom Tyler did. Like champ Roger Hirsch did. Like MANY THOUSANDS like you did. SO Mail coupon NOW!
MAIL COUPON IN TIME FOR FREE OFFER!
BOTH FREE FOR QUICK ACTION!
1. Photo Book of STRONG MEN
2. MUSCLE METER
Dept. HS-27
"Jowett Courses greatest in World for Building All-Around HE-MEN" —R. F. Kelley Director Physical
JOWETT INSTITUTE OF PHYSICAL TRAINING
230 FIFTH AVENUE, NEW YORK 1, N. Y.
Dear George: Please mail to me FREE Jowett's Photo Book of Strong Men and a Muscle Meter, plus all 5 HE-MAN Building Courses: 1. How to Build a Mighty Chest. 2. How to Build a Mighty Arm. 3. How to Build a Mighty Grip. 4. How to Build a Mighty Back. 5. How to Build Mighty Legs—Now all in One Volume "How to become a Mighty HE-MAN." ENCLOSED FIND 10¢ FOR POSTAGE AND HANDLING (no C.O.D.'s).
NAME AGE
ADDRESS
CITY ZONE STATE

New Styles Demand Smooth, Flat Tummy
Amazing New French Undergarment Girdle Makes You Look Your Best in New Fashions
MOST FLATTERING TUMMY CONTROL EVER CREATED
Wear TUMMY-TRIM with or without a girdle. TUMMY-TRIM is an entirely new kind of lightweight girdle. Its extra FLATTENING pressure is due to the criss-cross design plus a new strength elastic that s-t-r-e-t-c-h-e-s and adjusts automatically to shape your figure. Solid comfort! Better, more healthful posture! Exquisitely made! TUMMY-TRIM will actually improve your figure instantly and continue to better it day by day. The lacy trim completes its all-feminine picture. The four extra-length detachable adjustable garters are scientifically placed for comfort and to glamourize your legs.
Old fashioned girdles spoil your figure instead of improving it. Note how the "bulge" pokes out instead of being flat and graceful. No excuse now because TUMMY-TRIM holds you in.
Here's the modern, up-to-the-minute sylph-trim figure that TUMMY-TRIM will give you. A dramatic change to an eye-full dreamy figure of charm, grace, and desire.
10 DAYS FREE TRIAL
Order today. Send the coupon. Try on and wear your TUMMY-TRIM for 10 days . . . Test it! Examine it! If not 100% delighted with your new figure and the tremendous value, return for prompt refund of the full purchase price. Waist sizes 24 to 30, $2.98. Waist sizes 32 to 48, $3.98.
CUSTOM MADE FEATURES
• Automatically adjusts for perfect fit • Off or on in a jiffy • Lightweight . . . boneless • Extra strength, extra stretch, all-elastic Wonder-Web • Reinforced for long wear • Four 10-inch adjustable garters • Guaranteed to combine style and quality or no cost • Extra flattering—flattening • Girdle that walks with you . . . never will ride up.
FREE TRIAL COUPON
The S. J. Wegman Company, Dept. 117
836 Broadway, New York 3, N. Y.
RUSH my new TUMMY-TRIM three-in-one at once. If I am not thrillingly satisfied, I may return it after 10-day FREE trial for prompt refund of full purchase price.
Size .... (Waist size in inches)
☐ Send C.O.D. I will pay postman, on delivery, cost of the garment plus few cents postage.
☐ I enclose payment. The S. J. Wegman Company will pay postage. Same money-back guarantee.
Name ....
Address ....

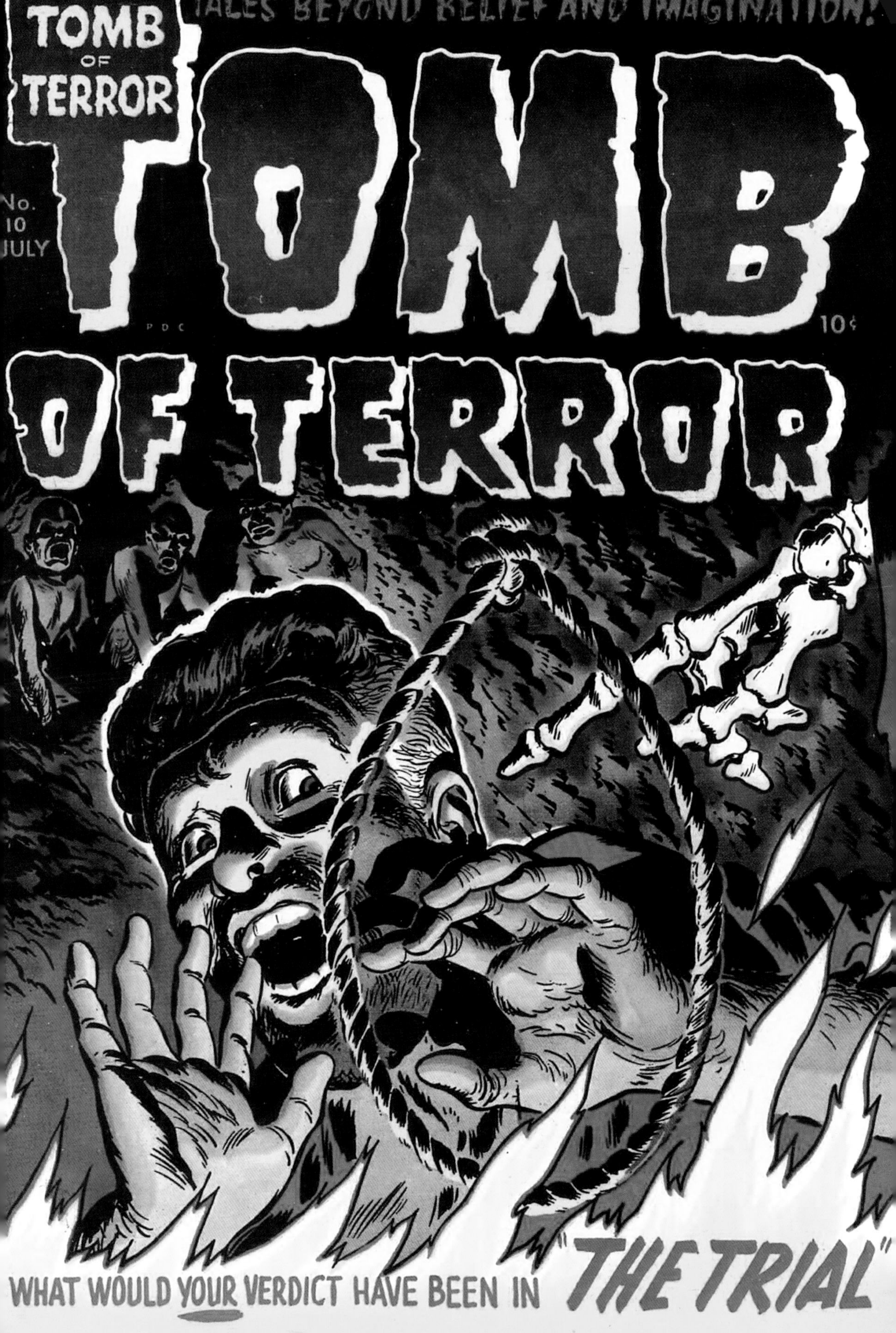
TALES BEYOND BELIEF AND IMAGINATION!
TOMB OF TERROR
TOMB OF TERROR
No. 10 JULY
PDC
10¢
WHAT WOULD YOUR VERDICT HAVE BEEN IN "THE TRIAL"

JUNIOR SPACE PILOTS
ON THE BEAM!
GIVEN!
BOYS! GIRLS! LADIES! MEN!
WE GIVE YOU CASH OR PREMIUMS!
I'M IN A HURRY TO GET BACK TO OUR EARTH BASE, PENNY, THE MAIL MAN'S BRINGING MY NEW CAMERA!
JUMPIN' JUPITER! YOU'RE SURE SIZZLING TH' OL' ROCKET TODAY, TED!
SAY! THAT CAMERA SURE IS SUPERSONIC! YOU MUST HAVE STRUCK A URANIUM LODE!
DIDN'T COST ME A DIME- JUST GOT IT FOR SELLING WHITE CLOVERINE BRAND SALVE!
HURRY AN' GET DE-PRESSURIZED!
MAIL COUPON
Footballs, Pocket Watches, etc.
Fishing Outfits . . . Flashlights . . . 1000 Shot Daisy Air Rifles
ACT NOW!
HURRY
I'VE EARNED A SWELL RADIO AND A TELESCOPE TOO! IT'S EASY SELLING TO YOUR FRIENDS - AND YOU GIVE 'EM THESE SWELL ART PICTURES-
THAT'S FOR ME!
TRAINING BASE
OUTTA MY JET TRAIL, MATES - I'M MAILING THE COUPON FOR THAT BIG NEW PREMIUM CATALOG NOW!
U.S. MAIL
R.T.
WE ARE RELIABLE!
Cameras, Corn Poppers, Speedball Cartoon Sets, Aluminum Ware, Blankets (sent postage paid). Mail coupon for SALVE and pictures to start.
ACT NOW
Ukeleles, Watches, Lovable Dolls.
WHITE CLOVERINE BRAND SALVE PRICE 35¢
OUR 58th YEAR
Alarm Clocks, Pen & Pencil Sets, etc. Mail coupon.
NU BRITE
LET'S GO!
MAIL COUPON!
GET BIG CATALOG!
Candid Cameras with carrying case, Telescopes, Watches (sent postage paid). SIMPLY GIVE pictures with White CLOVERINE Brand SALVE easily sold to friends, neighbors, relatives at 35c a box (with picture). Alarm Clocks, Pen & Pencil Sets, Bibles, Billfolds, Telescopes, Roller Skates, Blankets, Aluminum Ware, Record Players, Movie Machines (postage pd.). Rush coupon to start!
Guaranteed by Good Housekeeping
LET'S GO!
ACT NOW
Radios, Candid Cameras with carrying cases, Telescopes, Roller Skates (sent postage paid) . . . Mail coupon to start.
BE FIRST
KEYSTONE
Food Choppers, Carving Sets, Bibles. Mail coupon.
HIGH SCHOOL
WE TRUST YOU!
.22 Cal. Rifles, Archery Sets, School Boxes, Wallets. Mail coupon for SALVE and pictures to start.
WE TRUST YOU!
OUR 58th YEAR!
LOOK!
Footballs, Telescopes (sent postage paid). Boys', Girls' Bicycles (express chgs. collect).
LET'S GO!
ACT NOW!
Boys', Girls' Wrist Watches, Baking Sets, Typewriters, etc.
Lucite Dresser Sets, Cook Books, etc.
ACT NOW!
Red Ryder
OUR 58th YEAR - WE ARE RELIABLE! MAIL
MAIL NOW!
Wilson Chemical Co., Dept. 25, Tyrone, Pa. Date..........
Gentlemen:- Please send me on trial 14 colorful art pictures with 14 boxes of White CLOVERINE Brand SALVE to sell at 35c a box (with picture). I will remit amount asked within 30 days, select a Premium or keep Cash Commission as explained under Premium wanted in catalog sent with order, postage paid to start.
NAME .... AGE ....
ST. .... R. D. .... BOX ....
TOWN .... ZONE NO. .... STATE ....
PRINT LAST NAME HERE
Paste coupon on postal card or mail in envelope today

We've opened the doors to the TOMB OF TERROR once more. So come into the magazine that dares to be different!

And this month, we've got something new and startling to show off to you. It's a new twist in terror, a new thrill in suspense! And it's going to be a regular feature of the TOMB OF TERROR!

We call it our "Boo of the Month!" And we're going back to some of our most famous classics for our stories. But what we're going to do with them...well, you'll see for yourself.

Our first story in the series is called, "Noah's Argh!" You can guess where that came from, but from then on you;re in for a string of surprises straight through to the shocking climax.

But that's only one thing you'll find in this month's issue. There's a BIG JOKE that you just won't want to miss. You'll find out if A ROSE IS A ROSE. And you'll attend THE TRIAL of your life.

And keep us posted on YOUR feelings of the TOMB OF TERROR. Let us know if you think we're riding the right track to terror!

Write to:

TOMB OF TERROR
1860 Broadway
New York 23, N.Y.

TOMB OF TERROR, July, 1953, Vol. 1, No. 10, is published every other month by HARVEY PUBLICATIONS, INC., at 420 DeSoto Avenue, St. Louis 7, Mo. Editorial, Advertising and Executive offices, 1860 Broadway, New York 23, N. Y. President Alfred Harvey; Vice-President and Editor, Leon Harvey; Vice-President and Business Manager, Robert B. Harvey. Entered as second-class matter at the Post Office at St. Louis, Mo., under the Act of March 3, 1879. Single copies, 10c. Subscription rates, 10 issues for $1.00 in the U. S. and possessions, elsewhere $1.50. All names in this periodical are entirely fictitious and no identification with actual persons is intended. Contents copyrighted, 1953, by Harvey Features Syndicate, New York City. Printed in the U. S. A.

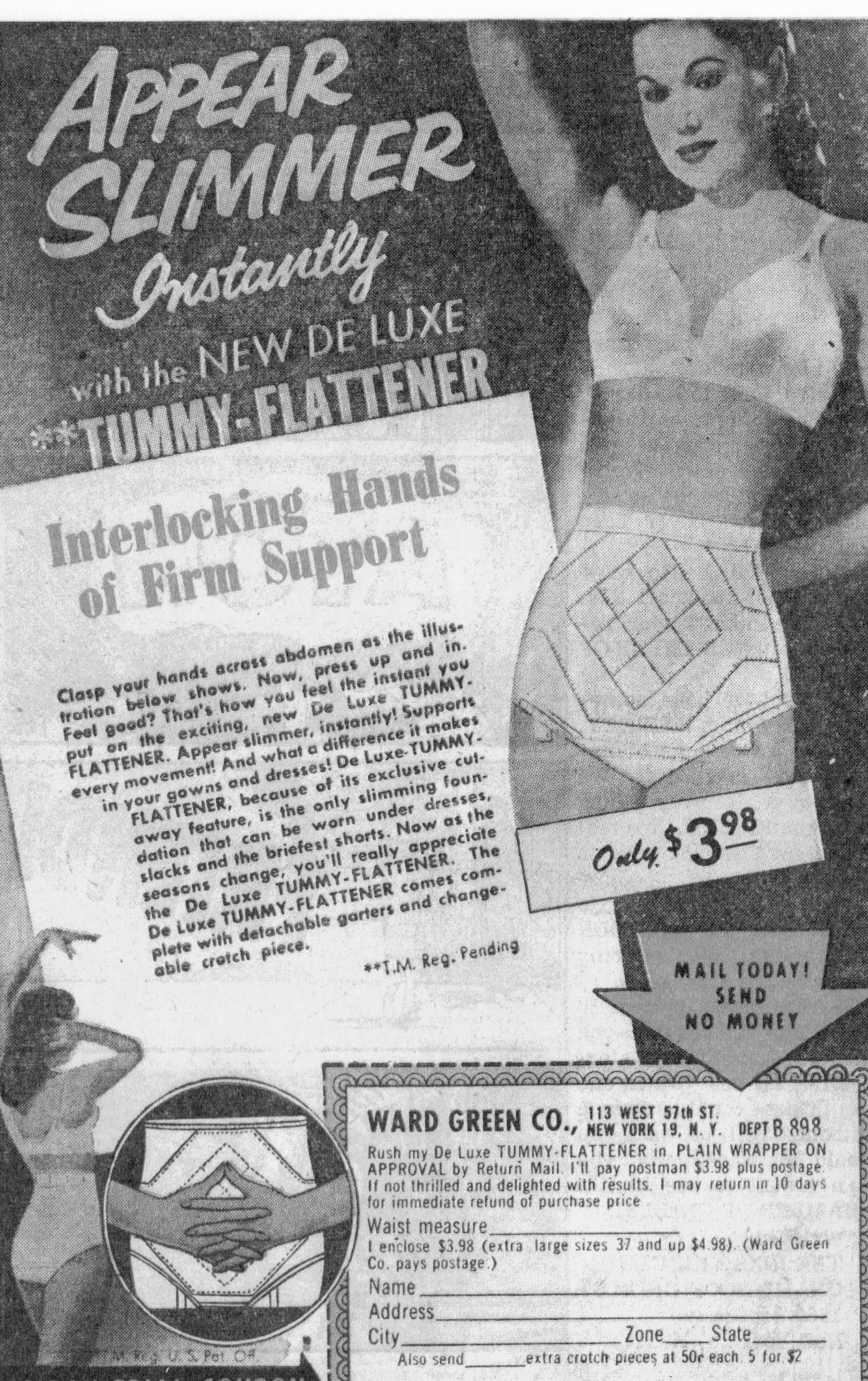

APPEAR SLIMMER Instantly
with the NEW DE LUXE
**TUMMY-FLATTENER
Interlocking Hands of Firm Support
Clasp your hands across abdomen as the illustration below shows. Now, press up and in. Feel good? That's how you feel the instant you put on the exciting, new De Luxe TUMMY-FLATTENER. Appear slimmer, instantly! Supports every movement! And what a difference it makes in your gowns and dresses! De Luxe-TUMMY-FLATTENER, because of its exclusive cut-away feature, is the only slimming foundation that can be worn under dresses, slacks and the briefest shorts. Now as the seasons change, you'll really appreciate the De Luxe TUMMY-FLATTENER. The De Luxe TUMMY-FLATTENER comes complete with detachable garters and changeable crotch piece.
**T.M. Reg. Pending
Only $3.98
MAIL TODAY! SEND NO MONEY
T.M. Reg. U.S. Pat. Off.
10-DAY TRIAL COUPON
WARD GREEN CO., 113 WEST 57th ST. NEW YORK 19, N. Y. DEPT B 898
Rush my De Luxe TUMMY-FLATTENER in PLAIN WRAPPER ON APPROVAL by Return Mail. I'll pay postman $3.98 plus postage. If not thrilled and delighted with results, I may return in 10 days for immediate refund of purchase price
Waist measure____________
I enclose $3.98 (extra large sizes 37 and up $4.98). (Ward Green Co. pays postage.)
Name____________
Address____________
City____________ Zone______ State______
Also send______extra crotch pieces at 50¢ each. 5 for $2

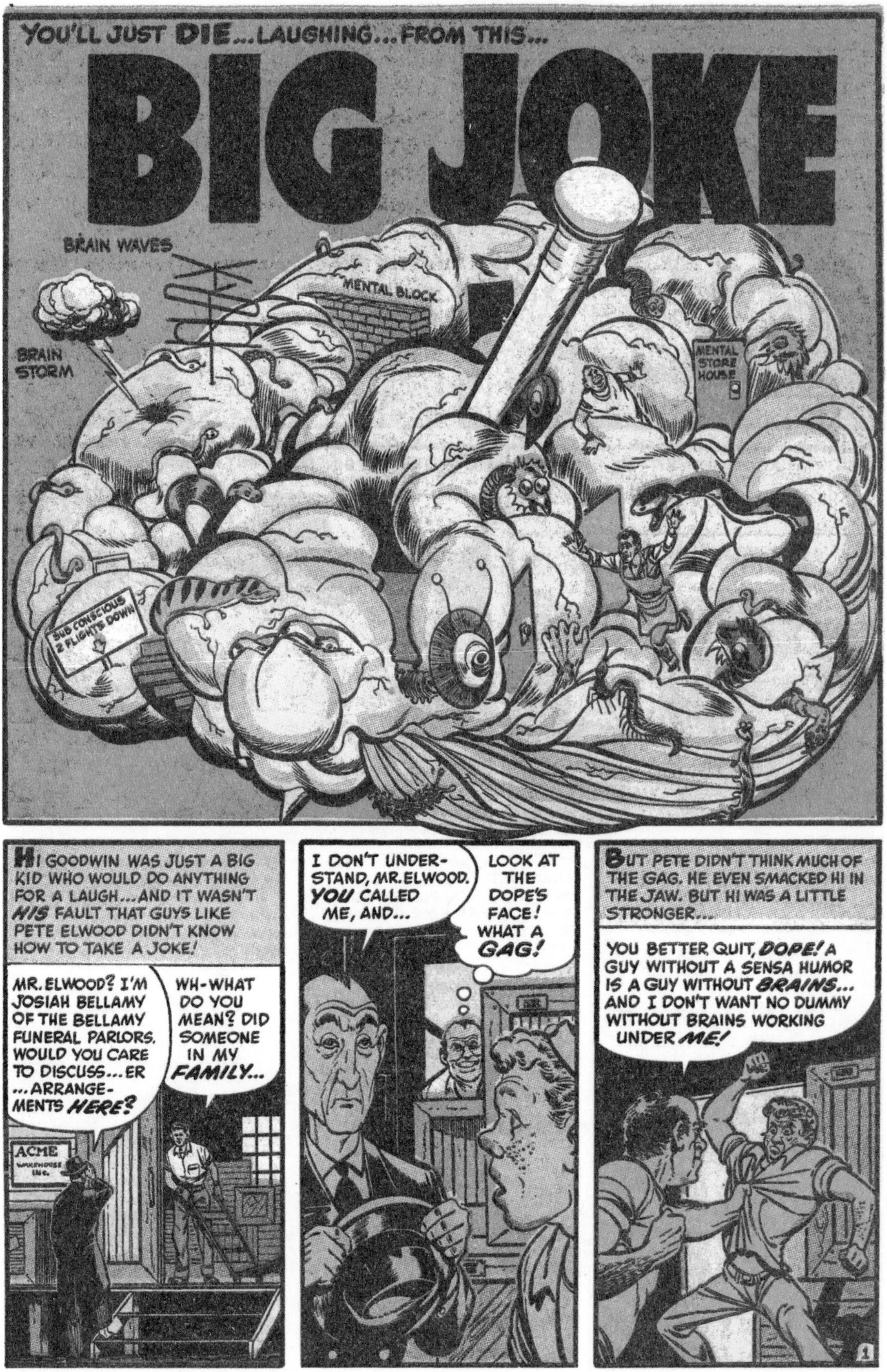

YOU'LL JUST **DIE**... LAUGHING... FROM THIS...

BIG JOKE

BRAIN WAVES

MENTAL BLOCK

BRAIN STORM

MENTAL STORE HOUSE

SUB CONSCIOUS 2 FLIGHTS DOWN

HI GOODWIN WAS JUST A BIG KID WHO WOULD DO ANYTHING FOR A LAUGH... AND IT WASN'T *HIS* FAULT THAT GUYS LIKE PETE ELWOOD DIDN'T KNOW HOW TO TAKE A JOKE!

MR. ELWOOD? I'M JOSIAH BELLAMY OF THE BELLAMY FUNERAL PARLORS. WOULD YOU CARE TO DISCUSS... ER ... ARRANGEMENTS *HERE?*

WH-WHAT DO YOU MEAN? DID SOMEONE IN MY *FAMILY...*

ACME WAREHOUSE INC.

I DON'T UNDERSTAND, MR. ELWOOD. *YOU* CALLED ME, AND...

LOOK AT THE DOPE'S FACE! WHAT A *GAG!*

BUT PETE DIDN'T THINK MUCH OF THE GAG. HE EVEN SMACKED HI IN THE JAW. BUT HI WAS A LITTLE STRONGER...
YOU BETTER QUIT, *DOPE!* A GUY WITHOUT A SENSA HUMOR IS A GUY WITHOUT *BRAINS...* AND I DON'T WANT NO DUMMY WITHOUT BRAINS WORKING UNDER *ME!*

SO THAT'S HOW JOE MELSNER GOT PETE'S JOB...
I'M..ER..JOE MELSNER. I UNDERSTAND I'M TO BE YOUR...ER.. ASSISTANT, MR.GOODWIN?
GLAD TO MEET YA, PAL. AND CAN THAT MR.GOODWIN STUFF. JUST CALL ME HI!

YOU AND ME'S GONNA BE REAL BUDDIES, KID. ESPECIALLY IF YOU GOT A GOOD SENSA HUMOR!
OH, YES INDEED, I HAVE, MR.. ER..HI! I'VE ALWAYS..ER..SAID THAT IT'S MOST IMPORTANT TO BE..ER..CON-GENIAL AT WORK!
HANDLE WITH CARE

THAT WAS HI'S PHILOSOPHY TOO... AND HE SHOWED HOW CONGENIAL HE WAS THAT VERY DAY! HE FELL BACK INTO A JUNGLE OF CRATES, AND...
PULL ME UP GENTLE, JOE. MY ARM... IT FEELS KINDA FUNNY!
JUST RELAX, HI. I... ER... I'LL BE REAL GENTLE!

JOE TRIED TO BE GENTLE, BUT HE MUST HAVE PULLED A TRIFLE TOO HARD...
OWWWW! MY ARM!
AAHHHHH!

EEEEHHH!
HEH-HEH! YOU CAN KEEP THAT ONE! I STILL GOT TWO LEFT!

SNAP OUT OF IT, KID. IT'S A JOKE! GO AHEAD... LAUGH!
GU-GU--OH.. PLEASE, NO, MR.GOODWIN. NEVER DO ANY-THING LIKE THAT AGAIN! I..I GOT A WEAK HEART! I...I CAN'T TAKE IT!

WHADDYE MEAN YA CAN'T TAKE IT? AIN'T YA GOT A SENSA HUMOR? AIN'T YA GOT A BRAIN? A GUY WITH BRAINS DON'T GET UPSET OVER A JOKE... YA HEAR?
2

NOW FORGET ABOUT IT AN' LET'S EAT! IT'S TIME TO KNOCK OFF FOR LUNCH.
OH, NO... NOT NOW. I.. I COULDN'T EAT AFTER THAT!

WHADDYE MEAN YA CAN'T EAT? YOU WANNA WORK WITH ME, YOU GOTTA BE SOCIABLE! I DON'T LIKE TO EAT ALONE!
WELL.. ER.. ALL RIGHT. GUESS I... ER... I'LL HAVE LUNCH, TOO.

I'LL TAKE A... EEEEAAAHHH!
WHAT'S THE MATTER NOW?

LOOK... IN MY SANDWICH.. A.. A.. DEAD M-MOUSE!
NO WONDER YOU DIDN'T WANNA EAT. HOW CAN A GUY WHO BRINGS A MOUSE SANDWICH BE HUNGRY. WONDER WHO --HEH-HEH- PUT IT THERE!

POOR JOE, HE JUST DIDN'T HAVE A SENSE OF HUMOR. HI TRIED TO GET A LAUGH OUT OF HIM, BUT THE MORE HE TRIED, THE MORE TERRIFIED JOE GOT. THEN ONE EVENING JUST BEFORE QUITTING TIME...

THE LIGHTS... MUST HAVE BLOWN A FUSE. OH, DEAR... WHERE WAS THAT FLASH-LIGHT?

HI MUST HAVE SPENT DAYS FIGURING THAT ONE OUT. IT WORKED REAL GOOD!

JOE MELSNER, YOUR TIME HAS COME! TAKE MY HAND AND TOGETHER WE WILL JOURNEY INTO THE LAND BEYOND!
NO... NO! GET AWAY! I DON'T WANNA DIE!

JOE BACKED UP SO FAST THAT BY THE TIME HI TURNED ON THE LIGHTS AGAIN...

CRASH
LOOK.. IT'S ME... IN A LUMINOUS COSTUME! YA DOPE! AIN'T YA GOT ANY BRAINS? GET AWAY FROM THAT WINDOW!

THAT'S LUCK FOR YOU. A GUY FIGURES OUT A *PERFECT GAG*, AND THEN A DUMB IMBECILE WITHOUT BRAINS RUINS IT ALL! HI COULDN'T EVEN GET A LAUGH OUT OF IT... MATTER OF FACT HE WAS PRETTY *SCARED* UNTIL...

NASTY SKULL FRACTURE... LOT OF BONE SPLINTERED... BUT WE'RE PULLING HIM THROUGH WITH SOME SPECIAL TECHNIQUES.

JOE COULD HAVE HAD HIS REVENGE THEN, BUT HE NEVER DID LIKE TROUBLE...

PLEASE, KID... DON'T TELL 'EM WHAT HAPPENED. I SAID IT WAS AN *ACCIDENT*, AND THE COMPANY WILL PAY YOUR DOCTOR BILL. I'LL LAY OFF YA WHEN YOU GET BACK!
OKAY, HI. JUST SO YOU LEARNED YOUR LESSON!

HI KEPT HIS WORD FOR A GOOD LONG WHILE, BUT THEN HE GOT TO THINKING...
GIMME A HAND WITH THIS CRATE, WILL YA, HI?
HE CAN HANDLE IT HIMSELF. EVER SINCE HE BOUNCED ON THAT DUMB HEAD OF HIS, I GOTTA *CRAWL* SOON AS HE OPENS HIS YAP!

I GOTTA SHOW HIM I'M BOSS AROUND HERE... AND THERE'S ONLY *ONE WAY* TO DO IT!

SO LATER THAT DAY...
HEY, JOE... OPEN THAT CRATE, WILL YA? I'M BUSY HERE.
SURE, HI.
HERE IT... *EEEYIII!*
HA-HA! STILL THE *SAME* JOE, AREN'T YA?
THAT OPERATION ON YOUR HEAD DIDN'T HELP... DID IT? *YOU STILL GOT NO BRAINS!*

JOE SHOULD HAVE BEEN TREMBLING... BUT AFTER THAT FIRST SHOCK HE WASN'T SCARED ANY MORE. HE JUST SMILED... KIND OF STRANGE...
I WAS HOPING YOU WOULDN'T TRY THAT STUFF AGAIN, HI... FOR YOUR SAKE!
HANDLE WITH CARE

WH-WHAT DO YOU MEAN, JOE.. FOR MY SAKE?
YOU SEE, HI, WHEN I WAS IN THE HOSPITAL, I FOUND OUT YOU WERE WRONG. I FOUND OUT I REALLY DO HAVE BRAINS!

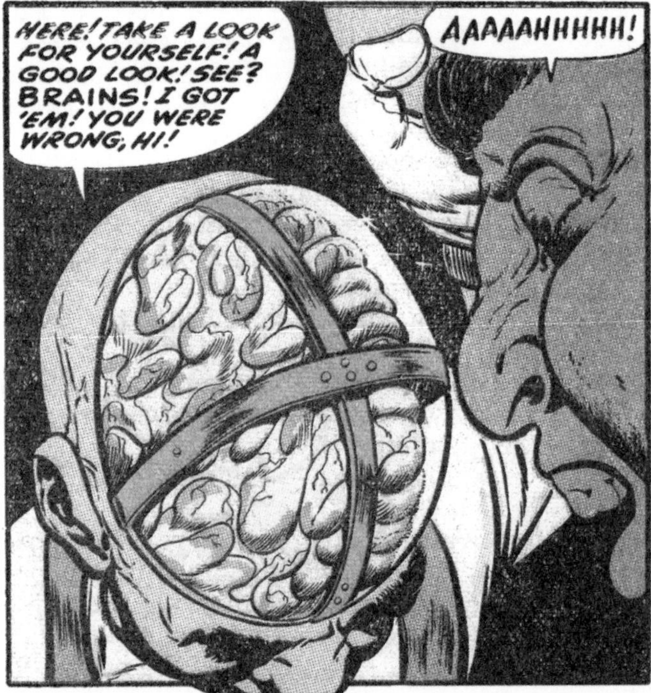
HERE! TAKE A LOOK FOR YOURSELF! A GOOD LOOK! SEE? BRAINS! I GOT 'EM! YOU WERE WRONG, HI!
AAAAAHHHHH!

THEY GOTTA TREAT ME EVERY MONTH, SO THEY PUT ON A REMOVABLE PLATE! NOW I KNOW I GOT BRAINS! GET IT? IT'S A JOKE, PAL... LAUGH! GO AHEAD ...LAUGH, DOPE ...LAUGH!
Y//////!

JOE SCREWED THE PLATE BACK ON AGAIN... AND THEN HE SMILED. BY THAT TIME, HI'S SCREAMING HAD ATTRACTED QUITE AN AUDIENCE...
BUH-- BUH-- GOOG--. GAAA...
WHAT'S THE MATTER WITH HIM?
CAN'T YOU TELL FROM THE WAY HE TALKS WHAT'S WRONG WITH HIM?

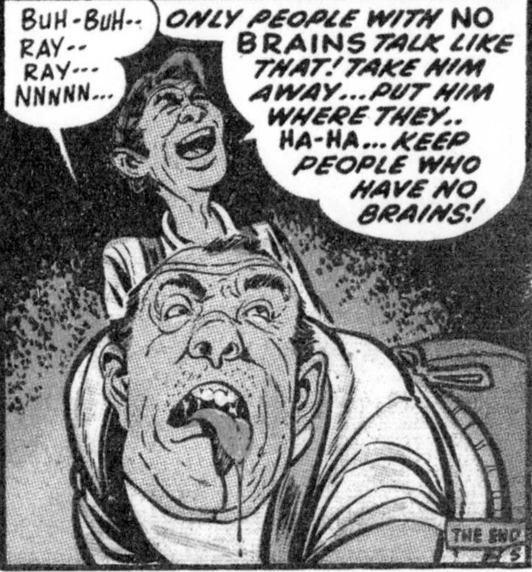
BUH-BUH-- RAY-- RAY--- NNNNN...
ONLY PEOPLE WITH NO BRAINS TALK LIKE THAT! TAKE HIM AWAY... PUT HIM WHERE THEY.. HA-HA... KEEP PEOPLE WHO HAVE NO BRAINS!
THE END

MURDER FOR SALE

The train hooted through the night's storm. Outside the rain beat down like hoof-beats. Inside the train, few people spoke.

The train halted now at a whistle-stop. A man dashed on leading a trail of muddied water. "Ticket, sir," asked the conductor.

The man obliged without saying a word. Then he walked through one of the cars and found himself a seat near the window.

There weren't more than five people in the car, each of them having a cherished seat near the window. But now a man was giving up his seat near the window. He was coming toward the new arrival.

"Mind if I sit next to you," he said.

The man just shook his head.

"How've you been, Pete?" the man asked the new arrival.

"How'd you know my name?" was the answer.

"Oh, I know even more than that," said the man, and he smiled.

"Like what?" asked Pete.

"Like what you're going to do... like how you got your new job."

"You sound smart, mister," said Pete. "If you keep talking, I'll be listening."

"Well, about five hours ago, you got a telephone call from a guy named Glisson. You never heard of him before. But he must have heard of you. He told you he had a job for you. Am I right so far, Pete?"

"Just keep talking, and I'll keep listening."

"He wanted you to kill a man for him. To kill a guy at the Percyville Station. He said he'd pay you ten thousand. You agreed. You picked up five thousand at the Biltmore Hotel. You'll pick up another five thousand there two hours from now. How'm I doing?"

"You sound like a pretty smart egg, mister," said Pete. "Your name's Glisson, huh?"

"Oh, don't jump to conclusions, Pete! Why don't you take a good look at me. Didn't Mr. Glisson say that the guy would be wearing a brown tweed coat. Isn't that the color of mine?"

Pete looked, and it was true.

"How about the color of the hat, Pete? Didn't he say it would be dark brown with an odd green plaid band? Just like mine, eh, Pete?"

Pete's breaths were coming in gasps now.

"And, Pete, remember what he told you would be the clincher? The scar on the right side of the face!"

The man turned his head, and Pete saw the scar! Then he got up.

"We're coming into Percyville now, Pete," he said. "I guess I'll be going."

The man was walking down the aisle. Then he stopped, and turned around toward Pete. "By the way," he said. "I never introduced myself. The name's Glisson!" And he walked toward the door.

WHY WE CALL IT
BLUE MONDAY
IT WAS SAID THAT CAIN WAS BORN ON A MONDAY...AND THAT IT WAS ON A MONDAY THAT HE KILLED ABEL!

THE CITIES OF SODOM AND GOMORRAH WERE DESTROYED BY FIRE BECAUSE OF THEIR UNNATURAL WICKEDNESS...ON A MONDAY!

IT WAS SAID THE JUDAS BETRAYED CHRIST...ON A MONDAY!

THE IDES OF MARCH...THE DAY OF JULIUS CAESAR'S DEATH...WAS A MONDAY!

BARROOM!
THE BRITISH DESTROYED THE SPANISH ARMADA...ON A MONDAY!

MARIE ANTOINETTE RODE TO HER DEATH...ON A MONDAY!

OUR CLASSICS HAVE BEEN FORGOTTEN --*TILL NOW!* SO IN THE INTERESTS OF *CULTURE*, WE GO TO THE BOOKSHELF AND TAKE OUT OUR *BOO OF THE MONTH* SELECTION, WHICH WE CALL...

NOAH'S ARG-H!

NO-AHH!

WHY DOESN'T SHE LET ME *ALONE*?
NOOA

AH!

SO NOAH GARNERED ALL HIS STRENGTH...AND WENT TO THE WOMAN WHO CALLED HIS NAME!
Y-YES, RHODA... WHAT IS IT?
COME IN HERE! WHY DIDN'T YOU COME WHEN I CALLED YOU?

I-I JUST WANTED TO BE ALONE!
THAT'S A SCREAM! YOU'RE THE CARETAKER OF THIS ISLAND... WHERE NOBODY LIVES... EXCEPT YOU AND I...AND YOU WANTED TO BE ALONE! WELL, MR. ALONE-- YOU HAVE A CHORE TO DO!

GO CHOP SOME FIRE-WOOD FOR THE STOVE! AND... HURRY BACK!
YES, RHODA, DEAR!

SO NOAH WENT TO CHOP WOOD! IT WAS DARK... BUT HIS HATE SEEMED TO LIGHT UP THE WOODS AROUND HIM!
WHY DID I MARRY HER? IF I ONLY COULD ESCAPE?!! BUT... HOW? IF I HAD A PLANE... OR A BOAT...?!!

A BOAT! WHY NOT? I COULD BUILD ONE-- AND SAIL AWAY!

I'LL BUILD A BOAT...WITHOUT HER KNOWING IT! I'LL FLOAT AWAY FROM RHODA!
2

THAT NIGHT... NOAH BEGAN TO PUT HIS IDEA INTO EFFECT, WHILE RHODA SLEPT... HE DID NOT!

AND IT WAS BY A STREAM FAR FROM THE HOUSE THAT NOAH STARTED HIS WORK!
AH! SO FAR... SO GOOD! BUT... I'VE GOT A LOT OF WORK AHEAD OF ME... MANY MORE NIGHTS OF WORK!

BUT NOAH WAS A HARD WORKER. AFTER MANY WEEKS HIS LITTLE BOAT BEGAN TO TAKE SHAPE!
SOON... VERY SOON... I'LL SAIL AWAY!

AND FINALLY NOAH COMPLETED HIS LITTLE BOAT!
FINISHED! TOMORROW NIGHT... I'LL SHOVE OFF!

AND THE NEXT NIGHT!
I'LL FINALLY BE ALONE! GOODBYE, ISLAND... GOODBYE, RHO...

BUT...
NOOAAH!

RHODA!
IT'S NOT YOUR AUNT TILLY! YOU STUPID MAN! DO YOU THINK I DIDN'T KNOW WHAT YOU WERE DOING...ALL THESE NIGHTS?!! I'VE WATCHED YOU!

BUT... YOU'LL NEVER BE ALONE! NEVER! NEV...
OH, NO!

WE'LL SEE... ABOUT THAT!
NOAH ... DON'T! I DIDN'T... NOOA-A-A...

SHE NEVER LIVED TO FINISH HER SCREAM. AND NOAH EASILY PUSHED HIS LITTLE BOAT INTO THE STREAM!
GOODBYE, RHODA! NOW... I'M ALONE!

AND HIS LITTLE BOAT SAILED DOWN THE STREAM ... AND INTO THE OCEAN!
SAILING...SAILING...OVER THE BOUND-RY MAIN...

HMM! IT LOOKS LIKE WE'LL HAVE SOME RAIN!
4

AND IT RAINED HARD!

AND THE RAIN BECAME A TEMPEST...

AND THE RAIN LASTED FOR MANY DAYS AND NIGHTS...

UNTIL FINALLY IT STOPPED IN A BLAST OF SUNSHINE!

I WONDER WHERE I AM? THE WATERS SEEM TO BE... RECEDING!

AND IT WAS THEN THAT NOAH REALIZED SOMETHING...

FOR NOAH WAS ALONE...REALLY ALONE... FINALLY ALONE...FOREVER! AND ALL THAT COULD BE HEARD WAS NOAH'S...
ARGHH
THE END

WITH THIS OFFER

EVERY BOY AND GIRL LOVES THESE CLEAN LITTLE PETS. DELIVERED HEALTHY AND SAFE IN A SPECIAL MOSS-PROTECTED PACKAGE.

Here's one of the most exciting toys you've ever owned. Just think — a baby turtle all your own. What's more, a real growing garden to keep him in, a garden you plant and grow all by yourself. You can teach him to recognize you when you feed him. Watch him swim — see how he pulls his head and feet into his shell when he's frightened. You can have turtle races — you can make a little house for him to live in — and all the time you can watch how the lovely, soft grass grows — see and smell the beautiful flowers. You'll amaze your friends with how much you know about animals and plants.

MAGIC ROCK GARDEN

Grows Real Grass & Flowers in 4 Days

only $1.69

HERE'S OUR OFFER

You pay only $1.69 for the rock garden and turtle . . . AND . . . you must be 100% delighted or money back. Only 3 orders to a customer with this special offer. Hurry Coupon!

FEATURES

Everything You Need

You get all these items — you don't need anything else. Plenty of Magic grass seeds . . . Magic soil, lovely flower seeds . . . Practical attractive container . . . Bright-colored metal butterfly . . . American Flag . . . Parasol that opens and closes . . . Simulated rocks. Plant food. Many other exciting features.

Magic Seeds in Magic Soil

A real growing Rock Garden — about 100 square inches of sweet grass and bright lovely flowers — for you to care for. When the flowers grow you can pluck a bouquet for your mother or friend. When the grass grows too high you will have to cut and trim it. And all the time you will have a beautiful garden you can be proud of and show off to your friends. You'll learn many useful things, too — it will even help you understand many things they teach at school.

10 DAY TRIAL FREE!

Honor House Products Corp. 15th Floor
1860 Broadway, New York 23, N.Y.

Rush my Rock Garden and live baby turtle at once. If I am not completely satisfied I may return the garden for prompt refund of the full purchase price, and I may keep the turtle ABSOLUTELY FREE. Price is $1.69

☐ Enclosed find $.................... in full payment.
☐ Send C.O.D. I'll pay postman, plus C.O.D. fee on delivery.

NAME..............................

ADDRESS..............................

HARVEY FAMOUS NAME COMICS

are loved by MILLIONS

Get your copies NOW at all Newsstands!

LOOK FOR THE HARVEY SEAL!

YOUR SYMBOL OF A TOP COMIC!

"Hey YOU SKINNY You look like SOMETHING THE CAT DRAGGED IN!"
the boys yelled as I dragged myself into the gym, says Jowett Pupil, Gleason R. Cleveland. Then I gained 70 lbs and made the football team.
CLEVELAND BEFORE 90 lb. Skeleton
GLEASON CLEVELAND AFTER JOWETT TRAINING 160 lbs. of Muscle
Come on, PAL, NOW YOU do as I did
in 10 EASY MINUTES of FUN a day
Get a NEW HE-MAN BODY
For Your OLD SKELETON FRAME!
I GAINED 60 LBS.
of SHAPELY MIGHTY MUSCLES
Mail the "ALL-FREE" coupon get this "AMAZING "SECRETS" Photo Book while you can.
FREE!
AMAZING SECRETS How to WIN MUSCLES like IRON NERVES of STEEL World's Great EXPERT Tells You How YOU Can BECOME An All-Around ALL-AMERICAN HE-MAN in 10 MINUTES of FUN A DAY IN YOUR HOME
PHOTO BOOK
FREE
while they last!
Now wouldn't YOU Like To Have A New Body Like Mine? I added
7 INCHES to my CHEST
3½ INCHES to each ARM
and to the rest of my body in proportion as YOU can
Yours John Sill UTAH
This Book will also show You HOW YOU CAN WIN $100.00 and A BIG 15" tall SILVER TROPHY (Your Name On It) as I have just done.
You'll LOOK like A Real HE-MAN!
WIN WOMEN AND MEN FRIENDS
You'll FEEL like A Real HE-MAN!
Full of New Strength and Self-Confidence
You'll ACT like A Real HE-MAN!
Win in Sports! Win Promotion, Praise, Popularity. Make More Money.
Let's go, young fellow, Now YOU give me
10 PLEASANT MINUTES A DAY IN YOUR HOME
LIKE SLIM JOHN SILL DID and I'll give YOU a New HE-MAN BODY as I gave MANY Thousands like You
NO! I don't care how skinny or flabby you are. I'll make you OVER by the SAME method I turned myself from a wreck to the strongest of the strong. Why can't I do for you what I did for MANY THOUSANDS of skinny fellows like You?
Develop YOUR 520 MUSCLES
Gain Pounds, INCHES FAST!
YES! You'll see INCHES of MIGHTY MUSCLE added to your ARMS and CHEST. Your BACK and SHOULDERS broadened. From head to heels, you'll gain SIZE, POWER, SPEED. You'll be A WINNER in EVERYTHING you tackle.
John Sill was a 125 lb Skinny Weakling
Before $1 price goes back
YOUR LAST CHANCE TO GET ALL 5 FREE!
PICTURE PACKED COURSES MILLIONS HAVE BEEN SOLD FOR $1 AND MORE
Just send me a dime for postage and handling
How to Build A MIGHTY BACK
How to Build MIGHTY ARMS
How to Build A MIGHTY CHEST
How to Build MIGHTY LEGS
How to BECOME A MIGHTY HE-MAN
How to Build A MIGHTY GRIP
ONLY MY 5-WAY PROGRESSIVE POWER SYSTEM BUILDS YOU 5-WAYS FAST SO YOU SAVE YEARS AND DOLLARS!
GEORGE F. JOWETT "Champion of Champions" 4 times Winner Perfect Man Contest
like John BECOME A MOVIE STAR HE-MAN
LAST CHANCE — ALL FREE COUPON!
1. Photo Book of STRONG MEN
2. MUSCLE METER 3. FIVE COURSES
DEPT. HS37
Tell Me How To WIN $100, etc.
JOWETT INSTITUTE OF PHYSICAL TRAINING
220 FIFTH AVENUE, NEW YORK 1, N. Y.
Dear George: Please mail to me FREE Jowett's Photo Book of Strong Men and a Muscle Meter, plus all 5 HE-MAN Building Courses: 1. How to Build a Mighty Chest 2. How to Build a Mighty Arm 3. How to Build a Mighty Grip 4. How to Build a Mighty Back 5. How to Build Mighty Legs—Now all in One Volume "How to become a Mighty HE-MAN." ENCLOSED FIND 10c FOR POSTAGE AND HANDLING (no C.O.D.'s)
NAME AGE
ADDRESS
CITY ZONE STATE
SAVES you YEARS and DOLLARS!!!
Mail Coupon in Time for FREE offer and PRIZES!

How 'BLACK BEAUTY' TURNS AN ALSO-RAN into "VIDEO VIC!"

JOE BONOMO
World's Strongman. Hercules of the Screen. International Authority on Health & Strength.

DEVELOP REAL POWER

INCREASE YOUR STRENGTH • BUILD YOUR BODY

FREE
3 CABLE
'BLACK BEAUTY'
EXERCISER
(Worth 3.95 alone)

BECOME AN ALL-AROUND WINNER

WIN FRIENDS • GAIN POPULARITY • BE A SUCCESS

LOOK AT WHAT YOU GET!

This big action-packed 3-CABLE COURSE is literally packed with dynamite . . . every word batted out for you by Joe Bonomo himself. Many of today's strongmen paid $25.00 for these same instructions as a personalized mail order course. You get it now for only $2.95 . . . including Joe Bonomo's famous *'Black Beauty'* 3-CABLE EXERCISER as a FREE gift to you. Don't wait! Act RIGHT AWAY!

Free SMCA Membership Card
FREE membership in the Strongmen's Club of America also included to those who act right away!

STRONGMEN'S CLUB OF AMERICA Dept. HR
1860 Broadway, New York 23, N. Y.

JOE BONOMO SHOWS YOU HOW!

Why grope in the dark always wishing? Why let other guys run off with the best of everything? Specially when you CAN be the most popular fellow in your class. Just let mighty Joe Bonomo and Black Beauty show you how easy it is. Think of it! Just a few minutes a day is all it takes to put you in the LEADER-WINNER-ATHLETE class . . . "tops" in popularity.

Scientific? And how! Just wait and see!

Joe Bonomo's big action-packed Cable Course is loaded with dynamite . . . 96 complete pages that tell you how . . . hundreds of photos, diagrams and charts that show you how. Your "Black Beauty" 3-Cable Exerciser (given to you FREE) is designed by Joe Bonomo himself . . . the world's strongman and "hercules-of-the-screen." You can be sure of the best. But, don't wait! Act right away!

Bernarr Macfadden says:

"As an instructor in muscle building you should stand at the head of the list Many of your pupils already attest to your ability in building better bodies. I can recommend you most highly Here's wishing you all possible success!"

Jack Dempsey says:

"I consider your Course tops for all-around physical development—power strength—endurance. The secrets and short cuts you reveal with your system of body development are miraculous and I cannot endorse your course too highly."

CUT OUT THE DREAMING!

Strongmen think fast . . . act fast! Now that you've made up your mind . . . do something about it quickly! Get going! Send your order in right away!

ACT NOW FOR FREE OFFER

STRONGMEN'S CLUB OF AMERICA
1860 Broadway, Dept. HR
New York 23, N. Y.

MAIL THIS SPECIAL ORDER

Okay, Joe! Rush me your famous 96 page Cable Course and include FREE your "Black Beauty" 3-Cable Exerciser plus membership in the SMCA—no dues, no fees. If I am not 100% satisfied, in any way, I can return within 30 days for full refund.

☐ I enclose $2.95 in full Ship prepaid.
☐ Ship C. O. D. for $2.95 plus postage

PLEASE PRINT PLAINLY

Name__________ Age_____
Address__________ Weight_____
City_____ Zone___ State____ Height_____

Foreign & APO's (Except Canada) $3.95 with payment in full.

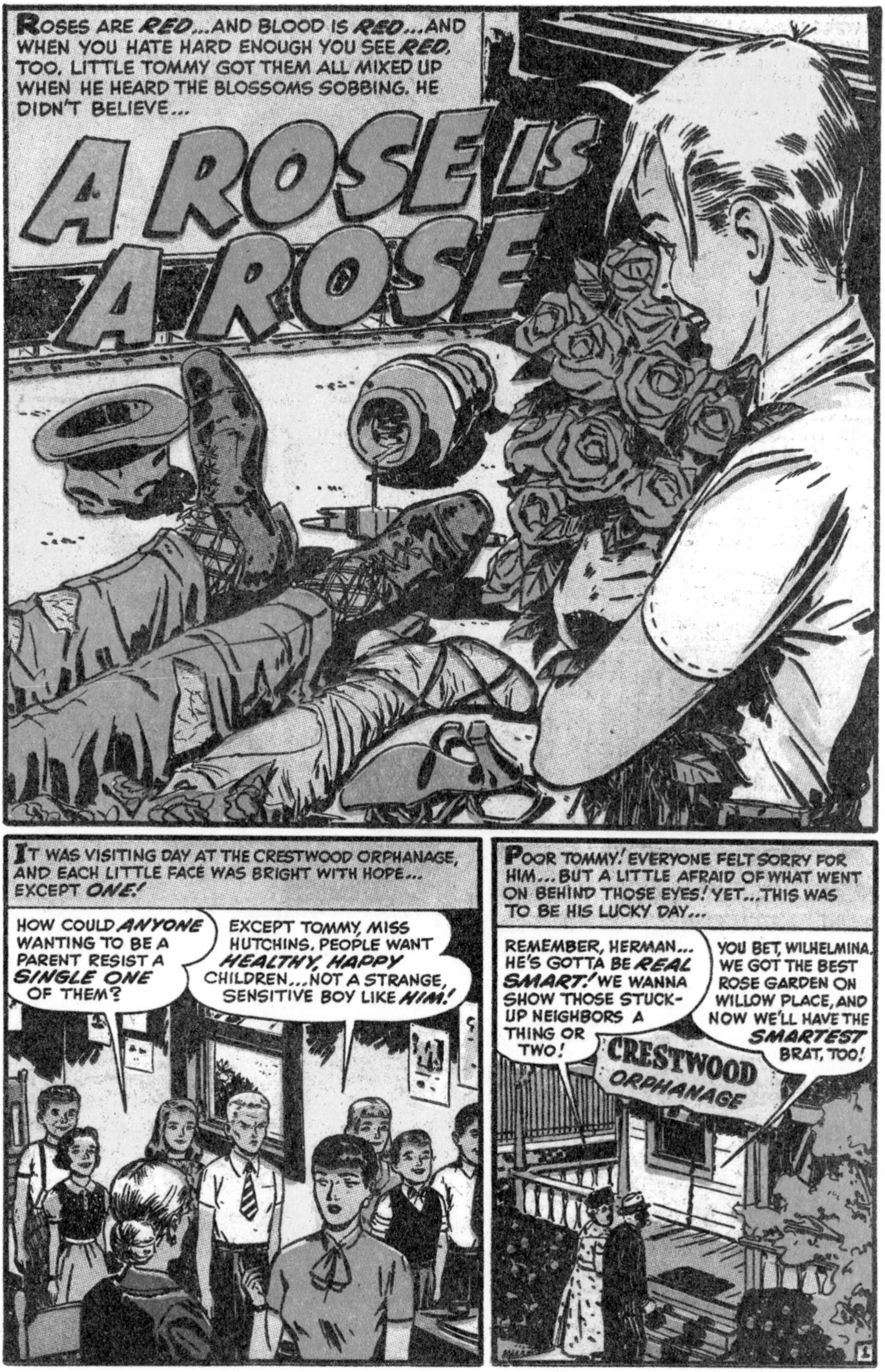

ROSES ARE *RED*... AND BLOOD IS *RED*... AND WHEN YOU HATE HARD ENOUGH YOU SEE *RED*, TOO. LITTLE TOMMY GOT THEM ALL MIXED UP WHEN HE HEARD THE BLOSSOMS SOBBING. HE DIDN'T BELIEVE...

A ROSE IS A ROSE

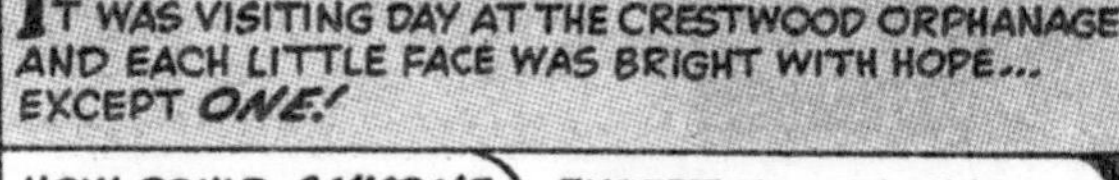

IT WAS VISITING DAY AT THE CRESTWOOD ORPHANAGE, AND EACH LITTLE FACE WAS BRIGHT WITH HOPE... EXCEPT *ONE!*

HOW COULD *ANYONE* WANTING TO BE A PARENT RESIST A *SINGLE ONE* OF THEM?
EXCEPT TOMMY, MISS HUTCHINS. PEOPLE WANT *HEALTHY, HAPPY* CHILDREN... NOT A STRANGE, SENSITIVE BOY LIKE *HIM!*

POOR TOMMY! EVERYONE FELT SORRY FOR HIM... BUT A LITTLE AFRAID OF WHAT WENT ON BEHIND THOSE EYES! YET... THIS WAS TO BE HIS LUCKY DAY...

REMEMBER, HERMAN... HE'S GOTTA BE *REAL SMART!* WE WANNA SHOW THOSE STUCK-UP NEIGHBORS A THING OR TWO!
YOU BET, WILHELMINA. WE GOT THE BEST ROSE GARDEN ON WILLOW PLACE, AND NOW WE'LL HAVE THE *SMARTEST* BRAT, TOO!
CRESTWOOD ORPHANAGE
1

WE'RE LOOKING FOR SOMETHING... I MEAN WE WANT A KID THAT'S GOT A LOT ON THE BALL IN THE... ER... MENTAL DEPARTMENT, IF YOU KNOW WHAT I MEAN!
I SEE. YOU... UH... PUT A PREMIUM ON INTELLIGENCE?

YEH, THAT'S IT! WHO'S THE BRAINIEST KID IN THE OUTFIT?
WELL, LITTLE TOMMY IS REALLY QUITE PHENOMENAL. AN IQ OVER 200!

HOWEVER, HE'S RATHER ODD! NOT THAT THERE'S ANYTHING WRONG WITH HIM, BUT HE'S FUNNY ABOUT BIRDS AND FLOWERS... TREATS THEM AS IF THEY WERE LITTLE CHILDREN!

HE PROBABLY IDENTIFIES HIMSELF WITH THEM... AND GIVES THEM THE LOVE HE REALLY WANTS OTHERS TO GIVE HIM!
I GETCHA! BUT WE'VE GOT JUST THE THING FOR HIM! YOU SHOULD SEE OUR ROSE GARDEN!

TAKE HIM, HERMAN! I CAN JUST SEE THEM SNOOTY NEIGHBORS WHEN HE GETS THE HIGHEST MARK IN THE CLASS. THEY WON'T CALL US STUPID THEN!

THE PAPERS WERE SIGNED, AND HERMAN AND WILHELMINA DROVE OFF WITH THEIR "BARGAIN!"
I'M REALLY VERY GRATEFUL TO BOTH OF YOU, MOMMY AND DADDY! I HOPE I LIVE UP TO ALL YOUR EXPECTATIONS.
GET THE LINGO, WILHELMINA! JUST WAIT TILL THEY GET A LOAD OF THIS!

I UNDERSTAND YOU LIKE FLOWERS, TOMMY?
AND THEY LIKE ME, TOO! I CAN TELL BY THE WAY THEY MAKE SOUNDS WHEN I COME NEAR THEM!
HUH?
2

HEY... I DON'T LIKE THIS. THAT KID SOUNDS NUTS!
DON'T BE SILLY. HE'S JUST A LITTLE CRACKED ABOUT FLOWERS ... BUT SO ARE WE IN A WAY! HE'LL BE OKAY!

YES, TOMMY WAS OKAY... HE TRIED HARD TO BE A GOOD SON, AND WHEN HE FOUND THAT HIS PARENTS WANTED HIM TO GET HIGH MARKS, HE GAVE THEM JUST WHAT THEY WANTED!

HE'S ABSOLUTELY INCREDIBLE, MRS. SANDERS! YEARS AHEAD OF THE OTHER CHILDREN! I'VE NEVER SEEN A MIND LIKE HIS BEFORE!
OPEN SCHOOL WEEK

HA-HA! DID YOU SEE THEIR FACES WHEN OLD REYNOLDS SPOKE ABOUT OUR KID?
I CAN JUST HEAR THEM CALLING US DUMB NOW... IN A PIG'S EYE!

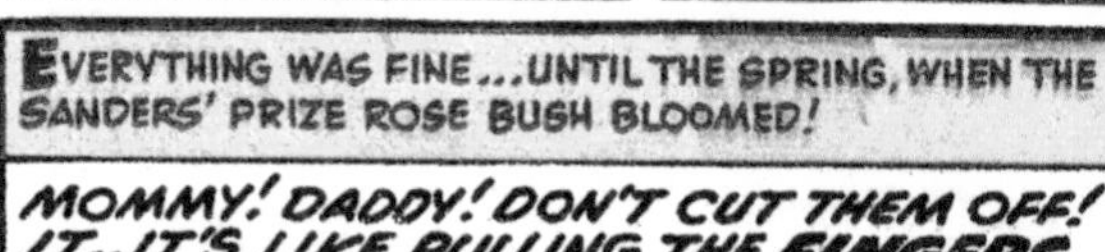

EVERYTHING WAS FINE... UNTIL THE SPRING, WHEN THE SANDERS' PRIZE ROSE BUSH BLOOMED!

MOMMY! DADDY! DON'T CUT THEM OFF! IT.. IT'S LIKE PULLING THE FINGERS AND TOES OFF A PERSON!
WH - WHAT?

SHUT UP, YOU CRAZY BRAT... BEFORE THE NEIGHBORS HEAR YOU! YOU WANT 'EM TO THINK WE'RE RUNNING A LOONY HOUSE HERE?
I'LL KEEP SCREAMING TILL YOU STOP! WAAAAAA!

ALL RIGHT... IF YOU WON'T SHUT UP, I'LL SHUT YOU UP!

NO MATTER WHAT YOU DO TO ME, I WON'T LET YOU HURT THEM! I... I CAN HEAR THEM CRYING WHEN YOU TRY TO PLUCK THEM!
LET ME HANDLE THIS, HERMAN!

WAIT! YOU'RE RIGHT, TOMMY! I CAN HEAR THEM CRYING, TOO!
YOU...YOU CAN?

CERTAINLY...BUT THEY'RE CRYING WITH JOY! THEY'RE SAYING... PLEASE PUT US IN VASES...IT'S SO NICE AND WARM AND COZY INSIDE!
GOSH...THEY MUST LIKE YOU EVEN BETTER THAN THEY LIKE ME. I NEVER HEAR THEM TALKING ...JUST CRYING!

NOW YOU MAKE THEM HAPPY AND CUT SOME, TOO...TO PUT IN VASES!
YOU...YOU'RE SURE THEY WON'T DIE INSIDE?

OF COURSE THEY WON'T. THEY'LL GROW BIGGER...AND HEALTHIER!
YOU SURE DID A JOB ON HIM. I GOTTA HAND IT TO YOU.

ONLY ONE THING, WON'T THE KID SEE THEM BLOSSOMS FADE?
DON'T WORRY, AS SOON AS THEY START TO WILT WE'LL THROW THEM AWAY AND PUT NEW ONES IN THEIR PLACE!

WILHELMINA'S PLAN WORKED PERFECTLY UNTIL ONE EVENING, WHEN TOMMY WAS RESTLESS...
I'LL THROW THESE IN THE GARBAGE PAIL AND THEN WE'LL GET THE FRESH ONES. AS SMART AS THE KID IS...WE SURE ARE SMARTER!

THEY...THEY DECEIVED ME! THEY MADE ME KILL MY LITTLE BROTHERS AND SISTERS! THEY'RE REALLY CRUEL, CRUEL PEOPLE!

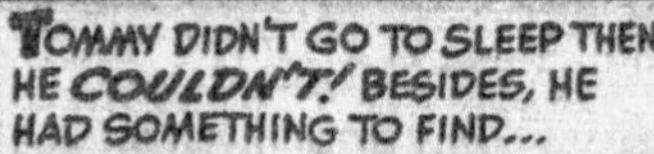
TOMMY DIDN'T GO TO SLEEP THEN. HE COULDN'T! BESIDES, HE HAD SOMETHING TO FIND...

HE LOOKED EVERYWHERE FOR IT...

UNTIL FINALLY...
I'VE FOUND IT!

AND THEN TOMMY MADE USE OF HIS NEW-FOUND POSSESSION...
ARGGGG
EEEEEEEEEEEEEEEEL
NOOOOOOOOO

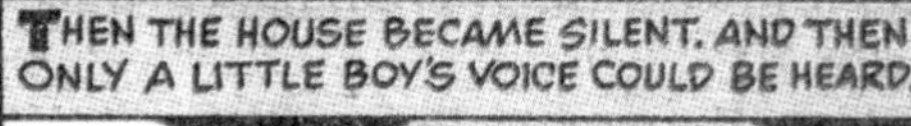
THEN THE HOUSE BECAME SILENT. AND THEN ONLY A LITTLE BOY'S VOICE COULD BE HEARD.

SEE, MOMMY AND DADDY. HAVEN'T I BEEN A REAL SMART BOY NOW?

DON'T YOU JUST LOVE TO BE IN THOSE VASES? IT'S SO NICE AND WARM AND COZY INSIDE!
THE END
5

THE BIG IDEA

Peter Wilson's door was thrown open.

"Pete," the man shrieked to the attorney, "a guy just confessed to the murder! Barney will be free!"

Wilson at first didn't feel the impact of the words. It didn't sound possible. Then the wonderful meaning hit home.

"What?" was the first thing that came to his mind. "Talk fast! What happened? Talk fast!"

"This guy just came to Barney's house.. He told everything to Barney's wife. Said he just couldn't see an innocent guy go to the chair, even if it meant his own death! Sounds crazy, but that's it!"

A smile parted Peter Wilson's lips.. "Lennie," he said, "I guess you just have to believe in miracles!"

"But, Pete," said Lennie, "we've got to work fast. We've got only ten minutes before Barney's supposed to burn!"

Peter Wilson didn't move.

"Pete, aren't you going to call the prison? Pete, we've only got ten minutes!"

Still, Peter Wilson didn't move.

"Pete, Barney's wife called me just this second. She's depending on you."

Finally, Peter Wilson had something to say. "Lennie, I've just had a big, wonderful idea! Do you know what kind of story has come our way? Do you realize that we're sitting on the biggest yarn of the century?"

"Pete; what are you talking about? We've got to move fast!"

"Take it easy, Lennie. Let me tell you my idea."

Lennie knew there was no other way. You couldn't turn Peter Wilson's mind. He sat down and listened.

"No one has ever known what it really means to walk that last mile. No one knows what a guy really thinks of during those last moments. But the world would pay a fortune to learn! And we'll have that information to sell.... if we only wait a few moments."

"Pete, you're crazy! We can't pull anything like that! We've got to save Barney!

"Shut up! We'll save him all right, don't worry. But we'll make plenty out of it, too!"

"But, Pete, suppose we don't figure correctly? Suppose we call too late? Pete, we've got to call now!"

"Stop acting like a fool, Lennie, and take it easy. We've still got three minutes to go. We'll just wait another minute and a half. By the time they get to him, he should be midway in his walk."

Lennie knew it was useless to argue. He took it easy, he kept silent, and he watched the clock's second hand spin around.

"OK, Pete, it's time. Call, Pete, call!"

Peter Wilson was still calm. He walked to the phone, picked up the receiver and dialed seven numbers. Then he waited for the buzz...but got only a...busy signal!

STRANGE SUPERSTITIONS

IN 1891, A SEAMAN WAS SWALLOWED ALIVE BY A WHALE. HOURS LATER, WHEN THE WHALE WAS KILLED AND THE GREAT BODY CUT OPEN, THE MAN WAS FOUND CURLED UP IN THE STOMACH, STILL BREATHING! HE LIVED TO A RIPE OLD AGE!

GUIDING TRAVELERS THROUGH THE DARK STREETS OF CHUNG-KING, CHINA, IS A MAN WITH A LIGHTED CANDLE STUCK IN HIS SKULL. THE HOLE FOR THE CANDLE IS BORED THROUGH THE TOP OF THE HEAD ALMOST TO THE BRAIN ITSELF!

THE WALLS OF MEKNES, IN MOROCCO, HAVE REASON TO WAIL IN THE WIND. ENTOMBED WITHIN THEM ARE 50,000 SLAVES... THE WORKERS WHO BUILT THE WALLS! THE RULERS THOUGHT THE DEAD BODIES WOULD STRENGTHEN THE WALLS!

WHAT WAS THE VERDICT OF THE TRIAL!

...THERE IS NO ESCAPE FOR THE GUILTY, EDDIE KING! YOUR BLOOD-STAINED HANDS HAVE BROUGHT YOU TO THE *FIRES OF TORMENT!*

NO--*NO!* I'M *INNOCENT!* I DEMAND A FAIR TRIAL!

A PLASTER SAINT? NOT *ME*, EDDIE KING. I DIDN'T BELIEVE IN MAKING MONEY THE *HARD* WAY. AS A LAWYER OF SORTS, I KNEW MANY A PERSON WITH A... *SOILED* PAST WHO WOULD PAY TO KEEP IT QUIET!
LOOK, THOMPSON, EITHER YOU BRING THAT GRAND AROUND OR I'LL SPILL *EVERYTHING* TO THE COPS!

WHO WERE YOU TALKING TO, EDDIE? YOU LOOK AS IF SOMEBODY POISONED YOUR FAVORITE CAT!

NOBODY IN PARTICULAR, HONEY, JUST A... *CLIENT!* IT'S NOTHING FOR *YOU* TO BOTHER YOUR PRETTY HEAD ABOUT!

CAROL STEVENS WAS MY GIRL--AS SWEET AND TRUSTING A KID AS EVER CAME OUT OF DAYTON, OHIO! SHE KNEW NOTHING ABOUT MY "CLIENT", EXCEPT THAT THERE WERE *LOTS* OF THEM...

STICK BY ME, CAROL--NO MATTER WHAT HAPPENS. A MAN IN MY BUSINESS SOMETIMES NEEDS A LITTLE HELP...
YOU KNOW I'D DO ANYTHING FOR YOU, DARLING. YOU CAN--OH, THERE'S THE DOOR-BELL!
RING!

I WENT TO THE DOOR AND...
SILVERA! WHAT ARE YOU DOING HERE?
YOU SHOULD ACT MORE SOCIABLE TO AN OLD FRIEND. LET ME IN OUT OF THE RAIN--I WANT TO *TALK* TO YOU!

SILVERA WAS A CHEAP THUG WHO HAD GOTTEN INTO TROUBLE--UNTIL I HELPED HIM OUT...FOR A LARGE *"FEE."* HE PUSHED INTO THE LIVING ROOM...

SAY, TAKE IT EASY!
WE HAVE AN OLD SCORE TO SETTLE, EDDIE...FOR EVERY PENNY YOU DRAINED FROM ME! I CAME HERE...

--TO KILL YOU!
EDDIE! LOOK OUT! HE'S GOT A *GUN!*
SILVERA--YOU FOOL!

I SAW *DEATH* STARING ME IN THE FACE...AND I LEAPED TO FOIL IT!
SOK
YOU'RE DUMBER THAN I THOUGHT!
BLAM!

WE GRAPPLED FOR ONLY A FEW SECONDS...AND THEN...
YOU PICKED ON THE WRONG...
OHHHH!
THUD!

HE--HE'S *DEAD!* THE BANG ON THE TABLE DID IT! I DIDN'T KILL HIM--YOU SAW THAT, CAROL--*I DIDN'T KILL HIM!*
BUT WHY, EDDIE--WHY DID THIS HAPPEN? WHO IS HE?

FIFTEEN MINUTES--AND I WAS CAUGHT UP IN AN ECONOMY-SIZE NIGHTMARE! I TOLD CAROL THE WHOLE DIRTY STORY...
...WE SHOULD GO TO THE POLICE, EDDIE...IT WAS AN ACCIDENT!
AND HAVE THEM ASK ABOUT MY FRIENDSHIP WITH SILVERA? I'M TAKING THE FIRST TRAIN TO PHILLY! COME WITH ME, CAROL --I NEED YOU NOW!

CAROL WAS GOOD, CLEAN--AND HONEST--BUT SHE WAS SOLD ON ME! IT DIDN'T TAKE MUCH TO CONVINCE HER...
EVERYTHING'S SHOT TO PIECES NOW! BUT I CAN MAKE SOME NEW CONTACTS WHERE I'M GOING!

BUT SUDDENLY THE WHOLE WORLD CAVED IN AROUND ME! I FELT THE TRAIN LURCH--AND THEN CRASH INTO A MILLION BITS! EVERYTHING WENT BLACK AS THE ACE OF SPADES...
YAAAAAA

I WAS DEAD...BUT I DIDN'T REALIZE IT!
WH-WHAT'S HAPPENING? WHERE AM I? CAROL! DON'T LEAVE ME! YAAAHHH!

I WAS BEING TOSSED AROUND LIKE A LEAF IN A STRONG WIND--AND THE FACES...THEY MADE MY FLESH CRAWL AND WHEN I CAME TO, IT WAS WORSE...

WHERE AM I? THOSE.. PEOPLE.. I...I... MUST BE GOING MAD!

THEN I KNEW...
MY DEAR MR. KING, YOU ARE PERFECTLY SANE. YOU ARE MERELY WHERE YOU BELONG--IN THE BLACKEST DUNGEON OF HELL...RESERVED EXCLUSIVELY FOR MURDERERS!
BUT THAT COULDN'T BE! I--I'VE MADE CROOKED DEALS IN MY TIME--BUT I NEVER KILLED ANYONE! SILVERA'S DEATH WAS AN ACCIDENT!

OUR RECORDS INDICATE THAT YOU KILLED ONE RAYMOND SILVERA ON--BUT WHAT DOES IT MATTER? WE ARE SELDOM WRONG HERE, MR. KING...

BUT YOU ARE WRONG THIS TIME! I WANT A TRIAL TO PROVE I'M INNOCENT--A FULL TRIAL WITH ALL THE TRIMMINGS!

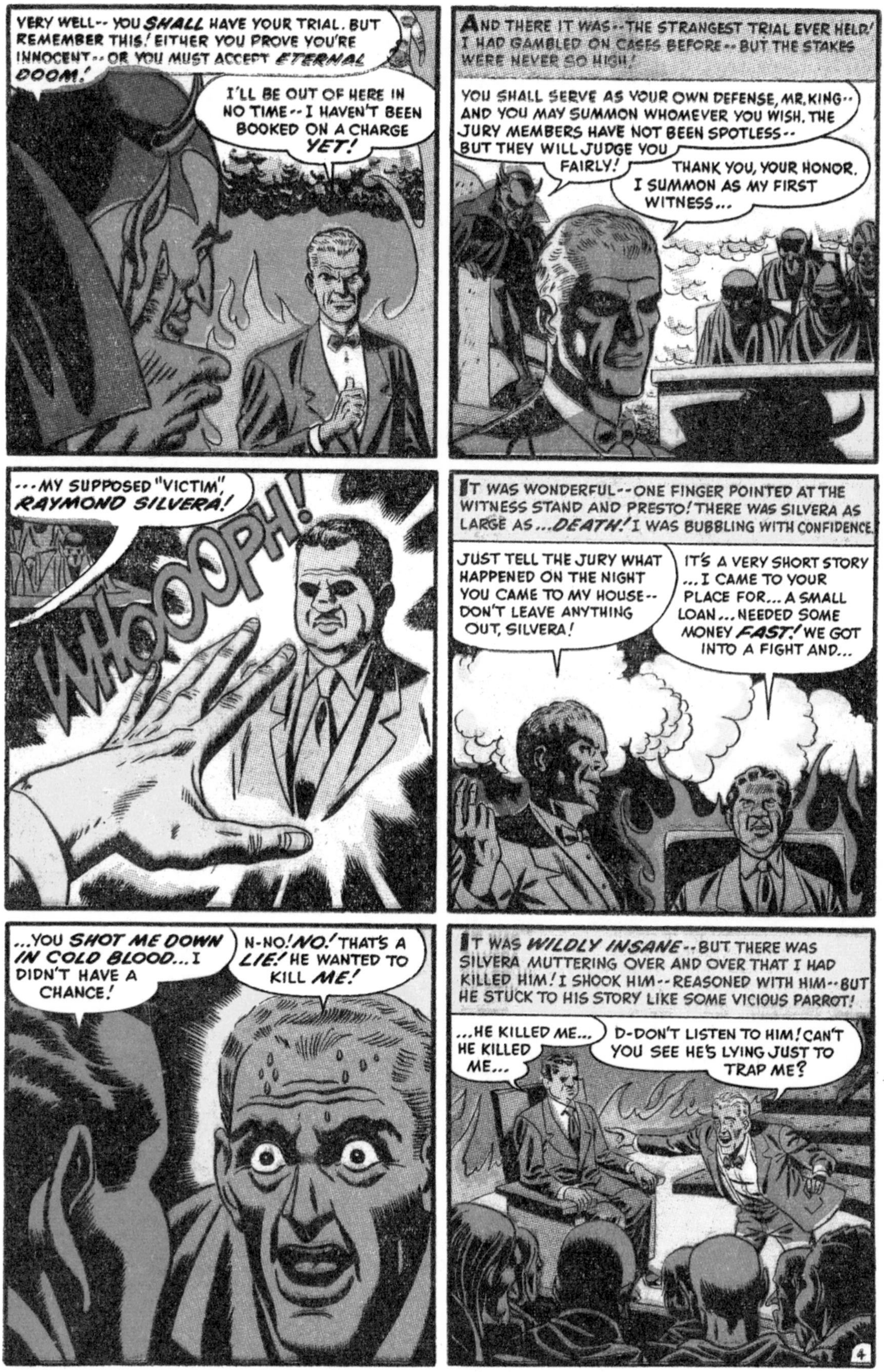

VERY WELL-- YOU *SHALL* HAVE YOUR TRIAL. BUT REMEMBER THIS! EITHER YOU PROVE YOU'RE INNOCENT-- OR YOU MUST ACCEPT *ETERNAL DOOM!*

I'LL BE OUT OF HERE IN NO TIME-- I HAVEN'T BEEN BOOKED ON A CHARGE *YET!*

AND THERE IT WAS--THE STRANGEST TRIAL EVER HELD! I HAD GAMBLED ON CASES BEFORE-- BUT THE STAKES WERE NEVER SO HIGH!

YOU SHALL SERVE AS YOUR OWN DEFENSE, MR. KING-- AND YOU MAY SUMMON WHOMEVER YOU WISH. THE JURY MEMBERS HAVE NOT BEEN SPOTLESS-- BUT THEY WILL JUDGE YOU FAIRLY!

THANK YOU, YOUR HONOR. I SUMMON AS MY FIRST WITNESS...

...MY SUPPOSED "VICTIM", *RAYMOND SILVERA!*

WHOOOPH!

IT WAS WONDERFUL--ONE FINGER POINTED AT THE WITNESS STAND AND PRESTO! THERE WAS SILVERA AS LARGE AS ...*DEATH!* I WAS BUBBLING WITH CONFIDENCE.

JUST TELL THE JURY WHAT HAPPENED ON THE NIGHT YOU CAME TO MY HOUSE-- DON'T LEAVE ANYTHING OUT, SILVERA!

IT'S A VERY SHORT STORY ...I CAME TO YOUR PLACE FOR... A SMALL LOAN... NEEDED SOME MONEY *FAST!* WE GOT INTO A FIGHT AND...

YOUR STAR WITNESS SEEMS TO HAVE FAILED YOU, MR. KING! IF THIS IS ALL YOU CAN OFFER...
NO--WAIT-- THERE MUST BE SOMETHING-- SOMEONE WHO...

SUDDENLY A HAPPY BRAINSTORM HIT ME...CAROL HAD BEEN THERE THAT NIGHT--AND SHE COULD SAVE ME!...SHE WOULD WANT TO SAVE ME!
I'D LIKE TO CALL ONE MORE WITNESS TO THE STAND...MISS CAROL STEVENS!
AS YOU WISH... HAVE HER BROUGHT FORTH AT ONCE!

CAROL STEVENS TO THE STAND!
WHERE IS CAROL STEVENS?
CAROL STEVENS!

--WH--WHERE IS SHE? WHY DOESN'T SHE ANSWER? DOESN'T SHE KNOW SHE'S MY ONE LAST CHANCE? SHE COULDN'T LET ME DOWN AT A TIME LIKE THIS!

SILENCE--JUST STRANGE OMINOUS SILENCE--AND THEY ALL STARTED CACKLING LIKE A PACK OF FIENDS --THEN SOMEONE WHISPERED IN THE JUDGE'S EAR...
WHAT'S THE MATTER? WHAT'S HAPPENED TO HER? SHE'S GOT TO SHOW UP-- YOU CAN'T--

YOU ARE DOOMED TO REMAIN HERE FOREVER, EDDIE KING! CAROL STEVENS CANNOT BE SUMMONED TO HELP YOU!
BUT WHY? WHY?

AND THEN I HEARD IT...AND HERE I AM... ALWAYS WILL BE...ALWAYS...ALWAYS...
CAROL STEVENS IS... UP THERE...IN THE OTHER PLACE!
THE END

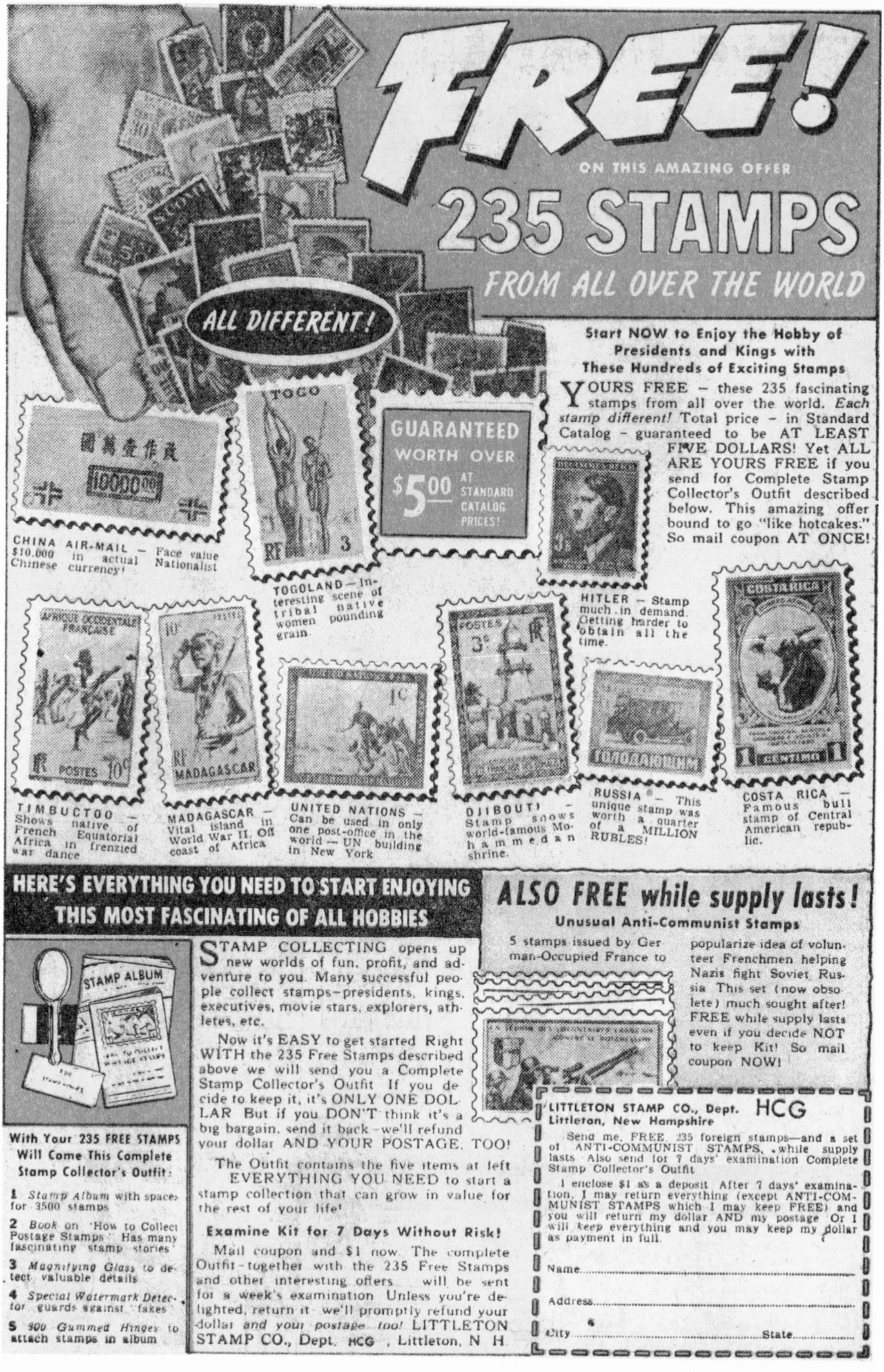
FREE!
ON THIS AMAZING OFFER
235 STAMPS
FROM ALL OVER THE WORLD
ALL DIFFERENT!
Start NOW to Enjoy the Hobby of Presidents and Kings with These Hundreds of Exciting Stamps
YOURS FREE – these 235 fascinating stamps from all over the world. Each stamp different! Total price – in Standard Catalog – guaranteed to be AT LEAST FIVE DOLLARS! Yet ALL ARE YOURS FREE if you send for Complete Stamp Collector's Outfit described below. This amazing offer bound to go "like hotcakes." So mail coupon AT ONCE!
GUARANTEED WORTH OVER $5.00 AT STANDARD CATALOG PRICES!
CHINA AIR-MAIL – $10,000 in actual Chinese currency! Face value Nationalist
TOGOLAND—Interesting scene of tribal native women pounding grain.
HITLER – Stamp much in demand. Getting harder to obtain all the time.
TIMBUCTOO – Shows native of French Equatorial Africa in frenzied war dance
MADAGASCAR – Vital island in World War II. Off coast of Africa
UNITED NATIONS – Can be used in only one post-office in the world — UN building in New York
DJIBOUTI – Stamp shows world-famous Mohammedan shrine.
RUSSIA – This unique stamp was worth a quarter of a MILLION RUBLES!
COSTA RICA – Famous bull stamp of Central American republic.
HERE'S EVERYTHING YOU NEED TO START ENJOYING THIS MOST FASCINATING OF ALL HOBBIES
STAMP ALBUM
With Your 235 FREE STAMPS Will Come This Complete Stamp Collector's Outfit:
1 Stamp Album with spaces for 3500 stamps
2 Book on "How to Collect Postage Stamps." Has many fascinating stamp stories"
3 Magnifying Glass to detect valuable details
4 Special Watermark Detector guards against "fakes"
5 300 Gummed Hinges to attach stamps in album
STAMP COLLECTING opens up new worlds of fun, profit, and adventure to you. Many successful people collect stamps—presidents, kings, executives, movie stars, explorers, athletes, etc.
Now it's EASY to get started Right WITH the 235 Free Stamps described above we will send you a Complete Stamp Collector's Outfit. If you decide to keep it, it's ONLY ONE DOLLAR. But if you DON'T think it's a big bargain, send it back – we'll refund your dollar AND YOUR POSTAGE, TOO!
The Outfit contains the five items at left EVERYTHING YOU NEED to start a stamp collection that can grow in value for the rest of your life!
Examine Kit for 7 Days Without Risk!
Mail coupon and $1 now. The complete Outfit – together with the 235 Free Stamps and other interesting offers will be sent for a week's examination. Unless you're delighted, return it – we'll promptly refund your dollar and your postage too! LITTLETON STAMP CO., Dept. HCG, Littleton, N. H.
ALSO FREE while supply lasts!
Unusual Anti-Communist Stamps
5 stamps issued by German-Occupied France to popularize idea of volunteer Frenchmen helping Nazis fight Soviet Russia. This set (now obsolete) much sought after! FREE while supply lasts even if you decide NOT to keep Kit! So mail coupon NOW!
LITTLETON STAMP CO., Dept. HCG
Littleton, New Hampshire
Send me, FREE, 235 foreign stamps—and a set of ANTI-COMMUNIST STAMPS, while supply lasts. Also send for 7 days' examination Complete Stamp Collector's Outfit.
I enclose $1 as a deposit. After 7 days' examination, I may return everything (except ANTI-COMMUNIST STAMPS which I may keep FREE) and you will return my dollar AND my postage. Or I will keep everything and you may keep my dollar as payment in full.
Name
Address
City State

Uncle Bernie's FUN SHOP
BUY NOW at our Low Low PRICES!

THE ALL-FAVORITE MONEY MACHINE!

It's thrilling fun to be a magician! But it's twice as wonderful to be a money-making magician, to baffle all your friends and family. With this amazing money machine you can perform real, mystifying magic. Think of the excitement when plain sheets of paper are placed in the machine, and as the rollers revolve, **OUT COMES HONEST-TO-GOODNESS MONEY**. There's a magic trick, of course, that only you will know. You'll be one magician in tremendous demand to perform your money magic! The whole family will find this remarkable money-maker thrilling entertainment. Rush your order NOW. **SEND NO MONEY.** Remit with order and we pay postage or C.O.D. plus postage.

NEW! SENSATIONAL! A Terrific Toy Set

8 METAL CAR "ACTION FLEET"

- **Bell clangs . . .**
- **Taximeter registers . . .**
- **Windows Go Up and Down**
- **Windshield wipers move . .**
- **Gun moves and Bangs.**

Fascinate the youngsters with hours of fun and action. Imagine — every car WORKS in the line of duty! 1 car with working windshield wiper, 2 cars with windows that open and close, 1 police car with gun that bangs and recoils, 1 ambulance with ringing and swaying bell, 2 taxis with meters that register fare, 1 fire chief car with bell that rings and sways. All 8 cars made of durable steel . . . rubber wheels cannot come out . . . bottoms completely enclosed . . . all new Two-tone and metallic finish . . . all differently colored. SEND NO MONEY. (C.O.D., you pay postage. Remit with order, we pay postage.)

Terrific Value! Only $2.98 COMPLETE

AMAZING • EXCITING • IT'S TELEVUE!

SUPER DELUXE

ELECTRIC MOVIE PROJECTOR

SHOWS REAL MOVIES

- A BIG SHOW "Little Red Riding Hood"
- A REAL PROJECTOR! Bright Red Plastic!
- A COLORFUL THEATRE with Screen!
- COMPLETELY SAFE! Any Child Can Operate

Imagine Only $2.98

COMPLETE Projector, One film and Screen!

EXTRA FILM
3 FILMS ONLY $1.00
SNOW WHITE
THE OWL AND THE PUSSY CAT
JINGLE BELLS
THREE LITTLE PIGS
JACK AND JILL
RIP VAN WINKLE
TOM THUMB
ROBINSON CRUSOE
HOUSE THAT JACK BUILT
WINKIN WILLIE

Now any child can show the most exciting movies at home with this streamlined TELEVUE Projector, complete with colorful theatre and screen. The bright red plastic projector is safe and simple to operate — nothing to get out of order. Think of the fun of watching your favorite come to life on the theatre screen! This Super Deluxe Projector will mean big movie parties for friends and family. You boys and girls will be fascinated with the Big Movie Shows, and running movies all by yourself is the greatest treat of them all! **SEND NO MONEY.** Remit with order and we pay postage or C.O.D. plus postage.

Hi! I'm LANA! the Doll whose HAIR YOU CAN WAVE!

FREE HAIR WAVE KIT

A wonderful new doll in washable rubber Wonderskin whose hair is so lifelike it can be waved in any style and rewaved just like your own. A perfect playmate for the "Junior Mother" of the house. Complete with real Hair-wave kit which consists of . . . plastic curlers . . . rubber waving bands . . . waving end papers . . . plastic comb . . . and bottle of hair wave lotion. *LANA* is 11 inches tall. Her soft cuddly body which can be bathed will give the "Junior Miss" an almost real baby sister to play with.

SEND NO MONEY — C.O.D. you pay postage and handling charges. Remit with order we pay postage.

SEND COUPON!

NOVELTY MART, Dept. 110
59 East 8th Street, New York 3, N. Y.

Gentlemen: Please send me the following:
Enclosed find: ☐ Check or M.O. ☐ C.O.D. plus postage

☐ LANA $3.98
☐ Action Cars $2.98
☐ Money Machine $1.98
☐ T. V. Projector $2.98 (3 Films $1.00)

Name____________________

Address__________ City__________ State__________